THE
BELONGING

LEANNE WOOD

THE BELONGING

Printed in Australia 2019
ISBN: 978-0-9953804-6-2

A copy of this publication can be found in the National Library of Australia.

DEDICATION

For my Mum, who continues to stand beside me.
And for my Dad and Aunt Valda.
You will always be in my heart and in my mind.

Where there is forever love, there is never-ending
love. Where there is never-ending love, there is life. And
where there is life, the possibilities are endless.

TABLE OF CONTENTS

TABLE OF CONTENTS

CHAPTER ONE

Robert Jackson took a deep drag of his menthol cigarette and for a few moments stared out the window at the tree-lined street beyond his lush lawn. A stale odour of perspiration shadowed him, leeching from his crumpled red T-shirt and khaki cargo shorts. He had not bathed in days. Puffs of smoke curled around him, as he raked his fingers through his hair, his bitten-down nails snagging in the brown curls.

Searching. He was searching for answers, his hands occasionally shaking as he took another drag. The street was quiet; it was always quieter during storm season. Sudden downpours birthed sauna-like steam, and a nebula haze wavered over the asphalt.

Humidity was high and the air suffocatingly heavy.

Inside, his house reflected the tatters of his existence – old newspapers, stained coffee mugs, discarded food scraps, and an overflowing ashtray engulfed his wooden coffee table, spilling onto the floor. In the kitchen, dirty dishes piled up in the sink. Tidying was the last thing on his mind.

Hopeless, everything is hopeless.

Despair seeped from his bloodshot eyes as he dropped to his couch. Cupping his stubbled face, he wondered what he should do. How does one escape misery? He was never able to master an escape before. His life was a total shambles.

Why did I insist she go? She could've waited. I should've gone with her.

Patience had never been one of Robert's strong suits; maybe because it was always so lacking from those he encountered. Ever since he was a young boy, he felt misplaced, shunted from one foster home to the next, he ached to belong, to feel loved. Yet, love never appeared as a boy. Now in his late-forties, that frailty had returned. A repeat of younger years; flawed, missing pieces and unanswered questions. Only this time he knew why. This time he was responsible.

In theory, things appeared so easy. Logic dictated, there comes a time in everyone's life when you have to face the past, when you have to accept what has happened in order to build a future. However, Robert cannot accept what has happened, nor can he push his memories back to that part of the brain where heartbreak and secrets hide. Forgiveness had no place in his heart. Overwhelmed by grief and guilt, he toyed with the idea of ending it all. No one would miss a person who never belonged.

Rising to his feet, he began to pace the room. His steps were slow, meandering, like a lion trapped within a cage. Moving towards the bookcase on the far side of the room, he glanced at a photo of the most gorgeous woman in the world. He dropped his chin, his chest constricting. He was a shattered man, his heart broken, his soul in tatters.

Why did it have to end? We were so happy.

Closing his eyes for a brief moment, he inhaled deeply remembering her soft floral perfume. From that first moment when their eyes locked, he knew she was special. An instant connection. When they kissed, he got butterflies, and knew there was no turning back. There was a rightness, a belonging. For the first time in his life, Robert felt love, *real* love.

Wrapping his arms around himself, he could almost

feel the softness and warmth of her skin next to his. If only he could feel that one more time. Taking a deep breath Robert inched forward, he could not help but be hypnotised by her vision. A picture told a thousand words – they were in love, their faces glowing with happiness. They had the world before them, a bright future, endless dreams…

Now it was all gone.

Julie was gone.

In the blink of an eye, she was no more.

Suffocating by the darkness of reality, the room contracted and expanded around him, like a living, breathing thing. Robert froze, muscles tense and feet braced apart. Everything began to spin. Overwhelmed by panic, he dropped his cigarette. Pain. Excruciating pain. Grabbing his pounding chest, his legs buckled, and he collapsed to his knees with a thud. Visions of Julie flashed through his mind.

Did she suffer?

Clutching his forehead with his left hand while maintaining pressure to his chest with his right was the only thing he could do to abate his agony. It felt as though thousands of nails were being hammered into his forehead. Sweat covered his brow, his heart thumping as he struggled for breath. Unable to maintain his balance, his body crumpled.

A heavy moan escaped his lips. The timber floorboards felt cool against his back. Uncontrollable panting surrounded. His vision blurred. Wild elephants stampeded over his chest as he fought for breath. It was imperative to gain control. *Stay calm. As still as possible.* It would pass. It always passed. This was not the first time. Echoes of grief besieged him as he stared at the ceiling praying for forgiveness and relief.

Five minutes passed. Then five more.

A pool of misery soaked the floorboards around him.

At last the pain began to subside. A dull ache enveloped his head as he massaged his temples. Wiping his eyes with shaking hands, he struggled to his feet, staggered across the room and hoped the worst was over. *What did I do to deserve this?*

Robert Jackson wanted answers.

CHAPTER TWO

Elsie Graham was perceived as an unsociable, nasty and at times hostile cynic. A disconnected recluse. The cranky cripple who lived on the hill surrounded by ever increasing foliage, and six-foot fences. But no one really knew Elsie; no one knew from where she came, or if she had family. Besides regular social calls from her community carers, no one came to visit. Secrets underlaid her actions, and beneath her callous façade beat a heart full of regret and fear.

One of Elsie's biggest fears was being alone, of getting sick and no one finding her. What if someone tried to break into her house? What would she do? Would she try to flee? In the dark she could trip down her staircase. What if she heard a strange noise or a breaking window in the middle of the night? Something that made the hair on the back of her neck stand on end.

Was eternal loneliness her punishment? Or, would she find forgiveness and understanding?

"Here kitty, kitty," Elsie called, shuffling around the kitchen. "Where are you, Tinkerbell? Come on, baby… Come to Mumma."

Elsie's eleven-year-old moggie with mattered ginger fur was her constant, precious companion. Together, they followed a routine. Every morning Elsie would rise, wander downstairs to the kitchen, and switch the kettle on. Tinkerbell would greet her with demanding cries, paws stretching up

Elsie's leg. While Elsie sipped her cup of tea, Tinkerbell would drink her morning milk but today the kitchen was silent.

Tinkerbell was missing.

Elsie feared the worst; she struggled for breath as she opened the kitchen door to her rear garden. She called and called and called again. Tinkerbell was nowhere to be found. Elsie worried something may have happened to her beloved companion. Taking a deep breath, she bit her lip. Her hands fidgeted in her cardigan pocket searching for a tissue to dry escaping tears.

Where are you?

"Here kitty, kitty." She squinted against the morning sun as she scanned the yard. "Come on, baby."

Tightness in her chest, heart pounding. "Tinkerbell, come on, baby… Here kitty, kitty."

On old bones and feeble limbs, Elsie moved down the stairs. Tired and wrinkled hands wrapped firmly around the handrail with every cautious step.

In her childhood Elsie had survived an acute attack of poliomyelitis. Years later a second phase to this disease had surfaced. Post-polio syndrome. Initial onset had been slow and steady, over time her muscle weakness had worsened. Joint and muscle pain, along with severe fatigue made life a challenge. The disease was insidious and unrelenting. Small activities resulted in exhaustion. At her worst, Elsie required the aid of forearm crutches to relieve weight on her weakening limbs and to prevent falls. Listening to her body and pacing her activities was imperative while rest periods were required several times a day. Her future appeared bleak.

I can't lose you… Oh please, I can't lose you. Without you, I have no one.

A trail of small footprints on the dew-ridden lawn showed the path Elsie took in her pink fluffy slippers. Faltering steps led her closer to the hibiscus while worry shrouded her. She prayed everything would be fine. Tinkerbell enjoyed lying in the garden near the hibiscus. Elsie stopped, frozen. Her eyes widened, shaking hands danced in front of her lips. Tears filled her eyes. A large hole sat beneath the hibiscus.

Elsie's world began to collapse.

"Tinkerbell… Come on, baby, here kitty… Come on, baby."

Elsie shook her head. Weak-kneed, she stumbled backwards, retreating to the house, heart racing as she fought back more tears.

A snarling rose from within the bushes. Something loomed within the darkness. Raising her hand to her face, she stared into the obscurity. A low growl. Elsie tripped backwards; her head cracked against the back wall of her house. The noise continued. Her head ached. Outstretched hands guided her sidesteps towards the stairs. Her eyes never lost contact with the garden. The bushes moved. Elsie flinched; her heart raced as she struggled to swallow. The growling continued. Reaching behind, she grabbed the handrail. Pushing herself beyond her normal physical capabilities.

Struggling up the stairs in a forward motion was difficult at the best of times. Scaling the same steps backwards while being overwhelmed by panic was a severe test of strength and near impossible. Puffing breath. Strained legs. Racing heart. Wide eyes. Shaking hands and painful moans. At last, Elsie made it to the top. Her legs ached. Sweat covered her brow.

She fumbled for the door handle, tried to catch her breath. Contact. With one firm yank she stumbled into her house. Elsie staggered to the kitchen table, and collapsed on the chair.

She was safe, but where was Tinkerbell and what was growling in the bushes?

CHAPTER THREE

Shirley Jones wanted nothing to do with her parents. In her eyes, those hideous people didn't exist. It wasn't her fault she was conceived to an impoverished family. Born with a fiery spirit and strong mind, as a young child she dreamt of escape. Determination and success would deliver fortune and greatness. One day she would have it all. She would be free.

That day never arrived.

Shirley was a thirty-nine-year-old single mum with a screaming brat. Resentment and jealousy simmered below her smiling face. Struggling from one pay-week to the next was not a part of her plan. Things needed to change, and at last Shirley believed she'd found the answer to her problems. An unsuspecting soul sat clearly in her sights – a fortune for the taking.

Charging down the hallway, Shirley wiped her nose and continued to sneeze. Her allergies were playing up and she was in no mood for temper tantrums. Jai was supposed to be eating his breakfast, yet he was nowhere to be seen. The house was silent.

Her thundering footsteps bounced off the walls, and as she grabbed the doorframe, she hurled herself into the darkness of his bedroom, and flicked on the light.

"I told you to get up," she yelled. "We're going to be late if you don't get your butt into gear."

Jai wiped his eyes then covered his head with his blankets. "Where did you go?"

"Never mind where I went, young man. I told you to get up and I meant it."

Shirley dragged the blankets from the bed and smacked Jai over the head with the flat of her hand. His disobedience was infuriating. The boy cried out and grabbed his head. Glancing at her watch, she knew they were running out of time.

Jai frowned as he fought back tears, moaning as he glared at his mother.

Shirley stood with her hands on her hips, glaring back. "I said get up young man, and I am not going to say it again."

Before Jai had a chance to move Shirley snatched the young boy's arm and reefed him from the bed.

"Ouch! You're hurting me," Jai cried as his body hit the floor.

"I'll do more than get you out of bed if you don't get a move on," she said, holding up her hand. "Now get up and get dressed or you'll be wearing this hand on your butt, and next time it won't just be a tap."

A sobbing Jai huddled on the floor.

"Do you want a smack?" She waved her hand again.

Cowering at her feet, Jai's small body trembled. Tear-soaked eyes gazed up at her. "No."

"Then get up and do what you've been told without any carry on, otherwise I will give you something to cry about."

Sucking in his sadness, Jai wiped his eyes.

Shirley stormed from the room leaving behind her weeping seven-year-old.

In the laundry, her attention focused on her problem. If she didn't get a move on both of them would be late. Tingling returned to her sinuses, and itchiness spread to her eyes. Irritation spread while her anger grew. She finished what she needed to do and slammed the laundry door, rattling the handle to check it was locked.

"You've got two minutes!" Shirley snatched her handbag from the kitchen sink and drummed her fingers on the kitchen counter. Jai dashed down the hallway, shirt unbuttoned, shoes and socks in hand.

"I haven't had breakfast," he said, swinging into the kitchen.

"You were told to get up and have breakfast, you chose to stay in bed. Actions have consequences, young man. You can go to school hungry."

Opening the front door, Shirley brushed off her son's whining. In the car, his stomach growled as he put on his socks and shoes. Shirley ignored the noise. Licking her fingers, she reached over and swiped her hand across the top of his head as she attempted to flatten the cocky's peak in his hair.

They arrived at the school gate just as the bell rang. Jai opened the car door, climbed out and slammed it shut without looking back.

Shirley wound down the window. "I should be home when you finish school, but if not just go across to Robert's house."

Jai didn't acknowledge her at all.

CHAPTER FOUR

Veronica Reid's life had been a mixture of sunshine and pain. As a survivor, she liked to be in control. Life was too short to waste and she would do whatever it took to be happy.

When one door closes another opens. And if doesn't open, well, I'll take the goddamn window.

For Veronica it was time to move forward. She grabbed handfuls of clothing from the cupboard and tossed them into large bags. Sweat ran into her eyes, but she wouldn't stop. She had a job to complete. Determination propelled her forward. Everything would be gone before nightfall.

When Veronica set her mind to something, there was no changing it. Overflowing garbage bags covered the bed. Unwanted shoes were piled into old suitcases. The wardrobe stripped. Empty coat hangers clunked together. Veronica collapsed to the floor. Staring into the empty space, she wondered how long it would take her to remove all the unwanted items from her bedroom. It had to go. There would be no keepsakes. Redundant leftovers and materialistic reminders had no place in her life.

Tomorrow would be the first day of the rest of her life.

Veronica had lost her husband; it was time to find a replacement.

She dialled the telephone number scrawled on the paper she had been given. "Hi Robert," she said, toying with her hair. "I hope you get this message. My name is Veronica. I just wanted to let you know I'm looking forward to seeing you tonight. I hope you'll be there."

Veronica ended the call. Robert was such a formal name; she wondered if that was what he liked to be called... or maybe Rob. Rob sounded strong, protective, and adventurous, while Bob or Bobby gave the impression of a playful individual. Could he be all three? Formal when required, strong and protective of those he cared for while playful on occasion? Veronica licked her lips, and smiled. She looked forward to their meeting.

CHAPTER FIVE

Shirley sprang up the front steps, pushed the doorbell and waited patiently. It was mid-morning; the humidity was rising and the sun had bite. The door opened. "Good morning, Elsie, how are you today?" Taking a step back, she smiled. "Isn't it a wonderful day?"

Elsie looked up; her eyes hollow and blank. "I'm afraid not… something has happened," she said, turning her head, in an attempt to hide her tears.

Shirley leaned close and gently touched Elsie on the arm. "Oh, my poor dear. What's happened?"

"Tinkerbell is missing… I was nearly attacked." Elsie trembled as she raised her tearstained gaze to Shirley's.

"Attacked…? By who?"

The shock was apparently too much to bear. Elsie burst into tears and shook her head. "Not who… I-I don't know, something was in the garden."

"Oh my god!" Shirley gasped. "Tinkerbell is missing and you were nearly attacked? No wonder you're upset. I would be the same." Stepping closer, she again gently placed her hand on Elsie's arm, who continued to tremble. The poor woman was beside herself. "Come here, you're shaking like a leaf."

Shirley wrapped her arms around Elsie, feeling the sharp bony shoulders rise and fall between sobs. Her nose twitched as she inhaled Elsie's mothball odour. It was a scent that reminded her of her grandmother. Tears touched her eyes; she missed her grandmother deeply.

Like Elsie, Shirley's grandmother was reserved and appeared stern, but hidden beneath a hardened exterior was a gentle and loving woman who had passed away when Shirley was young. How she missed their conversations.

She rested her cheek on Elsie's shoulder. Stray cat fur embedded within the woollen fibres of Elsie's cardigan brushed against her nose and teased her sinuses. Drawing a quick breath in, she fought off her urge to sneeze. Itchiness scratched the back of her nostrils. She pulled back, and made a throat-clearing noise, but couldn't stop the sneeze. "Achoo!"

"God bless you, my child."

Shirley foraged through her bag for some tissues. "Oh, please forgive me, my allergies are playing up today." She blew her nose, placed the tissue back in her bag then hugged Elsie once more.

Shirley wanted Elsie to feel safe; it was her job to look after her. "Come now, let me help you inside. Everything will be all right."

She took Elsie by the arm, gently led her into the kitchen and eased the woman into a chair. "Now let me make you a nice cup of tea and you can tell me what happened," she said, reaching for the kettle. "I don't want you to worry, I'm here now and we'll get to the bottom of this. I'll find Tinkerbell." Shirley filled the kettle, flicked the switch, then leaned against the sink. "Now tell me everything from the start."

Elsie sat shaking her head, shoulders slumped, hands clasped on her lap. "I woke up as usual and came to make a cuppa, but Tinkerbell didn't show. She's always waiting for me in the kitchen, but this morning she wasn't here." She paused, looking up at Shirley. "I thought she may have been out under the hibiscus, so I took a wander outside and that's when it all happened."

Shirley looked out the back window then turned towards Elsie who began to sob. She drew nearer. "What happened?"

"I saw a hole then heard a noise, a growling noise. Something moved within the bushes." Tears seeped from Elsie's eyes as she placed her trembling hand over her mouth.

"You saw a hole… where?" Shirley's eyes widened, like Elsie, she placed her hand in front of her mouth. "Then you heard growling… in the bushes? Did you see what it was?"

Elsie dropped her head, her body trembled and she gasped. "No! I couldn't. I was petrified. The hole was under the hibiscus. Oh, my baby has gone. My poor Tinkerbell is gone." Rocking back and forth, she began to cry again. "Something has killed her."

Shirley draped her arm around Elsie's shoulder, and the old woman leaned into her warmth. "Thank you, my dear. I'm so glad I have you."

"Oh, Elsie, you do have me. I'm here for you and I understand why you're feeling this way. I would've been scared witless."

Shirley knelt in front of Elsie and took her hand. Their eyes met. "I'm so sorry for what you had to go through. Let me make you this cuppa and I'll go and check your backyard. I'll look for Tinkerbell. You need to calm yourself." She embraced Elsie. "Rest assured, I'm always here for you."

Shirley left Elsie sipping her tea then disappeared out the back door in search of answers. Where was Tinkerbell? What was the growling Elsie had heard coming from the garden?

CHAPTER SIX

Shirley walked slowly towards the hibiscus, scanning the bushes for any sign of something hiding.

"Here, Tinkerbell. Here kitty, kitty."

When she looked over her shoulder, she could see Elsie in the kitchen. The woman was clearly upset; her teacup clinked several times as she returned it to the saucer. At least Elsie was safe inside.

Turning her attention to the bushes she called a little louder. "Here, Tinkerbell. Here kitty, kitty."

She stopped, heart pounding. Her eyes locked onto something. Had Elsie seen what she could? Leaning closer she shook her head. The woman would have been beside herself. A growling noise in the bushes would have sent her into shock. Shirley stepped closer and moved to the right of the hibiscus. A wall of bushes ran along the fence line. Twigs and fallen leaves crunched beneath her feet with every cautious step. A slight breeze brought the bushes to life. A rustled warning entered her ears. She stood in the shadows assessing her next move.

"Ouch!"

Shirley snatched her face. Stinging warmth struck her cheek. Red crimson seeped. Fingers clamped over the burning wound.

"Are you okay, my dear?" Elsie squawked.

Shirley peeked through the bushes towards the house. Elsie was standing at the back door.

THE BELONGING

"Yep, I'm okay. Stay there. It's all okay. I just scratched myself."

Shirley was visibly annoyed. Trampling through the bushes was a waste of time. Tinkerbell wasn't there. No growling animal lay waiting to attack. Snapping branches from around her, she kicked leaves and dirt. What she had seen before was now out of sight. She returned to the house.

"Oh, my goodness, you have hurt yourself," Elsie said, opening the screen door. "Come here, my dear, let me grab a face cloth so I can take a look."

Elsie hurried out of the kitchen and returned moments later. "Take a seat and let me have a look, you're bleeding."

Shirley removed her hand and winced as Elsie placed the cool, damp cloth on her face and began dabbing gently.

"I'm so sorry. You should never have gone out there alone. You could have been attacked." Elsie ripped open a small envelope that contained a gauzed patch. "Here... hold that against your cheek while I grab some adhesive tape."

Shirley watched as the woman fumbled to retrieve the tape. "I'm sorry I couldn't find Tinkerbell, but I didn't see any growling animal either and there wasn't any sign of foul play so..." She shook her head, got up from the chair as Elsie began to weep. "There, there... don't upset yourself. Everything is going to be all right. Here, let me get the tape."

Elsie handed her the roll of adhesive tape. "I'm so sorry, my hands are shaking so much I couldn't find the end."

"It's okay. Look, it's only a small scratch."

Shirley pulled her hand away from her cheek and inspected the blood on the gauze. Flipping it over, she dabbed her cheek and inspected the volume of blood once more. A thin red line. The bleeding had eased so she placed the gauze onto the kitchen table. "See? Nothing to worry about, it's almost stopped bleeding and will heal in no time."

Elsie gave a half smile, bowed her head, her shoulders dropping.

CHAPTER SEVEN

Shirley sat on the couch next to Elsie. The pain in her cheek had subsided, she wanted to ease Elsie's concerns and distract her from her worries.

"Oh, before I forget, I wanted to let you know I'll be taking some staggered leave over the next seven weeks," Shirley said. "Head Office has instructed me to take it, so I decided it was best just to use two or three days every week so I can have long weekends. I can't go away, I have obligations. Jai is in school and to be honest, I would miss seeing you."

"Oh, that's lovely, my dear. I would miss you too." Elsie smiled.

"But I want you to know I'm going to continue my searching for Tinkerbell. I consider you both a part of my family."

"You are so kind. Thank you, my dear."

"It's my pleasure, Elsie, and I've asked that Robert be assigned to you while I'm away. Do you remember Robert? He filled in for me over the Christmas break last year."

"Yes." Elsie nodded, and turned to Shirley with a smile. "He's a lovely young man."

"I'm not sure if I told you, but he lives across the road from me. He lost his wife in a car accident." Shirley's voice softened. "The poor guy has been through so much, it's so sad... he's a wonderful loving guy, with so much to offer." Shirley shook her head then paused. Gazing into nothingness she smiled. "He gets on really well with Jai. I really like him."

Elsie leaned close and tapped Shirley on the knee. "And you would like to get to know him better?" She chuckled.

"I could think of worse things." Shirley blushed. "Doesn't everyone want a happily ever after?"

Elsie nodded. "Yes, everyone dreams of a happily ever after."

Shirley took Elsie's hand, and gazed into her sad eyes. "But I want you to be assured, I'm not giving up on Tinkerbell. I'll do everything I can to find her. I promise." Releasing Elsie's hand, she rose from the couch with a puzzled look on her face. "Have you searched inside the house?"

Elsie's eyes widened. "Oh no! I'm such a fool," she said almost apologetically, pressing her hands to her cheeks. "Maybe she's sleeping somewhere inside. I was in such a panic, the only thing I could think about was that wild animal in the bushes."

Gripping the edge of the couch Elsie groaned, as she attempted to stand.

"You sit and rest." Shirley reached out and grabbed the old woman's arm preventing her from standing. Elsie nodded and looked pensively towards her as she slumped back in her chair. Shirley followed, leaning forward she took Elsie's hand within hers. "I'll be back soon." She smiled, released her hold and disappeared into the hallway.

Upstairs the door to Elsie's bedroom was open. Shirley poked her head in. "Here, Tinkerbell. Where are you kitty?"

She stepped inside. There were so many places in which a cat could hide. Under the bed, she discovered dust-covered boxes – large and small. Leaning over the dresser, she peered into the darkness and inhaled years of mustiness.

She reached down, fingers covered in dust. Tiny particles filled the air, allergies stirred. Eyes itched. A long, sharp gasp was quickly followed by an explosive sneeze. Shirley flapped her hands and knocked Elsie's handbag to the floor, bits and pieces strewn all over the floor. Shirley scooped up the contents, shaking her head and wondering how much stuff could be shoved into one relatively small bag. Tissues, lipstick, a notepad, old shopping dockets, pens, a purse and a bank book.

I wonder how much money she has.

Looking over her shoulder she listened, everything appeared quiet. She stared at the purse.

Just a peek.

A hesitant glance over her shoulder; her head buzzed with possibilities as to how much money would be inside. A little pressure. The cool metal slid between her fingers. The purse latch clicked. Shirley's eyes widened. She couldn't believe the number of fifty-dollar notes stashed within the gold satin lining.

Oh wow!

Snapping the latch closed, she threw Elsie's purse back into her bag.

Oh my! The woman is loaded.

She thought nervously about her next move. Her hands shook as her fingers spread over the course-textured bankbook. The yellow cover screamed at her to be opened. Another quick glimpse over her shoulder. Stomach knotted. Heart pounding. *Now or never*. Her breathing was rapid and shallow. Silence lingered. If she didn't look, she would never know. If she never knew, she would always wonder. Nervousness changed to excitement as she flicked the pages. Shirley gasped. Her eyes popped wide.

Oh my gosh!

She threw the bankbook into the handbag, placed it onto the dressing table and left the bedroom. Had she read the figures correctly? She was not game to take another look.

Oh, my goodness. Oh wow. I hope she doesn't notice. Oh wow, she has a fortune.

Closing the door behind her, Shirley continued her search. "Tinkerbell, here kitty… Come on, Tinkerbell."

A hurried walk through the other rooms, but Tinkerbell was nowhere to be found. She returned downstairs.

Elsie straightened on the couch, and Shirley frowned and shook her head. Elsie's body slumped.

"I looked everywhere. In all the possible hidey-holes. I'm sorry Elsie… I can't find her." Shirley placed her hands on her hips and rocked slightly from side to side. "But I'm not giving up. I'll make flyers. I'll post them around the neighbourhood. Someone will know something. We'll find her. I promise."

Elsie nodded as tears appeared in the corner of her eyes; she bowed her head and slumped back into the couch.

"Oh, and I need to apologise," Shirley said. "I had a small incident upstairs… when I was looking behind your dresser. I accidentally knocked your handbag to the floor. It was open so everything fell out. I picked it all up and put it back in your bag, I just thought I'd let you know. I didn't want you to think I was up there snooping."

Elsie nodded and gave a half smile. "Thank you, my dear. I don't know what I would do without you."

CHAPTER EIGHT

Robert flicked his hands and wiped his sweaty palms down his pants as he walked into the room. Strangers stared. Robert paused. His heart pounded in his chest so loudly he feared others would hear. Sweat covered his brow and the urge to vomit rose deep from within his gut. Invisible hands wrapped around his throat. Tugging at his tie he struggled for breath.

What the hell am I doing?

He feared large crowds and was terrified of speaking in public.

Fold-up wooden chairs sat arranged in a circle in the centre of the room. A few people stood talking, sipping on cups of tea and coffee in the far corner. Curious eyes turned to him. Doubt scratched his mind.

Maybe I should just turn around and go home.

Out of luck. He'd been spotted. A woman waved. Trapped. He'd thought too long, moved too slow, and now it was too late to turn and run.

The woman approached with a welcoming smile. "Hi, you must be Robert," she said, extending her hand in greeting. "My name is Veronica. Would you like to grab a tea or coffee?"

Nodding politely, Robert followed her to the corner where the others stood chatting. Male and female, young and old, some appeared sad, others too difficult to read.

THE BELONGING

Blank expressions made it impossible to gauge their feelings. Robert swallowed nervously. Maybe, he shouldn't have come. Maybe the whole exercise would prove a waste of time.

Before he had a chance to make a quiet exit, an older lady approached. "How are you doing? We'll get started shortly."

Robert placed his cup on the table and turned towards Veronica. "I don't think I can do this. This really isn't me." He looked to the exit then turned back to her. "I think I might go."

His pace was quick as he walked towards the door, yet he didn't want to appear fearful. Once outside, he grabbed the railing and sucked in a lungful of air.

"Robert," a voice called. He turned to find Veronica at the door. The woman was persistent. "It's always scary the first time. The first meeting is always the hardest. I know, I've been there myself. You don't have to speak, no one will force you to do anything you don't want to."

Robert stared at Veronica's inscrutable smile. She had caring eyes, but was she telling the truth? Would he feel pressured into speaking? His stomach churned as he raked his fingers through his hair. "Five minutes, I'll give it five minutes."

Veronica nodded. "You will be fine."

As he followed her inside, Robert wondered if he had made a mistake.

CHAPTER NINE

The circle of people sat quietly. Robert fidgeted on his chair and nervously scanned the faces of those next to him. Turning his attention to Veronica he was overcome by a profound feeling of recognition. An instant chill. Robert shuddered. Had they met before? For a moment he thought they had. She appeared familiar.

Impossible.

Robert rubbed his stubbled face and returned his focus to the floor as Veronica's words played over in his mind.

The first meeting is always the hardest.

"Okay, I think we should get this meeting started," an older lady with grey hair announced. "First of all, I would like to welcome our new member." She paused and looked around the circle with a smile. Robert could feel the heat of his face flushing pink, but remained still. The woman continued. "This is a grief support group, so anyone who is here for the AA meeting, well I'm sorry, but you may have taken a wrong turn." She chuckled and a couple shared in her joke.

Robert sat quietly contemplating his next move, glancing at the other people. Six, there were six of them in total. Six lives shattered by grief. How many more people suffered in silence? He wondered what loss his fellow support members had experienced. One by one, he imagined their stories. The older lady with the grey hair; Maria had probably lost her husband. Next to Maria sat Amanda, she appeared youthful and a little shy with her face partly hidden by her long, curly brown hair. Amanda appeared scared and had probably lost a grandparent.

A spare chair separated Amanda from Veronica, who was slim, attractive and possibly in her mid-to-late-thirties. She sat twirling a wedding ring. Veronica would have to have lost a parent or possibly a grandparent. Then came Steve, young and loud, wearing colourful clothes. Steve appeared an adrenaline junkie, passionate about life – a tall, athletic, and an outgoing-type who talked about base-jumping. Steve would have to have lost a mate while participating in an extreme sport. Another spare chair and lastly there was Walter, who sat quietly looking at the floor as if he didn't want to be there. There was no way to guess whom Walter had lost.

One by one, they introduced themselves. One by one, Robert's imaginary storylines were proven wrong. Maria had lost her husband, that assumption was correct. Young Amanda had a good reason to feel alone and scared; she'd had a miscarriage. Her parents were devout Catholics and no one knew the married man who lived next door had impregnated her.

Veronica had lost her husband to suicide. Steve had lost his beloved granny. And finally, the most shocking story was from Walter. Walter had lost a work mate. The poor guy never stood a chance against a two-tonne slab of concrete. Walter had witnessed the tragedy. The poor guy trembled when he spoke.

Grief was one of the most difficult challenges of life. Listening to their stories provided support and comfort. While the stories were different, the emotions were alike. Robert felt a sense of security and acceptance come over him. Sadness and loss linked them.

Maria's gentle voice interrupted his thoughts. "Robert,

would you like to speak?"

Biting his bottom lip, Robert studied their faces. Everyone had been willing to share their stories. Some had shed tears. All of them had concluded talking looking less burdened. It was a support group.

A problem shared is a problem halved.

Robert nodded. "Yes. I believe I will."

As he looked around the room, he wondered where he should begin. He cleared his throat and raked his fingers through his hair.

"I'm having a real hard time at the moment." His voice shook. He paused, chewed his bottom lip, and looked around the room. Everyone was silent. Robert rubbed his hand over his forehead then tugged at his shirt collar. "I have nothing to offer, like I'm being punished. I feel so lost, despaired, and yet full of questions. I'm so desperate to understand why this has happened, but there's no way to fulfil the answers. I'm told she was in the wrong place, at the wrong time. It was an accident. It was her fate, a tragedy outside of her control, predetermined by a supernatural power. What is fate then, but a cruel affliction?"

Robert paused again. He hated that his voice trembled.

Everyone will think I'm weak. A man shouldn't stumble and stutter.

Warmth rose within his body as he raked his hand through his hair again, attempting to regain composure. Looking around the room, he noticed Veronica with tears in her eyes. Walter wiped his nose.

"I'm sorry, I don't think I can do this." Running his hand down his face, he took a deep breath and exhaled. "All I know is my world and reason for existence has been shifted in an irreparable way. I don't belong, and to be perfectly truthful the only time I ever felt I belonged was with, was with…" His voice cracked. "I'm sorry. I'm not ready. I can't say her name. It's… I just can't."

THE BELONGING

Maria jumped to her feet. "Okay everyone, I think we'll have a five-minute break and when we return, we can talk about some coping strategies."

Robert bowed his head and breathed a sigh of relief.

CHAPTER TEN

Veronica wandered to the coffee machine, and Amanda glared across the room – her normal calm and pleasant demeanour disappeared behind narrowed eyes. Within seconds she was behind Veronica and had reefed at the woman's arm.

Veronica spun and pulled free from Amanda's grasp. "What the heck!"

"You need to tell him!" Amanda's finger hovered within inches of Veronica's face.

Veronica pushed Amanda to the side and scanned the room, Robert was nowhere to be seen. Only Maria remained seated in the circle of chairs and was oblivious to their confrontation. "I'll tell him, just not now."

Amanda's face reddened. "You tell him or I will." She stormed back to her chair.

Veronica straightened her blouse and sipped on her coffee. There was no way a young, uppity girl would tell her what to do.

How dare she threaten me. What a cow.

Veronica's eyes bored into Amanda's. The stare down began, but from the corner of her eye, she noticed Robert and Walter appear from the bathroom. They were chatting with Steve, who was standing near the front door. Maria sat quietly looking over a stack of paperwork. No one had a clue about the heated exchange.

Amanda shook her head.

Veronica returned a fierce look; she was determined not to be outdone by a little upstart. The staring continued. Maria finished arranging her paperwork as the guys approached the chairs. All were unaware of the tension.

Amanda sighed loudly, shook her head once more then lowered her eyes. Veronica smiled and placed her empty cup on the bench. Straightening her blouse again, she stood with her chin held high. She'd won.

Returning to her seat, she was pleased with herself. Amanda looked at Robert, shook her head then glared at Veronica.

Veronica's satisfied grin told Amanda all she needed to know – she had no intention of opening her mouth.

***

Maria led the discussions about coping mechanisms, and Amanda stared at the ceiling. Veronica remained silent, twirling her wedding ring. Robert surveyed the room, Amanda's staring left him puzzled, and he anchored his attention on her. When she turned towards Veronica, she appeared annoyed. Her eyes narrowed to crinkled slits forming an intense gaze. Her hands closed into fists as she leaned forward. Silently she mouthed the words, 'tell him'.

Robert wondered what he'd missed and if he'd read her lips correctly. Who was Amanda referring to? Why was she so annoyed? Everyone appeared okay before he went to the bathroom during the break. No one had mentioned any argument. Their exchange was over. Veronica turned her back on Amanda and focused on Maria, who continued to speak.

Maria's strategies were interesting. Steve sat listening and taking notes. Walter continually nodded, but never said a word. Amanda stared into nothingness while Veronica offered the occasional reassuring smile.

Time appeared to fly.

Maria placed her papers on the floor. "Well I guess that will conclude our session for tonight. Thank you everyone and I hope to see you next month."

Amanda snapped before anyone had a chance to move. "Can we have a minute of your time. Veronica has something she needs to say."

CHAPTER ELEVEN

Veronica's face reddened. She despised being put on the spot. "Sorry, yes… um, before everyone goes, I just wanted to remind you the purpose of our group is to offer a support network. For anyone struggling with grief…" She paused, glancing at Amanda who sat with her head bowed, then gave Robert a half smile. "Please feel free to talk and share your stories. Create a network with others who have had similar struggles. Life can be hard and, at times, cruel. I know talking about our problems really helps." She paused again, clasping her hands, she twirled her wedding ring. Tears shimmered within her eyes as she looked towards Robert. She gave a slight nod. "So, let's talk and help each other without judgement, while we can all be assured everything said in this group stays in this group. Our conversations or ranting, whatever it may be remain confidential. We all have a story to tell and I am always here to listen. Thank you and have a great evening."

Everyone, but Amanda clapped. Steve rose from his chair and stretched. The meeting was over.

Veronica sauntered over to Robert. "I hope you found our meeting helpful and my last comments offered you reassurance," she said, curling her hair around her finger. "We want members of our group to feel safe and secure that they can say anything without repercussions."

Robert edged towards the door. "I did, I do and thank

you."

"So, we'll see you next month?"

"Next month, yes… well I'd better be off. I'll see you then."

"I look forward to it." Veronica smiled as Robert disappeared through the front door.

Returning to the centre of the room, Veronica began to fold the chairs and stack them next to the wall. She was pleased with her evening.

"I want a word with you!"

Veronica jumped and spun to the raised voice. Amanda stood near the front door with her hands on her hips.

"You said you would tell him."

Veronica looked around nervously. They were alone. Amanda strode over. Veronica couldn't believe the girl had the audacity to talk back. She was like a yapping little dog who wouldn't go away.

"I did and I will." Veronica straightened and stood her ground. "I'm not talking about this anymore."

Amanda shook her head, her eyes widened as she leaned closer. "Well you had better because if you don't tell him, I will."

Her words, though whispered, were unmistakably threatening. She threw her bag over her shoulder and stormed out.

Veronica stood fuming, twirling her wedding ring.

CHAPTER TWELVE

Robert released a sigh as he walked into his house and threw his keys onto the entry table. He kicked off his boots then headed straight for the answering machine. Nervous energy twitched from within as he spotted the red flashing light. Pressing the button, he stood still, hands on hips.

"You have three new messages," the robotic voice announced.

"Message received today at nine fifteen AM."

The first message played: "Hi Robert, I hope you get this message. My name is Veronica. I just wanted to let you know I'm looking forward to seeing you tonight. I hope you'll be there."

Robert smiled as he recalled how Veronica had made him feel reassured during therapy.

"Message received today at eight twenty-nine PM."

The second message played: "Elsie here, dear. I was given your number. Shirley tells me you will be here tomorrow. Could you be a dear and pick up some paper towels? Thank you, dear. See you then."

"Message received today at nine thirty-three PM."

The third message played: "Hi Robert, it's Veronica, I hope you are okay. You did well tonight. I just wanted to check you made it home safely. Talk soon and take care."

Next on his machine, "You have one saved message."

Closing his eyes, he dropped to his couch. He knew the message well. He had listened to it a hundred times before. It always started with a cute giggle. "Hello baby, I can't wait to see you… I have some exciting news. Anyway, you know what to do. I'll see you soon. Love you, baby. Toodle-pip." And that was when it ended, they were Julie's last words. Her excitement and happiness clashed with his despair.

Robert had failed in his promise. He hadn't protected her like he said he would. It was because of his failing she never got the chance to share her amazing news. It was his fault. His sobs echoed around the room and he dropped his head to his hands.

Within grief therapy they talked about writing letters to those you had lost. The idea sounded ridiculous, but anything was worth a try. Robert knew there would be no forgetting. But if there were a chance to reduce the pain, it would be worth the effort. Taking a deep breath, he wiped his eyes and rose from the couch.

With pen and paper before him, Robert tapped his fingers on the table. There was so much he wanted to say, but where to start…

CHAPTER THIRTEEN

My dearest Julie,

Where do I start? If I asked you, I'm sure you would say at the beginning, so I will try my best. I want to tell you, I love you. I want you to know I will always love you. You are always on my mind and in my heart.

As I sit here with pen in hand, a million things tumble through my mind. It's been five months, three weeks, five days and fifteen hours. Please forgive me. Everything is a horrible soul-destroying nightmare and I don't want to be a part of it. I have no desire for the future. I want to go back, but I fear my emptiness is never-ending.

I miss you so much. We shared everything. Your dreams were my dreams. My dreams were our dreams. We lived with love and for love. Our belief was all people deserved dignity, respect, and love. Helping those less fortunate and cherishing moments was an obligation we thought everyone should embrace. With you, life had direction. Our dream was to one day open a café that would welcome those who experienced hardship and loneliness. It would be a safe haven where any person could feel they belonged. We knew it was a big dream, but it was ours. We were going to conquer the world. Without you it feels delusional, unattainable. I wish I could hold on to our dream and realise our vision, but I'm afraid I'm struggling. My dearest Julie, I'm struggling to simply survive, for without you there remains emptiness.

A dark space between memories and thoughts. And there's nothing I can do. You're gone. I'm lost. I don't know who I am any more.

I just came home from group therapy. I know you are probably shaking your head. I bet you never imagined me as a therapy sort of guy. The truth is, I feel like I'm drowning, like I'm a puzzle with missing pieces for you are no longer here. Oh, my sweet, sweet Julie, I miss you so much. Earlier, I sat in my car and screamed repeatedly. I screamed like I've screamed many times since you died. My throat was raw, but nothing compares to my heartache. I feel like I'm being punished. I don't want to be here. I don't want to live in a world where I don't belong. My yearning for you is merciless. My pain from missing you is insufferable. My desire to have you here is unimaginable. I listen to your voice every day. You say, "you know what to do." But the truth is, I don't know. Without you I'm lost. I feel I have no place in life. Without you there is no belonging.

I love you so much, Julie. I loved you from the first moment I saw you. I miss you every second of every day. I long to be with you. I would give anything to have you back, for living without you is impossible. At night I pray I may not see daylight. Just let me sleep forever. But in the morning my nightmare continues, for I wake and you are not here. I'm so sorry. It should've been me. I'm so sorry I broke my promise to you. I swore I'd protect you, and I failed miserably. I hope you can forgive me, for I don't know if I will ever forgive myself. Please know I love you with every sense of my being, and I'll love you and miss you until we meet again...

Love always and forever,
Robert

Staggered breath ransacked the silence as Robert stared blindly towards his confession. Trembling fingers released the pen. Eyes, puffy and hollow. Overflowing

THE BELONGING

sadness seeped from his nose. Ink stretched and blurred from tears. Unrelenting grief delivered in crashing waves. A slight reprieve, he sucked in air, gasping. Heaviness swirled. Memories stirred. Painful reality hit hard.

Catch it; catch it now, for without warning my breath will be stolen by heartache.

The endless cycle of darkness continued until finally there was exhaustion.

He removed a tissue from his pocket and attempted to pat dry his smudged words. Folding the letter, he placed it in an envelope before sealing it with a kiss.

For now, the tears had gone. All he could do was hope his misery would ease. With time and effort, he would begin to live again. And one day, it might be possible to dream once more.

CHAPTER FOURTEEN

Morning delivered scorching sun and high humidity. Enticing radiance, the shade of a frangipani tree. Robert stood transfixed, lost in emotion, mesmerised by the carpet of butter lemon and rich cream. Surrounded by a familiar scent, he closed his eyes and inhaled the Hawaiian essence of peach and pineapple. A slight breeze. Gentle warmth kissed his cheek. A faint whisper. A delicate hug, instant relief and soothing comfort. Reminiscent words, traces of her voice, *'my gorgeous man, the complete professional package.'*

Then silence.

Tingling rushed through Robert's body. His eyes sprang open. Dazzling sparks and intense glare. Running the palms of his hands over his eyes he glanced again. Tiny red orbs invaded. Blazing orange energy flashed, like thousands of glowing fireflies. He blinked, squeezing his eyes closed. A cold shiver; his body covered in goosebumps.

He opened his eyes. Spinning around, he tugged at his earlobe. He was alone, yet Julie's words played over in his mind. His chest rose and fell rapidly. Staunch determination returned. Robert inspected his nails, tucked in his shirt and straightened his tie. It was time to get to work. He would be every bit the professional package Julie said he was. Opening the gate, he stepped inside.

I can do this.

THE BELONGING

Purposeful steps propelled him forward. Thirty paces in, things changed. Overgrown bushes encroached on the cracked and uneven path forcing him to slow. His stomach churned. Doubt rose to his throat. Bitterness lashed his tongue. Robert swallowed hard, his mouth void of moisture.

Oh God, can I do this?

Had he made the right decision? Gone was the warmth of the morning sun. The air damp smelling and cooler within the shadows of the giant structure before him. His stomach flipped as he peered upward, his eyes following the giant pillars. He stopped, staring intently, as if the answers to his questions would suddenly appear.

Silence.

He wanted to move forward yet grief clung tight, unrelenting sadness restricted and dragged him into the shadows of blackness. Wiping sweat from his brow, he clutched his aching chest and thought about what he had, what he'd lost, and what life meant.

Robert had been the sole beneficiary to Julie's estate. In financial terms he was a rich man who never needed to work, yet he would give it all back ten times over just to have Julie with him. Money didn't buy happiness.

Am I doing the right thing?

He edged forward. Paused. Edged forward again. He had to try. Trudging up the pathway he thought of Shirley, maybe he shouldn't have agreed to taking on her shifts. Sure, it was the right thing to do. But was he ready? Would he look the fool if he burst into tears for no apparent reason? Shirley was a great friend; they'd known each other for years. She'd also been a close friend to Julie. Both women were of similar age, height and size, their hair colour the same shade of deep chestnut-brown. The only difference, Shirley's hair flowed half way down her back, while Julie's had sat to her shoulders. Because of this uncanny resemblance some people had believed them sisters.

Dissimilar personalities and conflicting beliefs added depth and greater understanding to their friendship, their closeness reflected within Shirley's devastation when she found out Julie had died. Through it all, Shirley's friendship remained steadfast. Without her by his side, Robert couldn't imagine how he would have survived. She'd assisted with funeral arrangements, together they'd selected Julie's coffin, ordered flowers, spoken to the celebrant and the funeral home. There had been so many moments where Robert had been on the brink of collapse and there Shirley was, offering kind words, handing over tissues, delivering meals.

She'd been his shoulder to cry on, his constant support. She was a true friend; she shared, cared and understood. She had even gone to the solicitors with him; both had been left in shock. Julie had left behind a healthy bank balance, share investments, superannuation and a life insurance policy.

Robert was sitting on a fortune, but he couldn't care less. He wanted no part of it. What joy was there in spending death money? In his mind, working hard was how one built wealth. He had to work. Working would distract. Working would pay his bills, provide a sense of achievement and pride.

At last, he was at the door. Straightening his tie again, he took a deep breath and pressed the doorbell. Waiting in silence felt like an eternity. At the community care centre, Elsie Graham was referred to as nothing more than a cranky, old, demanding duck. Robert smiled, wondering if she would greet him with a 'quack quack'.

Nerves began to build. Robert studied the monstrous door before him. It resembled something from medieval times, like a portal to another world arched at the top. Its solid panelling was painted black, the bottom peeling and dull, blistering with years of water damage. He wondered how many people would have passed through such a door. Elsie Graham lived in an old mansion. Placing his ear against the rough timber, he listened for any noise. He heard a painful groan and shuffling feet. This was his time to summon strength and take a giant leap of courage. In his mourning he had felt selfish. No one else had mattered; it was time to put someone else's needs before his own.

His hands trembled.

His heart raced.

Soon he would come face-to-face with Elsie Graham.

The latch clicked. The heavy wooden door creaked open.

Lingering unease filled his body.

A puffing Elsie Graham stood before him looking frailer than the last time they'd met. Her face made up with discreet powder, a hint of rouge highlighting her cheeks, her fine lips encircled with cherry red lipstick. She couldn't have been more than five feet tall. Her legs and arms appeared withered.

"Good morning," she said, extending her hand. "Sorry for taking so long, you are —"

"I'm Robert," he said, shaking her hand with enthusiasm.

"I was going to say you are early, young man."

"Yes, yes, I am, Mrs Graham. My apologies, I thought you were asking my name." He shifted from one foot to the other.

"I'm aware of who you are, we have met before." The old woman rolled her eyes and took a step back. "My body may be failing, but I have not lost my mind. I do remember you," she said. "And shall I remind you, Mrs Graham was my mother. You can call me Elsie."

Bowing his head, Robert swallowed nervously; he didn't want to get off on the wrong foot. Elsie Graham possessed a regal countenance and spoke with precise diction, carefully pronouncing each syllable. Her clipped and slightly posh accent made Robert feel like he was talking with the queen. She was like no other woman he had ever met. He admired her old-fashioned ways, but quickly recalled how with the use of words she could motivate and inspire hopes and dreams or bring things to a sudden halt.

Shifting his weight to the other foot, he looked to her and smiled. "I see you're still a keen gardener by the soil beneath your nails."

Elsie pulled her hand away and glared. "As I said, you are early. I certainly do not make a habit of walking around unbathed. I may be frail, Robert, but I am far from stupid." She paused and looked beyond him. "Did you see Tinkerbell? Have you got my paper towels?"

Robert tugged on the straps of his backpack. "No, I didn't see Tinkerbell, but I do have your paper towels."

"Well come on then, follow me, boy. I need to tend to my responsibilities." She turned, motioning for him to follow.

Robert stepped inside, closed the door and watched Elsie's shuffling gait. In the fourteen months since he had last seen her, she had changed, deteriorated. Gone were her bold arm movements, she was slower, stiffer, her head stooped while her shoulders slumped. Halfway along the hall, Elsie grumbled something. Robert continued in silence.

When he turned into the kitchen, he stopped.

Oh God, distraction. Let's plunge into Ground Hog day.

At first glance nothing had changed. It was like stepping into the nineteen-sixties. Standing with his hands on his hips, he watched Elsie totter over to the sink and wash her hands. That's when he realised, nothing had changed, but everything was different. Tears filled his eyes. Elsie moaned as she made her way to the oven. Robert's heart broke. Did she not see the checkerboard linoleum cloaked in dirt and grime curled at the edges? Was she unfazed by her turquoise cabinets covered with food slops and dribbles? Last time things were dated but organised and clean. Was she unaware

THE BELONGING

her world was falling apart? Pots and pans advanced from the stove, invading the counter, a spread of cracking cream laminate blanketed in tea stains and crumbs.

Robert's attention was drawn to the *piece de resistance* of the battle zone; a large saucepan-sized scorch mark to the right of the stove. Further afield, he noticed another change. The small wooden table for four had been relocated. It was now squeezed into the far corner. Two of the chairs were wedged between the table and wall making them inaccessible. Gouges in the wall behind indicated they had been moved in great haste or with little care. Sitting at the table would provide a direct view out the back door into the garden. It was a practical change. With a gentle cross-breeze it would be the perfect location on a hot day, especially in the afternoon when the rear of the house was sheltered by shade.

Robert wiped tears from his eyes then crossed his arms. Looking to the side, he tapped his foot and wondered what Shirley had been doing. Surely, the mess hadn't appeared in a couple of days. Everything would need a good clean.

For now, he would cast his annoyance to the side. Closing his eyes, he focused on his breath and listened to Elsie, his job was not to criticise clients but to assist. The woman was obviously doing her best. As for Shirley, he would deal with her when they next met.

Pots clanged and cupboards slammed. Was the woman going deaf? Robert opened his eyes and wiped the stream of sadness from his cheeks. The smallest of things reminded him of Julie. This time it was the clanging of pots. Julie had been the cook in their house and Robert had watched her prepare countless meals. They had laughed and joked together while she had chopped and peeled, stirred and served wonderful creations. Watching Elsie and inhaling the sweet aroma of apple pie and cinnamon brought back wonderful memories. Robert sniffed then sighed as he looked around the kitchen.

Pull yourself together.

"Can I do anything to help?" he asked, straightening his stance.

"You could make us a cup of tea and join me for a piece of pie."

"I can do that. You take a seat while I make the tea."

Robert rushed over to the sink, dampened a cloth and began to organise and clean the counter. Reaching into the cupboard, he grabbed the cups and saucers making sure they were clean. Elsie shuffled over to the table and leaned back, arms folded. Peering over the rim of her reading glasses, she watched as Robert placed the teabags into the cups.

"Have you grown taller or I'm just shrinking?"

Robert spun around, teaspoon in hand and laughed. "I don't know if you're shrinking, you came up to my shoulders last time I was here, and I'm still about one-eighty or just under six feet. It's probably my crazy curls. This humidity makes my hair a messy mop. I wish I had straight hair like you." He smiled and tapped the teaspoon into the palm of his hand.

"Oh no, your hair is a beautiful shimmery brown... and the waves... I remember..." She shook her head, tears rising. "I wish I had waves, better than stick straight grey."

"Oh, come on, you have an air of distinction. I think grey hair makes a person look stately." He smiled then turned back to the counter and began stacking the dirty dishes into the sink.

Elsie laughed. "An air of distinction? Stately? Oh, Robert, I'll take all the compliments. But old is old, shrinking is shrinking, and falling apart is falling apart. Today, I feel all three. I feel like I have one foot in the grave."

Robert stopped what he was doing and swept the floor with his foot. Death was a subject he wanted to avoid. Fortunately, the kettle clicked.

"Two sugars?"

"Yes, thank you. And will you have some pie too?"

"Thanks, that would be lovely."

Insisting she serve the pie, Elsie released a loud moan as she stood. Robert finished making the tea and took the cups to the table while she removed a dish from the oven and placed it on the sink. She cut her baked treat into segments, and handed Robert a plate. Seeing the steam rise and smelling the sweet mouth-watering aroma made his eyes light up.

"Thank you, thank you so much."

At the table, Elsie sipped her tea while Robert dug into the pie. The buttery base cracked beneath his spoon. He blew on the steamy contents to cool it then shovelled the sweet pie into his mouth.

"Oh wow! This is delicious, this is really delicious."

Elsie ate at a slower pace. The serving sizes had been the same, yet she had more than half left by the time Robert scraped his plate clean.

"You must have been hungry, young man."

Robert's face reddened in embarrassment. "Oh, please forgive my rudeness Miss... er, Elsie." He paused for a moment and placed his hand to his mouth releasing a loud burp. "Oh my. I'm so sorry. I do apologise."

Elsie laughed. "Another piece?"

"Another piece would be wonderful. I didn't realise how hungry I was. Please forgive me, it seems I left my manners at home this morning, along with my brain."

Elsie served another piece. Robert thanked her again and took his time eating before ushering Elsie out of the room so he could clean. Sharing the kitchen with someone had been nice. Maybe the day would be better than expected.

CHAPTER FIFTEEN

With the washing done and a shopping list prepared, Elsie and Robert sat in the lounge room to rest. It was the perfect opportunity for Elsie to talk about what had been happening since they'd last seen each other. Elsie offered Robert her condolences, while Robert reassured her everything would be fine with her missing Tinkerbell. It was the first time he'd had a conversation with anyone since Julie's passing where issues other than his own became the focal point. Elsie appeared to understand, and unlike others she didn't expect he should just move on and leave the past behind without a second thought.

"You can only do what you can do," she said. "Never feel you have to force yourself forward. Just take things slow, one second, one minute, one hour, one day. You'll get through it. The pain will ease. You just need to allow yourself time. I know you may feel like your world has stopped, shutting down and clamming up is easy, but life is continuing, Robert. People care and understand your pain. I know Shirley cares, her eyes light up when she speaks of you. I see the pain on her face when she talks about your loss. I feel the love in her words when she talks about wanting to see you happy."

Robert nodded. "She's a good friend."

Elsie looked at Robert with a grin then chuckled. "Sometimes you men fail to see what is clearly in front of you." She paused shaking her head. "I suspect she feels more than friendship young man, much more..."

Robert's cheeks flushed and he quickly stood. "Would you like a cup of tea, Elsie?"

"Oh, that would be lovely, young man. I must say I am a tad parched with all this talking."

Robert smiled. "I'll be right back."

In the kitchen, he flicked the kettle on and retrieved the cups and saucers, all the while thinking about what Elsie had said.

Did she know more than she was letting on? He'd never thought of Shirley in a romantic sense. Was he ready for a new relationship so soon after losing Julie? And with Shirley...

CHAPTER SIXTEEN

Robert arrived home pleased with his day. Returning to work and focusing on Elsie had afforded him time in which he'd been able to put his grief to one side. While Julie still shadowed his every thought, he'd managed to talk about her without bursting into tears. Elsie appeared well grounded; she had experienced the good and bad in life and come through it well. Her words of wisdom offered hope. Robert would return in two days, in the meantime he wanted a release. He needed to let Julie know what was happening and how he was feeling. Writing helped.

My dearest Julie,

It's been six months... six months to the day and not a moment goes by without you in my thoughts. I tried everything I could to avoid thinking about it, but nothing worked. It feels so much longer and yet it feels like only yesterday. If only things were different. I can't stop thinking about what might have been. I struggle greatly in this new life without you. Sleep eluded me something severe last night. I wish you were here to hold. I wish I could wrap my arms around you and inhale your beautiful sweetness. To be able to look at you and smile, to feel your warmth and loving touch.

Instead, I am the man who smiles at strangers and

pretends all is okay, but weeps alone. I look at photos of you and cry. I light candles in your honour and in the quietness of our bedroom, I grieve. I am the weak and empty man who sobs in the shower so nobody can see or hear. My dearest Julie, I don't know what to do. Life holds no joy; I'm simply surviving for I miss you so, so much.

I'm afraid my words may not encapsulate a vibrant enough image of you, my love. For you were my one true love, you embodied open-hearted kindness, you treated everyone as you found them, happy to give any person an opportunity, a helping hand, a lift up, you were the champion to the underdog. You never passed a homeless person without giving money. You would insist we stop and offer a ride to those older if it were raining, even if it took us out of our way. Your intentions were always towards goodness and honesty, acceptance and kindness. You taught me so many valuable lessons. You taught me that integrity should never be compromised. You taught me caring does not mean we care only when you feel like it, or when you can. We should never stop caring, even when it hurts.

When I held your hand, I felt your love. You made me feel anything was possible. Did you know my love? I wish I had told you more.

It doesn't matter where I am or what I'm doing; you are with me always. I think of all your wonderful qualities. I strive to be like you, to make you proud. I've tried to adopt your positive attitude, but I fear I'm failing in every sense.

With your loss I have experienced a feeling of isolation. I can't believe how many of my friends disappeared, I guess it's because they were uncomfortable or they did not know what or when was appropriate. Maybe they are afraid of facing death; they're scared of it happening to them and those they love. So, it is easier for them to stay away. To talk about death is to think about it, to think about death means we have to acknowledge that death comes to us all.

But not everyone has disappeared. Shirley has been amazing, a guiding light who has stood beside me. She acknowledges the hole in my life and understands my grief cannot be fixed or forgotten. I don't know what I would have done without her. Sometimes she just sits in the room with me, she's been there and witnessed my pain, tears, and emotional outbursts, never judging. Not once has she pushed me to do anything. I am so grateful for all she has done to make the worst days of my life bearable. I am thankful for her support, encouragement and friendship. I know should I need or want anything she is there. I know she misses you too.

I've thrown myself into work, trying to distract my thoughts. But distraction is only temporary. On a positive note, I've met a lovely lady. Now, now don't get the wrong idea. She's an older woman, and wise. In fact, she is old enough to be my mother. She has lived and she has lost. I find great comfort in our conversations. Elsie Graham, do you remember her? She came up in conversation about fourteen months ago. I didn't want to take on the work, as Shirley had told me how grumpy she was. We had spoken about her at great lengths, I wanted to be assigned to Mr Osborne, who I had cared for previously, but you insisted I put my concerns aside and help a woman in need.

She had been diagnosed with post-polio syndrome. I'm sure you should remember. Anyway, she's a lovely lady with a harsh attitude. Sounds a bit like the Queen. I think she puts on a show of strength because she knows her body is failing physically. There's something strange about her. I don't know why I feel a connection. Maybe it's because of the stories she shares; maybe it's because my emotional struggles resemble her physical ones. I don't know, but I'm glad we've met. She's down-to-earth, matter-of-fact and frank, and a 'real' person. There is nothing false about her and that's what I think I like. She says what she means and means what she says.

Being around her reminds me that as we get older, we reluctantly have to accept that our contemporaries may not stay with us as long as we would like them to. I am learning that life becomes more precious every day and we must be grateful for those we love. I hope you know how grateful I was to have you in my life. I hope you know how much I love you. I will always love you and I miss you with every fibre of my being. Until we meet again...

Love always and forever,
Robert

CHAPTER SEVENTEEN

The two days off work flew by. Robert managed to catch up with Shirley and even accepted a dinner invitation with her and Jai. Great neighbours were hard to come by. Ultimately, he decided it best not to confront her about the mess at Elsie's. He didn't like confrontation. He'd been lucky when Shirley and Jai moved in across the road. Jai reminded him of himself when he was younger. Talkative and wanting to please.

When Robert was a child, he wondered what it would be like to have family, real family. Although Jai had his mother, Robert wondered if the boy missed the presence of a dad. Did Jai wish for brothers and sisters, aunts and uncles plus cousins and grandparents just as Robert had done when growing up? He wanted to ask the boy but feared upsetting him; instead, he vowed to look after him. He would be the strong and supportive male role model a young boy needed. In every child there was an innocence that required protecting, Robert would be that protection.

The alarm went off before the sun appeared, and for Robert it had been another restless night.

Unbearable humidity crushed beneath shadowy darkness. Claps of thunder rumbled in the distance and lightning speared through the gloom. Robert cast his eyes to the sapphire sky as he dashed along the pathway. Swirling clouds had devoured light and blistering heat. Something had to give. Sheltering within the entrance of the front door, he glanced at his watch. Five minutes, he was five minutes early.

Dust danced as the wind picked up. Blinding particles attacked his eyes. Large raindrops teased, slow to start. Intensity snapped. Robert retreated closer to the door as the wind unleashed. Howling screams tore leaves from branches, limbs ripped from trees. More thunder. Louder. Closer. Jagged flashes lit the darkened sky. Rumbling shook the ground. Five minutes, in five minutes there would be no escape.

Air thick with heat created unsightly sweat beneath his arms. Robert plucked at his shirt, sniffed his underarm. A mix of cinnamon and vanilla burst through his damp shirt – his Old Spice was working well.

It was imperative he arrived on time and look presentable. A moment of silence then the sky rumbled again. Large drops beat against the pavement, heavier and heavier. Another boom of thunder, lightning lit up the sky. Torrential rain.

Thank God I came early.

A wall of water spilled over the top of Elsie's gutters, gurgled through her downpipes and gushed rivers that ran along her pathway. Robert would wait no more.

Adjusting his tie, he pushed the doorbell.

She can take me as I am or find someone else.

Within seconds the timber door swung open. Roaring wind slammed it against the wall. Elsie stumbled backwards as fallen leaves and driving rain chased Robert inside.

"Did you see her?" she screeched above the chaos, her eyes squinting as she frantically pushed past. "Did you see her?"

Thunder crashed. Driving rain hit Elsie, eyes squinting as she scurried out onto her pathway.

The woman's lost her mind.

A close flash of lightning, another loud clap. Robert dashed into the deluge and lunged for Elsie's arm. Jagged bolts ripped through the darkened sky; his fingers fumbled as his eyes scanned, a loud cracking noise filled his ears.

"Get inside," he screamed, snatching at her cardigan through the inescapable wetness. Reefing her arm, he dragged her back inside and slammed the door. Water pooled on the timber floorboards, gasping breath filled the air. Both were soaked.

"Look at you! You're drenched." Robert shook his head. "What were you thinking?"

Elsie stared with flattened hair and wiped her face. "My baby." She paused. Trembling hands danced in front of her lips. "Did you see her? She must be terrified. My poor Tinkerbell must be terrified. It's been four days," she said, ripping her soggy tissue in half.

Robert shook his head; his voice softened. "No, I didn't. I'm sorry, I didn't see her."

A shaking Elsie lowered her face and burst into tears. "Without her I'm lost. I have no one."

Robert placed a hand of reassurance on her shoulder. "Come on, it will be okay," he said, stepping closer.

Elsie collapsed against him and wrapped her hands around his waist. All he could do was embrace her, gently tap her back, attempting to calm. Elsie buried her faced against his chest, and he could feel her strained grip, hear her hitching breath yet he could do nothing to ease her pain. He just held her.

After a few minutes Elsie straightened and wiped the back of her hand across her wet forehead. Her steel-blue eyes were rimmed with redness. Elsie stepped back, lowered her head and turned away while Robert was overwhelmed by vicarious guilt.

I should've known she'd be worried about Tinkerbell.

"Let me help you get cleaned up, then we'll work out

what to do." Stepping forward, he gently took her arm and guided her towards the stairs.

With Elsie upstairs getting changed, Robert flopped to the couch and stared out the window. After a minute or two the pelting rain reduced to a patter. Swirling grey clouds replaced black-streaked skies. Shaking tree limbs relaxed to a gentle sway. The storm had passed, but Tinkerbell was still missing and Robert knew Elsie would return just as upset as when she'd struggled upstairs.

As he looked around the room, he noticed it was void of life, lacking in photos and contained little furniture. No wonder Elsie seemed depressed. Lifeless walls were covered in dated and peeling taupe wallpaper. The couch he sat on was worn, the contents of her bookcase were sparse and the dining table showed years of grime wiped over, but never polished clean. It was an unwelcoming and cold room. Blended beige. Bereft of colour. Where were all her memories? Where were all her photos?

Robert began to cry. He cried for the missing Tinkerbell, he cried for Julie, he cried for Elsie's lonely existence, he even cried for the parents he never knew and the childhood friends he missed. Depressing, the room was emotionless and suffocating. It absorbed happiness, smothered hope.

He wiped his eyes and pushed to his feet, escaping outside for a quick cigarette. Wet, hot, or windy, he didn't care what greeted him outside just as long as he could see colour and feel life.

Sucking in deep on his cigarette, Robert wondered what Elsie needed.

Hope. He knew exactly what to do.

CHAPTER EIGHTEEN

Elsie stumbled forward and grabbed the doorframe near the lounge. Her heart was racing, and her legs trembled. The kitchen table was at least another twenty paces away. Wobbly and exhausted, she would not give in. She leaned against the wall for a rest, wheezing.

Robert placed her cup of tea onto the table then returned with his own, pulled out a chair and sat. "I could help you if you like."

Elsie glared. "Did I ask for help?"

Robert shook his head and rolled his eyes. "Nope."

Elsie was fiercely independent. Robert knew this from his last assignment with her, so he sat silently watching as she struggled to the table. Finally, she dropped within the support of her forearm crutches. Robert grinned, then chuckled despite his efforts to hold it in.

Elsie released her grasp and her crutches fell to the floor with a thud as she turned to him. "What's so funny?"

"I'm sorry, I didn't mean to laugh. You just look like—"

"I look like what?" She glared again.

Robert's face reddened. "Like... like a praying mantis," he said, another laugh escaping.

Elsie raised her eyebrows and picked up her cup of tea. Slurping a few times, she returned her cup to the saucer. "A praying mantis." She leaned back, her mouth twitching as she looked to the ceiling. "A praying mantis," she repeated.

Robert nodded, trying to maintain composure.

A slight smile teetered on the edge of Elsie's lips. "Well I guess I've been called many things in my time, but never a praying mantis." She chuckled. "That's funny, a praying mantis." Elsie slapped her thigh and her chuckle turned to full laughter.

Ripples of gentle happiness echoed as Robert joined in.

Elsie leaned back on her chair and rubbed her chin. "I like you, Robert. Actually, I like you a lot." She stared into his eyes. "Do you know why I like you?"

Robert shook his head. "No."

"I like you because you say what you think, and I believe you are the type of man who wears his heart on his sleeve." Elsie smiled and took another sip of her tea before returning her cup to the saucer. She leaned forward and pointed at him. "And I like your frankness, your honesty. There are far too many people in this world who refrain from telling people the truth for fear of insulting or hurting others, when in fact if more people were forthcoming there would be far less issues." Elsie sat back in her chair and smiled. "A praying mantis." She laughed again.

Picking up a Scotch finger biscuit, Robert dunked it in his tea. "Thank you, Elsie, I certainly didn't say it to offend you. It's just what you looked like." He gave her a smile. "And I appreciate your honesty too. I think honesty is a rare quality these days, so many people are out to get what they want at any cost. They twist words and connive, mostly due to jealousy and greed. I seriously wonder what the world is coming to." He paused and ate his softened biscuit as Elsie finished the last of her tea.

Robert stood and walked over to the sink. "If there's one thing I can't stand, it's liars. Liars, manipulators and cheats." Slamming his hands on the sink, he turned around and faced Elsie. "Social media, people jumping on the Internet and airing their dirty laundry, bullying others, making derogatory remarks and disclosing private issues within a public forum. Then there are those who read these comments and gullibly believe every word."

Elsie shook her head as she searched her pocket for a tissue. "I don't own a computer and have no desire to own one. I don't own a mobile phone and again I have no desire to have one of those either. I think this technology will be the downfall of society. People have lost the ability to sit and talk, to read and write. I see it all the time. Everywhere I go, people walking around looking at their phones, in coffee shops looking at their mobile phones, ignoring the person they are with. No wonder relationships fail. Whatever happened to healthy communication? No one is happy being the person they are, they want to be someone else or have what others have." She wiped her eyes and placed her tissue back into her pocket.

"Talking about what people have," Robert said, returning to his seat at the table. "I want to do something for you. I noticed your lounge room could do with a facelift, a splash of colour and I was talking to Shirley on the phone while you were upstairs. I hope you don't think we were talking behind your back, but we were thinking we could paint it for you, only if you want us to. Something to cheer you up. Shirley also said she's made up some flyers for Tinkerbell. We're going to post them around the neighbourhood this afternoon. The forecasts say the rain should clear by then." He picked up his cup of tea.

Elsie's eyes lit up. "Oh! That would be wonderful. Thank you so much. Shirley, is such an angel. She said she would help find Tinkerbell, and she is, even in her time off. Oh, I'm so blessed to have you both in my life. Thank you."

Robert smiled and placed his cup of tea on the table. "It's our pleasure. How about we finish here and head to the hardware store."

Elsie nodded. "That would be wonderful."

***

A few hours of walking around had Elsie exhausted. She'd missed her nap but was pleased with their productive afternoon. Grocery shopping completed, colours selected and paint purchased. Shirley had called in for a few minutes to pick up a photo of Tinkerbell for the flyers and Robert had finished cleaning. It was time to rest. Robert and Elsie sat at the kitchen table. A hot cup of tea always helped Elsie relax.

Sitting across from Robert she studied his face, he'd become quiet since Shirley left and Elsie worried if his additional attention was simply a deflection from his own issues.

"Are you okay, Robert?"

Robert looked up from the floor. "Yep, sorry. I was just thinking."

He dropped his gaze again, picked up a napkin from the table and began to fold it, his hands gliding over the new creases. Elsie could see he was in deep thought. She sipped her tea and waited as Robert continued to fold the napkin.

Finally, he looked up. "I don't expect you'd understand." He shook his head and dropped the napkin to the table.

Elsie reached out and touched his hand; she was surprised by its coolness. Robert pulled away, the creases around his eyes deepened as he raked his fingers through his hair. Elsie leaned closer. "I do. I do understand the way you feel, more than you will ever know." Elsie sat her teacup down with an audible clunk, removed a tissue from her pocket and wiped her nose.

Robert remained silent; his eyes distant as he ran his

hand over his stubble and sighed.

Elsie studied his mournful face. Her heart ached as she gazed into hollow eyes surrounded by dark circles and shadowed by grief.

So many sleepless nights.

"Young man, you don't get to my age without experiencing hurt and loss. And I appreciate all you are doing for me, putting me before your own needs, but you need to do one thing for yourself before it's too late."

Robert looked at her with vacant eyes.

Elsie leaned forward with her hands flat on the table and fingers fanned. "You need to accept your loss of Julie, and release yourself from this blame, otherwise it will consume you. You need to let it go."

Robert's eyes widened; obviously shocked by the forcefulness of her words. Taking a deep breath, it was time for a change in tone. She touched his hand again. This time, Robert didn't pull away. Instead he sat still, staring eyes filled with tears.

She leaned closer. "I don't say this to be harsh, I have known loss and the finger of condemnation has firmly pointed towards me. For years the hands of darkness strangled my hope, and I was haunted by the demons from my past. But this is life. No one is perfect." She paused and shook her head. "We are our own worst cynics, and while we cannot change what has happened or forget the pain and sadness we have endured, we must learn to forgive." She paused again and gently squeezed Robert's hand. Robert nodded as tears flowed.

Elsie wiped her nose and sniffed back her sadness. "Forgiveness is incredibly powerful, Robert, it doesn't mean condoning, excusing or forgetting. Forgiveness opens our hearts to hope and peace, self-forgiveness allows us to move forward."

Robert pulled his hand away and readjusted his tie as he straightened himself on the chair. Picking up the napkin he recommenced his folding.

Elsie leaned back and smiled. "Birds." She picked up her teacup and chuckled.

"What?" Robert placed the napkin onto the table, pushing his hand on top he pressed on his folds.

"You and I are like two injured birds, you want to fix my wings so I can glide through life," Elsie said, taking another sip of her tea and smiling over the rim. The corners of her lips rose. "At my age and with my condition, gliding would be a wonderful gift. But I have to be realistic. The best this little birdie can expect is to hop and flutter. Maybe I'm an injured canary." She paused placing her teacup back on the saucer.

She gazed into his eyes. "But for you, Robert, you are young, your wings may have been damaged and you may have crashed, but your wings can be repaired." Elsie gave him a small smile. "For you, recovery is possible. You are an eagle, strong with a powerful heart. You, young man, can fly. You can glide and soar. You just have to have the courage to spread your wings. Looking back is holding you back. You need to look forward, to the horizon. Have faith, and you will take off."

Elsie didn't expect Robert would respond, that wasn't what she wanted. Her only hope was he would listen, that he would take on what she believed was so vital. Her biggest fear was he would leave for the day and never return. He had already expressed his concern with returning to work earlier than he had intended.

Would Elsie's words force him to retreat into his shell of grief and darkness?

A knock at the door interrupted their conversation. Robert jumped to his feet and rushed out of the room. It was five o'clock. Shirley had returned as promised. Jai was with her and proudly flashed the flyers for all to see.

"We're going to find your cat," he said, jumping up and down.

Elsie smiled then laughed as she saw the large gap when the boy opened his mouth. Shirley had mentioned how he'd recently lost his two front top teeth. The boy spoke with a slight lisp, spit sprayed through his excitement.

"Thank you, young man," Elsie said.

"Can we go, Mummy? Are you coming, Robert?" Jai tugged at his mother's hand. "Let's find Tinkerbell!"

Elsie followed them to the front door. Hope had returned. The rain had gone. She prayed for Tinkerbell's safe return as she closed the front door.

CHAPTER NINETEEN

Determination and perseverance ensued. Large bright yellow flyers were mounted to street poles, at traffic intersections, placed on bulletin boards, in supermarkets and near schools. Darkness was upon them as they stood in front of Shirley's house. Robert stretched then rubbed his legs trying to relieve his dull, burning aches. He'd enjoyed his afternoon. All three had joked and laughed. Shirley was warm and amiable; he was seeing her in a different light.

"Thanks for helping," Shirley said.

"My pleasure. Let's hope the flyers work and we find Tinkerbell for Elsie."

Shirley held her hands up and crossed her fingers. "Definitely. Well, good night, Robert."

"Good night, Shirley."

Stepping closer, Shirley leaned forward. Their closeness broken by Jai dashing out of the garden.

"See you later, alligator," the young boy yelled.

Robert stepped back and laughed. "In a while, crocodile."

Walking across the road, he looked over his shoulder as he heard their front door shut. Had it been Shirley's intention to lean forward and kiss him?

Elsie's words played over in Robert's mind as he curled up on his couch guzzling down a glass of bourbon and dry. It was his second within a matter of minutes. He wanted to drink, to drink and forget, and to sleep and never wake up. Hunger alarms rumbled from within his stomach, but what was food? Eating created no enjoyment. Eating sustained life, life prolonged suffering. He ignored the rumbling and poured himself another drink, tossing the empty bottle of dry to the floor.

Closing his eyes, darkness returned him to a time full of happiness, joy and hope. His breathing relaxed as he thought about that weekend he and Julie had driven to the country. He smiled, remembering the way she squealed when he dropped to one knee and asked her to marry him. Her face shone and eyes sparkled, as she literally jumped for joy, screaming, "Yes, yes, yes!"

Opening his eyes, he wished he could return to that day, he recalled her tears of joy as he placed his drink onto the table. Tingling energy rushed through his body as he thought about the excitement he had felt. It was like he had won lotto. He had been committed to his future dream. Life with Julie by his side. It was a day he would never forget. Nothing came close to the love he felt in that moment. But it wasn't just about the big moments. Slow dancing in the kitchen in pyjamas was way better. Snuggling in bed watching movies, acting like clowns and joking around, these were the things he missed most. The way Julie would pause a movie, so she would hear him speak, and when she got herself a drink she never failed to ask if he wanted one too. So kind and caring, her feelings reciprocated. They were perfect for each other.

Both had demanding jobs. He was a caregiver who looked after many people society shunned; those with disabilities, aging individuals who had been abandoned by their families. He was proud of his chosen career. A caregiver had a powerful impact on the happiness of others. Working provided a sense of belonging, relationships developed, Robert made a difference in the world. Julie complimented his caring nature; she was patient and caring, understanding and open-minded, affectionate and loving. A registered nurse whose good humour and emotional stability provided her with the ability to manage stressful situations and draw strength from heart-warming moments.

Common values enhanced their relationship, both agreed pay was important – after all money was a necessity – but money would never drive their decisions and choices. Physical and mental health, time spent with loved ones, being thankful for all they had. These were life affirming things that would deliver personal joy and satisfaction. And they did.

Robert's hand shook as he reached for his drink. Drowning his sorrows would achieve nothing except a major hangover. With eating there was no joy, but food would assist with clarity of thought. He needed to think about his future. Stretching out his legs, he tensed his muscles for a moment then relaxed as he drew in a long breath. It was time to put his drink down, grab something to eat and write a letter to his beloved Julie.

CHAPTER TWENTY

My dearest Julie,

It's been six months and one week since you left me, and my pain never seems to end. There is no escaping my denial. How does one accept what one wants most to reject? Am I going crazy? I go to call your name often. Half of my heart thinks you are going to come back, I am going to get a chance to save you. Last night you were in my dreams, your soft warm body nestled against mine. This morning I woke and for a moment I thought I could hear your voice in the other room. I lay still and listened. Silence. Reality. I broke down and cried for I was cold and alone, my heart heavy with grief.

I miss you my sweet Julie. I miss you more than words can say. I miss your smile, I miss your warmth, I miss your jokes, I miss your laughter, but most of all I miss your touch. I would give anything to feel you again.

Oh, how I miss you.

Do you remember our first real date at Bondi Beach? I was so nervous, but with one touch you delivered calm. It was in that moment I realised how special you were. I felt love, an instant connection and that scared me, but it was a feeling I couldn't ignore. I was drawn to you. I wanted to spend the rest of my life with you. Remember how we ate fish and chips on the steps in front of the pavilion. One squawking seagull quickly became hundreds of relentless scavengers. Swooping flashes of grey and white. Frenzied dive-bombers with bad attitudes forced us to retreat. I'd never laughed so hard or run so fast. We finished our feast on the seats within the foyer of the pavilion.

After lunch we strolled towards the rocks on the north end of the beach eating creamy chocolate hearts we'd bought at the kiosk. The beach was crowded at first, people of all shapes and sizes, colourful beach towels, scattered sun umbrellas, surfboards and children's toys. Warm sand beneath our feet. We were holding hands. The breeze, a refreshing mix of sea saltiness tinged with the occasional scent of coconut oil. We followed the sun, our footprints disappearing within the cool waves behind us.

At the rocks I was so afraid you would slip and fall. I wanted to protect you and, in the end, it was me who fell. I was so embarrassed. I thought you would give me the flick there and then, but instead you made sure I was okay and thanked me for leading the way, for allowing myself harm in order to protect you. In my pain, I felt like a hero. You had a way of making me feel special. I hope you know how special you were to me.

Oh, my dearest Julie, life without you is intolerable, I loathe my existence.

Today was extremely tough. I think I returned to work before I was ready. I'm not sure if I should go back. Tonight, I'm exhausted and broken. My world will never be the same. I'm like an outcast who belongs nowhere.

My only hope is you can forgive me. I promised I'd look after you. I promised I'd protect you. I failed. I love you with all my heart and I'll love you and miss you until we meet again...

Love always and forever,
Robert

CHAPTER TWENTY-ONE

Veronica spotted Robert walking into the coffee shop. She'd been waiting for nearly half an hour, and her patience had paid off.

"Robert!" Jumping to her feet she waved and beckoned him over. "Fancy seeing you here. Why don't you come and join me?"

Robert hesitated for a moment, appearing not to recognise her then smiled, returned her wave and wove his way through the tables. "How are you, Veronica? I've never seen you here before."

Veronica giggled and batted her eyes as her cheeks circled pink. "Oh, I'm wonderful." As she sat, she glanced at Robert then looked away coyly. "I come here all the time. I'm surprised I haven't seen you before either."

She paused as she studied his face, gently twirling her hair. Hesitation filled her mind. Was Robert the man for her? He'd looked different when they met at therapy. His eyes were kind and honest, yet a haunting greyness tinged the blue, heavy circles reflected grief and sleepless nights. Was he ready for love? Veronica licked her lips as she imagined his Herculean arms wrapped firmly around her waist. "Today must be my lucky day," she said.

Robert grinned and raised an eyebrow as he pulled out the chair opposite her. "Maybe it's my lucky day." He laughed as he sat, straightening his chair before picking up the menu.

The coffee shop was a cool hive of activity. People swarmed inside to escape the oppressive humidity. Busy workers came in and out, diners sat on comfy seats competing to be heard while plates and cutlery clinked. Waiters and waitresses delivered food and cleared tables. Slow-moving ceiling fans circulated the aroma of freshly-roasted coffee beans, and mouth-watering meals. Burgers, hot chips, fresh pastries, pasta, and toasted sandwiches. People wove past, the clinking noise softened, and tables became vacant. Both enjoyed their meals and relaxed into a deeper conversation over coffee.

"So, tell me about you, Robert," Veronica said, moving the table number that blocked her direct view.

"Tell you about… about myself." Robert stiffened and cleared his throat. "Um… where do I begin?"

"From the start." Veronica smiled before leaning close. Raising her eyebrows, she licked her lips.

"Um… um… er…" Robert's face coloured, picking up a napkin he began to tear and pluck at the tissue. Veronica sat silent. After a few moments he dropped the remains of the napkin, scraped the tissue pieces into a pile and took a deep breath. He looked towards her. "Um… Well… I'm afraid… I'm afraid my life isn't all that exciting. I… my childhood was spent in foster homes." He paused, looked away momentarily then cracked his knuckles. "By the time I was a teenager, I'd lived in five different homes."

"Wow." Veronica shook her head and pressed her fingers to her lips.

Robert shifted in his chair and placed his elbows on the table as if trying to steady himself. Leaning forward, he began to tap his fingers against the table. His eyes furrowed and his gaze darkened. "As a… as a child, I always felt like I was living on a tightrope. Love was a four-letter word found in the dictionary. Cuddles and signs of affection were void." Sadness scratched, Robert's voice cracked and words abandoned. He shook his head, curled then uncurled his fingers before he recommended tapping. The pause this time was longer, and it seemed Robert was struggling to get the words out. Veronica glanced down to the tap-tap-tap of Robert's fingers against the table – a nervous tic, of sorts. It was clear he was having difficulty in divulging such personal information, but whatever it took to make him feel comfortable around her, she'd do. An encouraging smile, divulging her own information to make him feel more at ease. He cleared his throat, gave a nod that was more to himself than to her.

Veronica gave a half smile. "I'm sorry, Robert. I don't mean to upset you. We could talk about something else if you like."

"It's, it's okay. I was just thinking about some wise words a friend said and how I need to implement them into my life." With another slight nod he took a deep breath and straightened. "There was always a reason. I mean… when I was sent to a new home… there was always a reason, I was, I was either… Nevermind." He shook his head. "It doesn't matter. As they say, the past is the past. Can't change it…. Can we?" Robert cleared his throat and leaned back in his chair. Lowering his head, he focused on picking at his nails.

An awkward silence followed. Veronica blinked repeatedly and bit her lower lip attempting to hide her tears. "Oh, Robert, it must've been so difficult."

Robert looked up and rubbed his fingers together. "Yeah… it was. But there was no point in getting angry or frustrated. So I vowed that when I got older, I'd create a loving family and I'd *never* abandon those I loved. My adult life would represent everything I'd missed in my childhood."

Veronica leaned forward. The sincerity in his voice

had her fighting back tears.

"Oh, Robert, that's so sweet and I'm sure your dream will come true, probably when you least expect it. As for your experience, it would certainly be a motivator."

Robert nodded and edged closer. Placing his hands on the table, he raised his eyebrows and released a loud sigh. "I can't believe I'm telling you all this… Maybe… maybe it's those wise words tapping at my mind." He gave a nervous laugh. "My biggest regret would be the disappointment of not knowing my parents. I tried to find them when I was about twenty, not to lay blame or to abuse them, but to simply ask why. Was there a reason they didn't want me? Surely, there had to be a reason." Pushing back on his chair, he sniffed and wiped his eyes. "Oh, wow that chilli was hot today."

"Delayed reaction?" Veronica smiled.

Robert chuckled, looked towards her and shook his head. "Yeah, something like that."

"It's good to talk and release, Robert. Everyone needs to talk at some stage." Veronica smiled again. "As for chilli, I don't eat it much so I generally blame the onion." She paused and her smile quickly disappeared. "Back to what you were saying, I'm sure there was a valid reason. So many people have to give up their children, not because they want to but because circumstances dictate, they must. I'm sure that was the case with you and I'm sure they've missed you as much as you've missed them."

"Maybe, I try not to think about it. It's too depressing."

"I imagine it would be depressing, but I'd want to know too."

Robert smiled. "It wasn't all bad though. Of course, there was a stigma attached to being a foster child, and changing places made it hard to make friends but one of the greatest friends I ever had was when I lived in a foster home at Maroubra. Kenny, the boy next door. Most of the kids in the neighbourhood wanted nothing to do with him, but not me. He was like no other kid I'd ever met. Everyone said he'd been dropped on his head as a baby. You see he wore callipers on his legs, shiny metal poles firmly secured by thick leather straps. He'd march around like a determined robot. I was always so jealous, I thought about stealing them from him when he slept so I could be a robot too." Robert gave a weird, uncertain chuckle.

Veronica's eyes widened and her mouth opened as she sank into his words. She wasn't sure why the sudden shift in his behaviour and the willingness to tell all, but she welcomed it all the same.

Robert shook his head and his face reddened. "Oh what… No, no, no! You think I took them. I never did."

Veronica chuckled and tilted her head to the side. "Are you sure?" Her eyebrows raised.

Robert's face reddened. "Oh, I'm sure. I never did, cross my heart."

Veronica stared and rolled her eyes, her cheeks swelled and the corner of her lips curled. A slight giggle. Then through her nose, spluttering snorts. Rambunctious laughter filled the air. Tears leaked from the corners of their eyes.

Robert coughed and caught his breath, gazing towards Veronica who had retrieved a handkerchief from her handbag and was wiping her eyes.

Shaking his head, he smiled. "Oh, that was funny and poor, Kenny, was hilarious. Balance was not a strong suit; he would hit the deck with grace, brush himself off and stagger back to his feet as if nothing had happened. I left Maroubra when I was about seven years old. I always wondered what happened to him."

Robert took the final mouthful of his coffee as he relaxed back onto his chair and looked around the cafe. Most of the patrons had left. A couple staff stood near the cash register. "I think I should make a move," he said, glancing at his watch, "I've bored you for long enough and it looks like they want to close up so they can make preparations for the lunchtime rush."

Veronica pouted. "Oh bugger. I was enjoying myself and you haven't bored me at all. I've loved our little chat. It's been so nice getting to know you and I haven't laughed so much in a long time." She paused and smiled. "Maybe we could do this again some time."

Robert nodded. "I'd like that." He returned her smile.

CHAPTER TWENTY-TWO

Robert jumped out of his car and strolled to his letterbox with a spring in his step. Talking to Veronica had been nice. He felt relaxed while in her company, but he worried he may have revealed much more than he intended. Looking at the colourful flowers in the garden he shrugged away his concern, overall the experience had been positive. Time had flown by and during that time he hadn't been able to dwell on his current issues. It was wonderful to talk and think about something other than the heartache he felt. Veronica was refreshing.

He spotted Shirley working in the garden across the road.

"Hey, Robert, how are you?" She waved and walked towards the road. "I was wondering if you would like to catch up for a meal?"

"I'd love to, Shirley, but I just finished having brunch with Veronica."

Shirley waited for the cars to pass and hurried across to him. "Veronica, the woman you mentioned from grief support? What are you doing with her? She's just going to mess with your emotions and hurt you."

"Come on, Shirley, you don't even know her. Don't go getting all jealous on me." Robert laughed as he lifted the lid on the letterbox and retrieved his mail.

"Jealous! I'm not jealous, I just don't want to see you

getting hurt."

"I won't."

"Good. So how about dinner tonight?"

Robert laughed again, stepped closer and wrapped his arm around her shoulder. "Oh, my goodness girl... you are persistent."

Shirley giggled, nuzzled her face into his chest and looked up from under his chin. "So, I'll take that as a yes. I'll bring over pizza."

"Okay, I'll do dinner. I actually want to talk to you about work."

"Work?"

"Yeah, I think I may have gone back too early."

"Elsie's not giving you a hard time, is she?" she said, chuckling.

"No." Robert shook his head and gave a half smile, as he flicked his mail in his hands. "I'm just finding it difficult. How can I care for someone else when I don't feel I can look after myself properly?"

"Oh, come on, I'm sure you're doing fine."

"I'm not so sure," he said. "I'm going to take the rest of the weekend to weigh up my options. I still have lots of leave I can take." He paused and looked beyond Shirley. His eyes staring, slowly his lips curved upwards. His smile widened. Shirley reached up and clicked her fingers in front of his face.

"Well, something has made you happy."

Robert chuckled and smiled again. "Like I said, I just enjoyed brunch with Veronica."

Shirley rolled her eyes.

"Come on, Shirley, you'd really like her if you met. We had a great chat about my childhood. She's a great listener and sensitive."

Shirley shrugged.

Ringing from the house cut through the silence. "I'd

better go," Robert said. "That's my phone. So, I'll see you tonight at about six," he yelled, dashing off.

CHAPTER TWENTY-THREE

Shirley stormed across the street. She jammed her key into the door, pushed it open then slammed it shut behind her. Sucking in a deep breath, she clenched her hands into fists. Her eyes narrowed, as she glared down the hallway. All was silent. Jai was nowhere in sight.

She kicked the wall. "Argh!"

Shirley strode to her bedroom, loud thuds echoing in her wake. Throwing herself onto her bed, she sobbed thinking about how Robert had discussed his childhood with Veronica.

Who's this Veronica? I've known Robert for years; he's never mentioned anything about his childhood. Why is he telling her?

"Are you okay, Mummy?" Jai whispered.

Shirley jolted upright and jumped to her feet, wiping the tears from her face.

Jai shifted from one foot to the other. "Mummy."

"Don't Mummy me. Have you done the dishes like I asked?"

Jai shook his head. "No."

Shirley snapped and yanked him to her. "Do you ever do what I tell you?" Grabbing his chin, she flung his face upwards. "I'm asking you a question, young man."

Jai stared, his body trembled as her other hand tightened around his arm. Without a word, Shirley released her grasp. Jai reeled back and dropped to his knees, cowering in the corner with his hands over his head.

Shirley stomped her foot and stepped closer to the boy. "I asked you a question."

Jai flinched but lifted his chin. "Yes."

"Well it seems to me you don't. It seems to me that you need to be taught a lesson. And punishing you like I was punished when I was your age might just make you think twice before you ignore my requests," she said, stepping closer. She pulled the boy to his feet.

"I promise I'll listen! I promise I'll be good! Please, Mummy, please…"

Shirley ignored his pleading as she dragged him to the corner of the dining room.

***

Jai stood still with his feet slightly apart. Arms straight. Muscles strained. The weight above his head was becoming unbearable. Hot sun streamed in through the window, blinding rays of brightness challenging his ability to focus. He closed his eyes. Thirst invaded. A lawn mower started, he hoped it might be Robert. Maybe Robert would come to his rescue. Fading footsteps. Shirley left the room. The washing machine clunked as the spin cycle engaged. Jai remained still and hoped his mother would end his punishment. His tiny arms burned. The back door slammed. Opening his eyes, he relaxed his arms. The door creaked. Arms stiffened. He stood to attention. Silence in the street. Shafts of filtered light flashed around the floor. Dullness invaded the room as his shadow slowly shrunk. Pressure. His bladder cramped. Stabbing.

"Mummy."

"What?"

"I promise I'll listen. I promise I'll be good."

THE BELONGING

"You've promised before."

"But, Mummy…" Jai looked to the floor. Soft panting escaped his lips. Sweaty palms. Strained fingers. "I need to pee."

"I need a lot of things, doesn't mean I'll get them." Shirley glared at Jai and shook her head. She turned and left the room.

Jai stood still, fearing he would drop his arms. The heavy book slid within his fingers, as he readjusted his hands. It was impossible to hold on any longer. Jai closed his eyes. Warmth trickled down his legs. A strong urine smell entered his nose. Tears seeped from his eyes and down his cheeks.

Shirley returned. Gold liquid glistened. Thundering footsteps approached. Pounding hit his head, as the book flung from his arms.

"Get to your room, you filthy boy!"

Jai burst into tears and dashed away.

CHAPTER TWENTY-FOUR

Unperturbed by the events of the afternoon, Shirley pranced across the road with take-away pizza. Her reflection in the glass of Robert's front door made her smile. A white, lacy off-the-shoulder top with denim shorts and sneakers was the perfect choice – a hint of skin, flirty, fun and playful. If he asked about Jai, she would say he wasn't well.

Robert loved Mexican pizza. Shirley loved red wine. The two were a perfect combination and disappeared in no time. Strolling outside, Robert lit a cigarette. Shirley followed closely behind. Looking up at the stars, he took a deep drag and blew the smoke up into the air.

"Do you think she's watching us?"

Shirley stepped close and held his forearm. "I don't know, but I'm sure she'd want us to be happy."

Robert coughed and pulled away, tossing his cigarette in the ashtray. "I think we should go and check on Jai," he said.

"Oh, you don't have to do that," she said, biting her nail.

"I know I don't have to. I want to."

"But he's probably asleep."

Robert ignored her words as he walked towards his driveway with Shirley scurrying behind.

"It's late. I'll get him to call by tomorrow. Maybe we

could go to the park together." Tugging Robert's hand, she urged him to stop, but Robert looked over and shook his head. Flicking his hand, he dismissed her resistance.

"I'll be less than five minutes. He'll appreciate my visit."

Sliding her key into the front door, Shirley hoped her son would behave.

"Jai baby, Mummy's home. Are you awake? Robert's come over to see how you're feeling," she said, making her way down the hallway closely followed by Robert. Dropping her hands to her side, she spread her arms wide and stopped, turning back to Robert.

"Maybe he's sleeping."

"I thought I heard his TV when we came in."

Silence.

"I can't hear anything."

Robert nudged her to keep walking, and she did with clenched teeth.

One wrong word and he'll find out about punishment.

Both looked into the darkened room. A large mound of blankets covered the boy's body. Stillness.

"Hey buddy, it's Robert. I just came to check on you." He stepped into the bedroom. Shirley stood to the right of the door with her hands on her hips, as Robert crept closer to the boy's bed. Light from the hallway lit his path. Jai's bedroom was furnished on a meagre budget; a tattered toy box sat beneath the window, a small single bed ran along the wall. Unlike other children Robert had encountered, Jai's bedroom was always tidy. He stepped closer. The boy remained still beneath his Batman quilt.

"Are you okay, buddy?"

"Yep."

"Your mum said you were tired and not feeling too good."

"Yep."

Robert leaned forward and gently tapped the quilt. "I'll catch up with you later. I hope you're feeling better soon."

"Yep."

Shirley tiptoed closer and squeezed Robert's arm. Dipping her head, she indicated they should leave. Robert nodded, gave her a smile and followed her back to the hallway. They returned to the front door without saying a word.

"Thanks for a great evening. I'll see you tomorrow," Shirley said as she closed her front door.

Strolling to her bedroom, she was met by Jai returning from the bathroom.

Placing her hands on her hips, she stood legs apart blocking the boy's path. She leaned close and glared. Jai stepped back. Shirley edged forward. There was no way to escape. Jai's back was firmly against the cool wall. His body trembled. Her finger hovered in front of his face. His eyes widened.

"What happens between these walls, stays between these walls."

"Yes, Mummy." Jai nodded.

"If you want a better life, one full of fun and holidays you have to do what I say."

"Okay, Mummy."

"Do you understand me?" Her voice raised as her finger pointed.

"Yes, Mummy."

"Well don't say you haven't been warned. Open your mouth, spoil my plan, and I'll sew it shut."

Jai stared, unblinkingly, as he raised his hand and gently placed his fingers to his lips. Tears welled in his eyes.

Shirley stepped to the side, unblocking the hallway. "Now get to bed."

Jai dashed into his room.

The next morning Shirley spotted Jai creeping up the hallway.

"What are you doing?" she yelled.

Jai flinched, stopped in his tracks then walked to her bedroom door. "Nothing, Mummy."

"Yes, you were."

"I… I was…"

"Well, spit it out! What were you doing?" Her voice raised as she edged forward. "I'm asking you a question."

"I… I had an accident." Jai's eyes darted around the room as he jiggled from foot to foot. "I was going to put my sheets in the laundry. I wanted to see if the door was unlocked."

"I told you to keep out of the laundry. I'm working on something. Go and get your sheets and bring them to me. Get yourself some breakfast, brush your teeth and hair, and get dressed. Remember our little chat from last night?"

"Yes, Mummy."

Jai dashed off and returned with his sheets.

CHAPTER TWENTY- FIVE

My dearest Julie,

It's been six and a half months since the angels took you. I want you to know you have never left my thoughts. We never had the chance to talk about what we'd do if we lost one another. Would we expect the other to carry on? Would we want them to find another partner, to rediscover happiness? I wish I knew what you expected. Life is cruel. You were stolen. I don't want to do anything you would view as wrong. I promised I'd make you happy, that I would never prove a disappointment. I pledged my love for you and only you. Yet, now I find myself in a predicament. Do I try to move forward with someone else? Would you consider this an act of betrayal? I promise I will never forget the wonderful time we shared. You were the first person who made me feel as though I had purpose, that I belonged, and for that I will be eternally grateful. I will always love you.

My thoughts are so confused, my reactions delayed. Driving home this afternoon, I unintentionally ran a red light and narrowly avoided an accident. Needless to say, I burst into tears. What a fool I must have looked, shaking like a mad man as I sat on the side of the road. I can't think clearly.

I want you to know I have met someone. Someone wonderful, her name is Veronica. She understands me, she understands the pain I feel...you see she lost her husband. He committed suicide, an unimaginable experience. To lose a loved one because of an accident is one thing, I don't know how she can accept she lost him by his own hand.

I don't know where things will go. I don't know what feelings she has towards me, if any. I just know we are good for each other. It's nice to talk with someone who can relate to my pain, rather than those who feel they should tell me how to deal with it. I wanted you to know that I have asked her out for coffee tomorrow. I hope this doesn't upset you, please know I am not looking to replace you. No one will ever come close to you, my dearest Julie. But I feel as though I have been slipping backwards lately and I know you wouldn't want me to fall into darkness. I think Veronica can help me and I'm determined to do better. I love you, Julie, and I'll love and miss you until we meet again...

Love always and forever,
Robert

CHAPTER TWENTY-SIX

Robert flung a large garbage bag to the floor and with one continuous swipe all the rubbish on his coffee table disappeared. An unexpected phone call sent him scurrying. A visitor would soon arrive. They wanted to talk to him about something important. What had to be said could not be said over the phone. It required privacy.

Sweat ran from his brow. Ragged breath escaped his lips. Fingers fumbled. Clothes and magazines were sent flying. The spare bedroom, his new dumping ground. Its door would remain closed. Scrambling. Picking up and throwing. Windows opened. In the kitchen, dirty dishes were stashed out of sight. In the bathroom, old towels cleaned surfaces, new towels were hung. Fresh clothes on. Old clothes hidden away. A splash of Old Spice to his cheeks and neck. One last sprint around the house, his arm waving above. Air freshener hissing through the air. Inspections complete. Mists of the Hawaiian breeze struggled to remove the lingering odour. His house stained with smells similar to a pub after closing time. It was the best he could do. He hoped it was enough.

First impressions count. I don't want her to think I'm a pig.

Crazy thoughts ran through Robert's head as he stood at the back door staring at the cigarette between his fingers. Happiness, excitement, followed by nervousness then panic. Was he doing the right thing? Why had he agreed to the visit? What happened if things became awkward? The doorbell rang. His head jerked. Tossing his cigarette into the ashtray, he straightened himself and dashed to the door. Snatching the handle, he flung the door open.

"Hey, how are you?" He smiled and stepped back.

"I'm great, how about you?"

"Yeah, good. I'm good. Why don't you come in."

Stepping to the side, he pointed the way. His visitor brushed passed as he turned to lock the door. Across the street Shirley stood in her front yard, hand saluting above her forehead. Robert closed the door on her prying eyes and followed his guest inside.

"I must say, I was surprised to hear from you."

His visitor turned and smiled. "Oh, I hope you didn't mind me phoning."

"No, not at all." The corner of his lips rose. "Would you like a coffee?"

"A coffee would be lovely, thanks."

Robert disappeared into the kitchen, leaving Veronica in the lounge room. Steam billowed from the kettle. Cups and cutlery clinked.

"How do you have it?" he asked.

"White with two, thanks." Veronica scanned the room and ran her finger along the top of the coffee table inspecting for dust.

A few minutes later Robert returned with their coffee and placed them on the table. He sat and gestured to the couch. Veronica crossed the room in a couple of strides and sat beside him. She picked up her coffee, took a sip then returned the cup to the table.

"Oh, thank you, that's perfect." Leaning close, their arms brushed and thighs touched.

Warmth rushed through Robert's body and he began to sweat. Besides Shirley, he had not allowed another female inside his house since Julie's passing, fearing it would reflect poorly on his character and all involved. Self-tortured thoughts churned within his mind; his body stiffened. Was he wrong? It was not too late to move. To create distance and establish boundaries.

Nausea filled his gut, as he glanced towards a photo of Julie on his bookcase. Gripping the arm of the couch, he slid forward and picked up his cup. His face remained expressionless, giving Veronica no clue to his mood. Space. A few mouthfuls of coffee gave him time to think. Returning his cup to the table, he pushed back and leaned into the armrest. Their bodies no longer touching. Folding his arms, he looked at Veronica.

"You have a nice house, it smells of tropical fruit with a hint of coconut."

Robert bit the inside of his cheek and laughed. "It's air freshener."

"Well it's nice, not many men worry about keeping their house clean and tidy and smelling nice. You should be proud. You have a lovely home."

Robert nodded and smiled. Both relaxed into their conversation. Veronica said she had been thinking about him. She'd enjoyed meeting at the coffee shop. Robert surprised himself with his reaction to her comments, without any thought he told Veronica he'd been thinking about her too. Sipping his coffee, he worried she may have taken him the wrong way.

Veronica looked away momentarily. "I wanted to talk to you about something," she said.

"Oh okay." Uncrossing his arms, Robert straightened on the couch as his interest stirred.

"I wanted to, I wanted to—"

A knock at the front door interrupted her words. Veronica slumped as Robert jumped to his feet. "Hold that thought, I'll be right back."

Veronica remained seated as he left the room. Within

seconds, he returned with another woman.

"Shirley, meet Veronica. Veronica, meet Shirley, my neighbour from across the road."

Both women smiled but remained silent. Robert glanced between the two. "How many eggs did you say you needed, Shirley?"

"Just three. I'm going to bake a banana and walnut cake. We all love it so much. I was going to ask you over for afternoon tea."

"Oh, that would be lovely, thanks. Let me go check. I'm sure I have some."

Veronica continued her silence, casting a sceptical eye as Robert went into the kitchen. Shirley stood near the doorway glaring at her stylish opponent. Glowing skin, unblemished make-up, high cheekbones. The woman was glamorous. Push-up cleavage perched over her low-cut blouse. Her pant-suit had a tailored look. The woman radiated class. Shirley shook her head and tucked her hair behind her ear. The woman had salon-perfect hair and nails.

"So, it was you I saw crawling around in the dirt on my arrival," Veronica said looking at her perfectly manicured nails. She raised her eyebrows and smirked. "I have a gardener to deal with the mess."

Shirley glared at her, then glanced down at her dishevelled appearance. Dirt-covered baggy clothes were no competition. Stepping back, she jammed her weathered hands into her pockets. She hated Veronica already.

Robert returned with the eggs. "Did you want to stay for a coffee, Shirley?"

"No thanks, maybe later. I'll give you a shout out when the cake is ready."

She turned and walked towards the door without another word. Robert walked behind her. Veronica remained seated.

At the front door, Shirley stopped and turned to Robert.

She leaned close and placed her hand on his shoulder. "I know you've got her waiting, but can I have a quick word?"

"Sure."

Robert ushered Shirley onto the verandah and pulled the door behind him.

Shirley glanced over her shoulder. They were alone. "I don't know what to do with Jai. He's so disobedient lately, and now he's taken to wetting the bed." She frowned and bit her lip.

Robert's eyes widened, reaching forward he gently touched her arm. "Do you want me to talk to him? Maybe he's being bullied or something."

"Thanks, but no thanks. I don't want to embarrass him. I just thought he might have said something to you. I'll have a chat with him. I'd appreciate it if you could keep this to yourself and just let me know if he says anything."

"Of course, of course I will." He gave a half smile and rubbed her arm.

Shirley leaned forward and kissed his cheek. "Thank you, Robert. And thanks again for the eggs."

"My pleasure."

Robert returned to the lounge room and took his seat next to Veronica before picking up his coffee. "Sorry about that, you were about to tell me something?"

Veronica looked at him. A smear of lipstick sat on his cheek. She glanced at her watch. "Yes, yes, I was, but I just remembered I have an appointment. Maybe another time." She rose to her feet.

"Oh, okay." Disappointment etched on Robert's face as he returned his mug to the table. Escorting her to her car, he wondered what she was going to say before their interruption. The sparkle in his eyes faded as he watched her drive down the road in her flashy white sports car. The woman was intriguing. He wanted to know more.

CHAPTER TWENTY-SEVEN

Immersed in darkness, Robert sunk into his couch and ran his fingers gently over his whiskered face as he reflected on Elsie's words. She was right, he was alive whether he liked it or not. Life was for living. Maybe Veronica's visit had given him the shove he needed. If nothing else it had forced him to tidy up. The world *was* full of endless opportunities and he had important decisions to make regarding his career and personal life. Was he ready for another relationship? Was he game to put his heart on the line? Julie had been gone for less than seven months. Would he be judged harshly if seen smiling with another woman?

Robert flicked on the light, and strolled around the house. Everywhere he looked there were 'two'. Two dressing gowns behind the bedroom door. In the wardrobe her slippers still sat next to his. Two toothbrushes reminded him of their mornings together in the bathroom. His and hers matching towels. Matching pyjamas. There was no escaping the reminders. Was it right to think of the future?

In the kitchen next to where the keys hung was a wall calendar showing their plans for the year. Coffee mugs displaying the words 'good morning handsome' and 'good morning beautiful'. Dropping to the kitchen chair, he cast his eyes over to an old-fashioned jar – a gratitude jar. Half full with hand-written notes, slips of paper detailing daily activities, acts of kindness, loving thoughts or things to be thankful for. Each note dated. They were supposed to be read at the end of the year.

Nausea churned in his gut as grief rose. Robert swallowed hard trying to maintain control. He raised closed fists to his forehead, his eyes squeezed tight as he struggled to contain his seeping sorrow. Sitting in the corner and crying until he died would be easy. When was the right time to go through Julie's belongings? Would she approve if he removed her things? Was he emotionally ready to tackle such an arduous task? Julie would always live on within his heart. Was it necessary to dwell over physical items?

What do I do?

***

Elsie paced back and forth glancing out her front window. An earlier walk around her backyard proved fruitless. Hope was fading. Where was Tinkerbell? Over two weeks had passed. Would a reward achieve results? Reefing at her blinds, she scanned her front path and shook her head. *Where is he?*

Last week, he had left her stranded. Telephoned in sick. Elsie pounded her crutches against the floor as she thought of how she'd been left with no assistance. Movement on the path. Releasing the blinds, she grunted and thudded towards the door.

Do they want me to starve?

She snatched at the handle, flung the door open and stepped forward. Heat struck her face. "You're—"

"Pleased to see you." Robert smiled and looked at his watch. "Oh, and look, I'm on time. How are you, Elsie? Sorry about last week."

Overcome by the humidity, Elsie stumbled back and

leaned against the wall. Robert grabbed her arm as she squinted at her watch. "I hope you haven't brought anything contagious with you." Jerking her arm free of his grasp, she straightened her crutches, turned and shuffled along the hallway.

Robert closed the door and followed. "Nope, nothing contagious, feeling much better thanks. I suspect it was just a case of food poisoning with the runs. Shirley made me a cake. I thought it tasted a little strange, but you know me, when I have an appetite." He laughed and his cheeks flushed pink. "Only joking, although it did taste a little strange. It was probably something else."

They continued to the kitchen and Elsie dropped to a chair. Robert stood in front of the sink; arms crossed over his chest.

"I see you have a new tie." She pointed.

Robert smiled, wiggled the knot close to his neckline and ran his fingers down the shiny red fabric. "It was a gift from Julie. She said wearing a tie made me look professional and snazzy. This one she called my 'power tie'. Do you like it?"

Elsie nodded and returned his smile. "It's extremely dashing, but you don't have to wear a tie while you're here."

"I know, but I like to."

"Even with this heat?" Elsie wiped her brow then slumped forward with her chin resting on her hand.

"Always for work, no matter what temperature."

"As long as you know it's your choice."

"I do and thank you. So now I'm here, would you like a cup of tea?"

"Thank you, that would be lovely." She leaned back in her chair.

Robert sorted out the kettle then leaned back against the kitchen bench, hands on hips. "Tell me, what's been happening. Have you found Tinkerbell?"

Elsie bowed her head. "No." Sobs broke from her as

she retrieved a tissue from her pocket, her face etched with sadness.

"Oh Elsie, I'm sorry you're going through this." Robert stepped close and wrapped an arm around her shoulder. She trembled beneath his touch.

She looked towards him, squinting. "I was thinking I should offer a reward."

"A reward?"

"I have the money."

"You may have the money, but…"

"But what? What good is money if I have nothing and no one to enjoy it with?"

Elsie had a point. Robert removed his arm from her shoulder, pulled the chair out next to her and sat. Elsie blew her nose and placed her tissue into her pocket. Puffy eyes stared back at Robert.

"If you think it will help. It could be worth a try," he said. "Someone has to know something."

The kettle clicked. Robert smiled and tapped Elsie's hand trying to provide reassurance. Springing from the chair, he returned to the kitchen bench. "I'll make the tea and you can tell me how I can help."

Rising steam. Teacups clinked. Sweet treats teased. Elsie slurped. Robert sipped. Moreish macarons devoured. Falling crumbs. Bellies full. A plan had been hatched. Elsie and Robert retreated to the lounge. Robert would print new posters. A reward of one thousand dollars would be offered for the safe return of Tinkerbell. Their conversation now centred on Robert's dilemma.

Elsie slumped on the couch and looked towards Robert fighting back tears.

"When my mother died, I wanted desperately to hold on. I placed everything into boxes. Determined never to let her go, I thought it would be disrespectful to get rid of her possessions." Glancing up to the ceiling, she shook her head. Tears shimmered in her eyes as she turned to Robert. "Do you know what happened?"

"No."

"Years later, in a moment of extreme loneliness, I opened the boxes. Her shoe collection had been ravaged by mould. Clothes attacked by moths. There was mice poop everywhere. I was heartbroken."

Robert leaned forward. "Oh, that's terrible."

"So, you see, Robert, holding onto her things never brought her back, never made her feel closer. You can't keep a person alive by holding onto stuff. But that's my experience, there is no right or wrong way."

Robert remained silent, as Elsie drew in a long breath.

"You never get over grief, it changes," she said, "but you never get over it. Many people mourn for years, some forever. And don't get disillusioned by the suggestion that time heals all wounds, it doesn't."

She paused; Robert sat motionless, tears brimming. Glancing down she noticed his legs jiggling. She gently placed her hand onto his knee and turned to face him, her voice only slightly above a whisper as he looked at her. "There's no easy way to say this, Robert. After one year you wish they would come back. With the passing of time you may cry less. But, after twenty years you still wish they would come back. The wishing never stops. You wish you could sit and talk with them. Hold them in your arms. Tell them you love them." She brushed away a tear. "Then you worry you can't remember their voice, but you will remember. You will always remember. Those you have lost will always have a special place in your heart."

Robert stood and walked around the room then sat, ran his fingers through his hair and stood again. With his hands behind his head, he paced the room. The muscles in his jaw twitched, shaking his head he appeared defeated by her words. He stopped, hands resting on the dining table, fingers drumming as though deep in thought.

"I'm sorry, Robert, I wish I could tell you differently. I wish I could hold those I've lost, apologise for my mistakes, and tell them I love them. I trust in God that—"

"Don't talk to me about God. If he exists, he's forgotten about me." Robert jerked his head and stared at her.

"But the Lord said—"

"Leave the Lord out of this! The last thing I need is to be force-fed religion." He glared at her like she was a criminal.

Elsie could detect anger and confusion in his voice. Slumping back into the couch, she watched Robert tug on the knot in his tie. Sadness clouded his features; he was suffocating within his grief. Elsie wanted to loosen his tie, clear all obstructions and allow him to breathe. Awareness would provide strength and courage to move forward with understanding and hope.

"I can't do this. I need a cigarette." Robert rushed from the room.

Elsie prayed.

CHAPTER TWENTY-EIGHT

Amanda stood and stretched as another grief support meeting concluded.

She was seething. Having watched Veronica's antics all night she was ready to explode. There was a time and place for meeting people, grief support groups were not pick-up places. Amanda was interested in the welfare of all members equally. A new face had joined them; Sarah had recently lost her father in a boating tragedy. She had survived when the vessel sank off the Sydney coastline. Her father's lifeless body had been recovered in the wreckage. Sarah was drowning in survivor's guilt. It had been her idea to go fishing. Amanda watched as Veronica hugged Sarah goodnight. She listened as she offered reassuring words and waited for everyone to leave. One by one – Maria, Robert, Walter, Steve and finally Sarah disappeared out the front door.

It was time to confront Veronica; she was sick and tired of the woman.

"I was talking to Robert earlier," she said with her hands on her hips. "He told me you met up for a meal and you've visited him at home."

"And? What's it got to do with you?" Veronica snapped.

"He tells me you meeting him was a coincidence, but I know better." Amanda raised her eyebrows and edged closer. "I know you heard him talking to Walter. He told Walter where he likes to eat. What did you do? Go there and sit from open to close? Did you wait like a dog on heat?"

"How *dare* you." Veronica glared, her finger thrust forward and she stepped toward Amanda as the woman stepped back.

"I know what you're up to. You can't wait to get you're claws into him. Just like Henry. He was a nice guy. You pounced. You pursued. And poor Henry never came back." Amanda's words got louder with every breath. "This support group isn't your husband hunting ground."

Veronica swung and slapped Amanda to the ground. "You need to mind your own business, or it will be *you* who never comes back."

Heavy breathing echoed. For a few seconds, Amanda remained on the floor clutching her reddened cheek. Veronica edged closer, hands on hips and snickered as though she was amused.

A kick.

"Ouch!" Veronica hunched forward, shoulders raised and head down. Her hands wrapped around her throbbing shin. Amanda bolted upright.

"You can't stop me from coming here and you can't stop me from opening my mouth. I will talk to whoever I like! Go on, I dare you. You try to stop me and we'll see what happens."

She stepped forward pointing her finger, eyes glaring. Veronica's feet slid back, her arms flung to her side, hands out palm up. She slowly stepped back again, her face paled. Stopping still, she placed her hands over her cheeks.

"My God, what have I done? Please forgive me, Amanda. I don't know what come over me." Tears appeared in her eyes, as she straightened her blouse and fluffed at her hair. "I'm so sorry. Please forgive me."

Amanda stood at arm length studying the woman's face, questioning the veracity of her words. Tears and a trembling softness suggested sincerity. Veronica took a slight step forward, Amanda's gaze broke, and focus dropped to Veronica's extended hand. Doubt interrupted their stillness. A brief glance upward. Just as she predicted. Gleaming brightness had replaced Veronica's tears. Flushed cheeks edged curving lips, a gentle scoff.

"You make me sick!" Amanda turned and stormed to the door. Grabbing the doorframe, she flung around. "I didn't see you hovering over Sarah. It's only the guys. You really do make me sick, Veronica. People experiencing grief are vulnerable and should be protected, not preyed upon. You should know this more than most, you told me your story."

As Amanda disappeared out the door, Veronica snatched at her finger and went to twirl the wedding ring that was no longer there.

CHAPTER TWENTY-NINE

Sleep consumed Robert, but the forefront of his mind was consumed by thoughts of Julie. A mosaic of mixed feelings. Coolness at first, he'd strolled into the kitchen barefoot wearing only boxer shorts. Darkness and silence, he'd peered out the window to the star-covered sky. Then from behind, instant warmth. Robert turned. Endless love radiated from within a glowing vision. Cautiously, he stepped forward wiping his eyes. The haze cleared. Warmth rushed through his body, instant ecstasy. Julie had heard his cries. She had returned and was standing in front of him, wearing her long blue dress and looking so beautiful with her hair tied back. But was she real?

Julie.

Reaching forward he touched her face. He could feel her and she reacted to his touch with the same captivating smile she had in life. She appeared peaceful and eager to talk, she acknowledged his struggles and said she was proud of him, that she wished they'd spent more time together. She said she loved him. Holding her hand, Robert told her he loved her too, and they hugged and kissed. They danced just as they had danced so many times before in the kitchen. Then he asked her to come back to bed. Stepping towards the door, he could feel her resist.

"What's wrong?"

Julie released her hold. "I can't go with you. You must

take the rest of your journey without me."

Sadness engulfed, as coolness returned.

Julie gave him a reassuring smile. "You have an amazing life before you, Robert, but I have to go now. I just wanted to see you for a little while and tell you my passing wasn't your fault. Please don't blame yourself. It was my time."

Crushing energy tore through Robert's chest. "But I don't want you to go." Devastation ripped through his body as he buried his face within his hands. Echoes of his sobbing filled the room as he clung to her every word.

"I don't want to go either but I have to, my love. And I want you to move forward, free of guilt. You must believe. Believe in the future, Robert. Know that love never dies. And trust in your heart. A woman is coming into your life. You will love her and she will love you."

Robert reached for her, struggling to find her hand. He couldn't let her go, not again. Pressure restricted.

"Julie, don't go. Julie!"

"Toodle-pip, my love."

A glowing light. Release. Physical ease followed by peace and gratitude. Extreme comfort overwhelmed Robert and his heart brimmed with love. Julie was gone, but she was okay. On his lips, the softness of her kiss. Around his torso, a slight tingle from the warmth of her hug. Her voice was just as he remembered. He smiled and wiped his eyes. Had buried grief visited him in a dream? Was it real? A visitation perhaps? Was Julie an angel, a spirit, a messenger from God? Pulling the blankets up around his neck, he recalled every word and every feeling. Julie was okay and even after death she offered her love, reassurance and support. Robert would remember their encounter for the rest of his life. Relaxing into the softness of his mattress, he squeezed his eyes closed and wrapped his arms around himself.

"Toodle-pip, my sweetheart. Until we meet again."

***

Battering rain and blustery winds woke Veronica before daylight. Typical, meteorologists had predicted clear skies with medium to high temperatures and moderate humidity. She slammed her hands along the side of her body.
Blasted weather.

If the forecast were wrong, her plans would be useless. Robert was on the top of her mind and she was eager to spend time with him. Today was the day she was going to ask him out. She wanted to skip the traditional movie, dinner and drinks for something a little more original. Why would anyone want to spend an initial date confined to a prolonged period of darkness? Movie theatres were germ carrying, overcrowded, airless quarters. The thought of people shovelling handfuls of popcorn into their mouths and slurping drinks made her shudder. Then there was the after-movie chitchat. More valuable time wasted by the compulsion to discuss a movie that had just robbed you of two precious hours. Trying to blow, suck and inconspicuously pick popcorn shards out of your teeth. The thought was sickening.

Robert deserved better.

She deserved more.

In her plans, there would be no movie and definitely no popcorn. Her plans would be interactive and magical. It would infuse innocence, embrace Robert's inner child, and draw them together. Getting outside calmed the nerves and provided a different perspective. With an element of adventure and added excitement, it would be a date to remember.

All she needed was for Robert to say yes.

***

THE BELONGING

Repetitious ringing broke through Robert's dream – muddled then gone. Blinking his eyes, he struggled to focus. The ringing continued as he stretched and yawned. Daylight, a glimmer of blue sky through his blinds. Lunging across to the bedside table, he fumbled to pick up his phone.

"Hello."

An instant smile.

Robert ran his fingers through his hair as he listened. Today was a rostered day off work. In fact, he wasn't rostered to work for a few days.

"Yep, sounds nice, but I've just woken." He yawned and stretched again. "Oh sorry. An hour, I could be ready in an hour. Sounds good, I'll see you then."

He jumped from his bed and raced into the shower. First impressions counted, it was imperative he tidied his house and made himself presentable.

The doorbell rang. Flutters of nerves filled his stomach as he rushed to the door and opened it.

"Good morning," he said, high spirits eking into his voice.

Veronica curtsied. "Good morning to you too." Her nose crinkled as she smiled back and stepped closer. "Are you ready for an adventure?"

Robert nodded. He could feel a tingle in the depths of his stomach. "I am, but what did you have in mind? You only mentioned fresh air." He watched her closely as she spoke.

Veronica raised her eyebrows and tossed her hair. "I did, I did. Getting outdoors enhances mental health and positivity. It's just what the doctor ordered. You can call me, Nurse Veronica." She giggled and leaned forward, wrapping her hand around his elbow. Licking her lips, she gazed into his eyes.

A sense of overwhelming calm swept through Robert, her fingers gently caressing, sensual and purposeful. Was she the woman Julie spoke of? A sense of calm stability replaced his flutter of nerves.

"Well let's get this show on the road, Nurse Veronica. As suggested, I have my sunscreen on and my hat in my back pocket."

Robert had never been in a sports car, relaxing into the plush seat, he inhaled the intoxicating smell of new car leather. Pure luxury, push button ignition, a stylish electronic dashboard and voice-activated controls. It was a pleasure he could get used to. Unlike his old beat-up Ford, this engine purred. Watching Veronica change gears, he could tell she loved to be in control and appreciated the finer things in life. Stretching his feet out, he rubbed his hands together.

A street sign, a hint of where they were headed. Robert grinned, he felt more alive than he had in a long time. Today was different from yesterday. Today, was the first day of the rest of his life and he was determined to make the most of it. Sitting in silence, he thought about his dream and Julie's words. The car slowed. Ahead the traffic lights were red. They stopped. Veronica leaned over and pushed a button. A slight breeze, all the windows opened, a gentle humming sound, within seconds the roof retracted.

Veronica turned to Robert and smiled. "I think it's time for your hat."

Before he had a chance to respond, the lights turned green. Veronica placed her foot to the floor.

Robert's body pressed back into the seat. "Oh, my goodness!" He laughed. He snatched his cap in fumbling hands and placed it on his head.

As Veronica sped along the freeway, their laughter continued.

Robert could feel Veronica's excitement as she latched her arm around his. Fond memories swept through his mind as his pace increased. He felt awakened and excited. The last time he'd been to an underwater aquarium was when he was seven years old. He and Kenny had travelled to Manly on the ferry and spent the day at Manly Underwater World and the beach. Walking through the underwater tunnel Veronica remained close, occasionally jumping when large sharks appeared. To Robert it was a magical underwater adventure, like walking under the sea with so many creatures swimming above. Narrow tunnels provided closeness, few people, and a relaxed pace provided time to talk, to get to know each other. By the time they exited, both were hungry.

The day was far from over. Veronica had made lunch reservations.

A gentle breeze cooled the air as they strolled along the green foreshores of Sydney Harbour. A good walk always worked wonders, especially after an exquisite seafood lunch. Robert smiled. Veronica was full of surprises and like no other woman he'd ever met. He slowed his pace allowing her to edge slightly in front. A quick glance, a raising of his eyebrows followed by a nod. Veronica was appealing to the eye. She stopped. Resting against the railing, she turned to him and pointed towards the Harbour Bridge.

"How do you feel about heights and just over one thousand, three hundred steps?" She giggled as she watched Robert's reaction.

The fluttering within his stomach returned. "Are you serious? We're going to climb the bridge?" Robert grabbed the railing to steady his sway and looked at Veronica who stood smiling and nodding.

Both gazed up to the top of the giant structure. For Robert, the steps were of no real concern, but the height. Panicked thoughts raced through his mind, his knuckles whitening as his grip tightened around the railing.

What if I freeze or become dizzy or faint? A man shouldn't fear heights.

Sucking in a large breath, he straightened his stance,

wiped his brow and looked towards Veronica. "Are we really going to do this?"

Veronica nodded. "If you're game. We're booked in for the twilight tour. We'll journey up and along the Bridge's outer arch on the Opera House side until we hit the top. After a celebration at the summit, we cross the spine of the Bridge to the Darling Harbour side where we make our descent."

Robert sucked in another large breath.

I can do this.

"If I'm game?" he said, placing his hands on his hips with his elbows wide. "Of course I'm game, but if you're starting to have doubts." Straightening his back, he focussed on Veronica and tried to ignore his prickling skin and pounding chest.

"Me? Doubts?" she said with a rush of confidence. "I don't have doubts. If I see something I want or something I want to do, I go after it. I don't let fear or doubt control me."

And with that, the discussion was over. They made their way to the check-in and watched a short preparation video on what to expect. With a safety briefing over and romper suits on, they were on their way.

For Robert, there would be no backing out. The tour would take three and a half hours. Through a tunnel to the stairs, they commenced the climb. Hooked-in the entire time, Robert felt safe. Initial steps were easy. They paused along the way, admiring the stunning views and glistening water. There were so many boats in the harbour, big and small, ferries, sail boats, runabouts and fishing vessels. Who wouldn't want to spend a summer's day on the water? The higher they climbed, the more insignificant the world appeared. Robert began to sweat, and nausea swirled as his fear returned.

Pedestrians resembled armies of busy ants; everyone had a place to go. Warm wind swept across his face; he swallowed hard and bravely continued. Although his earlier fears that they would be climbing up steep see-through steps with cars whizzing directly below had vanished, he could still feel the stiffening of his legs. No safety harness, no amount of handrails, solid gradual steps or positive self-talk would ease his fear of heights. His body became hot and sticky, pausing for a moment he smiled at Veronica, who looked fearless. Silently he wished he'd been able to leave his nerves back in the lockers. This was one of the most amazing yet frightening things he had ever done, but it was a challenge he was determined to complete.

"Oh wow, Robert, look at the sunset." Veronica tugged at his sleeve when he stepped next to her on the summit. She turned from left to right and back again. "It's incredible! You could almost forget everything up here. There's a calmness within its pastel palette that lifts your eyes and heart. Look around, it's magnificent. Not a cloud to be seen all the way out to the Blue Mountains! And look at the steel arches, the way the sun kisses them."

"Holy fairy floss, Nurse Veronica!" Robert chuckled then smiled as he looked around. Knuckles whitened as his hands gripped the railing. He was pleased to have made it to the top and thankful they could rest for a while.

Veronica laughed at his playful gesture. Edging close, Robert took her hand within his. Veronica flinched and turned. Taken aback, her shoulders stiffened. Robert smiled, looked into her eyes and gave her a reassuring wink. She relaxed. Their fingers interlocked. Their bodies close, but not touching.

"Nature is awesome," Robert said, "and I want to thank you, Veronica, for such a wonderful day."

Veronica stepped closer and wrapped her arms around his waist. Warm hands travelled across his back; her gentle touch soothing. Overwhelming calm swept through Robert's body, his mind was at peace, fears forgotten. Shadows faded within the disappearing sun. Worries of the past dissolved within the darkening sky. In the distance the evening star, a flicker of hope and happiness. Hundreds of steps to be taken, his journey was far from over. Veronica moaned and pulled him closer. Robert tensed and pulled away; his thoughts invaded by thoughts of Julie.

"We'd better go, the others are leaving," he said.

It was late, by the time Veronica pulled up outside Robert's house. He felt refreshed, but slightly saddened their day had come to an end. Plucking at his collar, he placed it to his nose and sniffed. Veronica giggled then burst into laughter, snorted then laughed again. She placed her hands to her cheeks. "Oh stop, Robert, you have to stop. My face hurts from laughing. You've had me laughing all day."

Robert chuckled and placed his hands to his cheeks. He hadn't laughed so much in a long time. "Mine too." He sniffed at his collar again. "Phew, I need a shower. I smell like I've been rolling around on a cattle farm."

Veronica giggled. "You should have seen your face." Her eyes widened as she became more animated. "You were like, oh no! What's that, what's that?" Bouncing around in her seat, she flapped her arms and wiped her hands over her face. Robert laughed at her antics. The woman was beautiful, kind, and honest. He wasn't sure what he felt, attraction, affection or just friendship. Whatever it was, there was a connection. He leaned close.

"I was relaxing, taking in the warmth of the sun with my eyes closed. I thought it was raining for a bit. But when the putrid smell hit and I opened my eyes I realised you should have put the top up." He pointed towards Veronica and chuckled. Their laughter erupted, echoing into the street.

Veronica slapped his leg. "I'm so sorry, I didn't realise until it was too late. I swerved, but the wind must have changed and that's why you got hit. I didn't feel it. But now I know, never drive with my top down behind a cattle truck." She released a slight giggle, despite her efforts to hold it in. "I'm sorry."

Robert smiled and released a loud sigh. "It's okay. I forgive you. Isn't poop supposed to be lucky or is that just bird poop?" He paused, reached over and took Veronica's hand within his. "Thank you, Veronica. Thank you so much. Today was just what I needed. You are what I needed. Reminding me I can have fun, that there is no shame in laughing and enjoying life. Of all people, you understand." He leaned closer and kissed her on the cheek. "Goodnight, Veronica."

Robert watched her drive off then strolled inside.

Was Veronica the woman Julie had spoken of?

CHAPTER THIRTY

Shirley dropped to the ground as the white sports car stopped outside Robert's house. Hidden within a fortress of flowering grevilleas, she peered across the road. She bit her lip and struggled for breath. Her rival had returned. Why? Surely, she had seen him enough. They'd spent the previous day together. She'd seen her drop him home late the previous night. Watching Veronica saunter along Robert's pathway and up to his front door made her feel sick to the stomach. The woman repulsed her.

The knocking echoed. Veronica studied her reflection in the glass, straightened and knocked again. A few minutes passed. Faint knocking continued. Shirley pushed herself to her feet. It was time for answers. Why was a seemingly high-falutin woman interested in a genuine and caring guy like Robert? Brushing herself down, she walked to her driveway.

"He's not home, but you're welcome to come over for a cuppa."

Veronica stopped knocking and turned with a hand to her forehead. "Oh, Shirley, it's you."

"Yes, Veronica, it's me. Robert's not home. Would you like to come over for a cup of tea or coffee?"

"I was supposed to meet him."

"He must have forgotten."

Shirley shrugged and turned her back, smiling. Robert

116

wouldn't be home for hours. A hurried click-clacking noise approached from behind.

Darn! She's coming.

Rolling her eyes, Shirley took a deep breath. A puffing Veronica confronted her as she whirled around. Overpowering scents of musk and vanilla swirled. Shirley sneezed and placed her hand below her nose.

Oh, my goodness, the woman owns a perfume factory.

Veronica bent forward and placed her hands to her knees trying to catch her breath. Her red sleeveless blouse pulled tight, brimming cleavage begging to escape. Shirley shook her head.

Darn woman looks like a snooty lady of the night.

She waited in silence for Veronica to straighten. After a few moments, the two women came face to face. Shirley thrust out her chest and smiled as she rocked back and forth.

Drawing in a long breath, Veronica tucked a lock of hair behind her ear. "A cup of tea would be lovely, thank you."

Shirley's lounge room was far from modern or fancy. Veronica cringed as she studied its pale ivory walls and shuddered at the sight of the old, worn furniture and cluttered bookshelves.

"Are you sure I can't give you a hand," she yelled towards the kitchen.

"No thank you, I won't be long."

Running her finger along the top of the table, she inspected the line of dust. "I don't know where Robert could be. I left a note on his front door telling him I would be over. Maybe it blew away in the wind."

"It could have." Shirley smiled as she poured the water into the cups. She knew exactly what happened to her note and where Robert was. Veronica hadn't asked if she knew. She simply said Robert wasn't home and her note was gone. They were statements, not questions. Returning to the lounge room she placed the cups of tea on the table and sat. Sitting opposite Veronica would enable her to study the woman's reactions. She wanted answers and there was no time like the present.

"Robert told me your husband committed suicide."

Veronica inhaled sharply then glared over the rim of her teacup, her face paled. "Yes, that's right." She placed her cup on the table and wiggled around on her chair.

"Can I ask how?"

"With respect, that's a private matter—"

"Oh no, I'm sorry. I didn't mean to sound unkind. How selfish of me."

Veronica glared. "No, no. Don't be sorry, I just don't feel up to talking about the past. I'm trying to move forward."

Shirley couldn't conceal her look of suspicion. Veronica picked up her cup, straightened and squared her shoulders before taking another sip. Returning the cup to the saucer, she raised her eyebrows. "Robert tells me you have a son."

"Yes, he's playing in his room."

"And the father?"

"Immaculate Conception." Shirley laughed, seeming unaffected. She'd experienced dealings with the likes of the Veronicas of the world before; it was imperative she chose her words wisely. Who did Veronica think she was? The woman was sickeningly obvious, spruced up in the latest fashion. Hair trimmed and styled, carrying a Prada handbag while prancing around in ridiculously uncomfortable high-heeled shoes. Robert didn't need a high maintenance wife; he needed a woman, a real woman. It was time to increase the heat.

"Robert said your relationship was going through a rocky patch. Is that why your husband did it?"

"I don't know." Veronica's eyes widened. Her face

flushed pink.

"I imagine it would be hard."

"Yes, extremely. And I imagine it would be hard raising a child alone."

Shirley smiled and leaned back in her chair wanting to appear unfazed. *Two can play this game.* "No, not really, we have great support. Robert loves Jai. I always joke and say he's like a father to him." She paused to study Veronica's reaction. The woman sat stiffly, legs together and heels slightly to the rear, hands clasped on her lap.

Shirley swallowed hard and shifted on her chair. Only once before had she witnessed such contempt. It was a moment she preferred to forget. Old memories rushed through her mind. Tugging at her top, Shirley struggled for air. She needed to escape. "Oh my, I forgot the biscuits." She rose from the couch. "I'll be right back."

In the kitchen, she tried to pull herself together. Fanning her fingers over the kitchen bench, she attempted to steady her breathing. Unable to remove the thought of Veronica's piercing eyes; cat-like and golden, they were alluring yet repulsive. Warm sunlight streaming through the window took her back to a time when she had seen similar eyes. She was eight, at the time her mother worked for the Rothchild family as a housemaid. Aurelia was the Rothchild's seven-year-old only daughter, for months the two girls had shared a secret friendship.

Together they sat on the floor, laughing and playing with Aurelia's dolls. It was a day that would change Shirley's life forever.

The door flung open; a sudden breeze followed by a loud bang.

"Aurelia, get away from that wretched scrawny girl, she's the maid's simpleton," snapped Lady Penelope Rothchild. Both girls dropped their dolls. Stepping into the room Lady Penelope stomped her foot and clapped her hands. "Get away from her now, before you catch something."

Shirley cowered in the corner as Lady Penelope edged closer.

"Aurelia, off your knees at once! Young ladies don't play on the floor. Animals belong on the floor."

Aurelia leapt to her feet and dashed from the room in tears. Shirley trembled beneath Lady Penelope's piercing glare, petrified and confused by the harshness of her words. Why would Lady Penelope berate and forbid a caring, joyful friendship? What was wrong with laughing and playing on the floor? And what did she mean by wretched, scrawny and simpleton?

Later that evening Shirley asked her mother why she had abandoned her. Why had she continued to make Aurelia's bed unperturbed by the commotion? Why had she remained silent to Lady Penelope's insults?

"Rich people have freedom and power, they demand respect. Social status determines friendships, there are some friendships you should never have," her mother said. "You can no longer see Aurelia."

It was a concept Shirley rejected, but she was young and vulnerable, powerless. The two friends never saw each other again. Shirley was devastated.

From that moment on, she vowed she would never be weak and submissive. One day she would be rich. When she grew up, she would choose her own friends. Sucking in a deep breath, she opened her eyes and picked up the plate of biscuits. It was time to prove a point. Veronica Reid was not Lady Penelope Rothchild. Robert was not Aurelia, and Shirley was far from the submissive eight-year-old.

With smiling determination, she returned to the lounge room. "Would you like a biscuit?" Extending her hand, she offered a plate of seemingly mass-produced disks of baked dough.

Veronica looked up from where she sat and raised her eyebrows. "Namebrand or Homebrand?"

"Top quality private label." Shirley smirked.

Veronica gave a dismissive wave of her hand. "No, thank you."

"So, what were we talking about?" Shirley asked as she took her seat. Picking up a biscuit, she took a bite and waited for Veronica to speak.

"You being a single mother."

"Oh yes, that's right and Robert being like a father to Jai. Actually, he's better than a father, he's there for the both of us, by choice." Shirley leaned back in her chair arms folded, a smile on her face.

Veronica threw her head back and laughed. "Oh my, you poor naive woman. Do you really think any man wants to be the stepfather? That's one of the most ridiculous statements I've ever heard. It's like believing a derelict with a pocket full of change is rich. Only a birdbrain would believe something so absurd." She glared at a stunned Shirley. "Don't fool yourself. Robert associates with you because you live across the road. He's not looking for an instant family. What Robert needs is a woman, a real woman with no baggage."

"How dare you!" Shirley jumped to her feet, dropping her biscuit to the table she thrust her chest out and froze, glaring at Veronica.

"How dare I, what?" Veronica sank back into her chair and brushed a piece of fluff from her shoulder. "Tell me, Shirley. How about you stop with the games and tell me what you're going to do?" Tilting her head to the side, her lips curved upwards then relaxed. Widening pools of blackness expanded within her piercing golden eyes.

Shirley clenched her hands, counted to ten then rubbed her hands together as she looked beyond her unrelenting enemy. In her younger years she would have stormed over and smacked the smile from her face. But now, she had Jai to think of, and her job. With an assault charge she would lose her job, everything she'd been working towards would be lost.

She took a small step and leaned forward. "First of all, I am not a birdbrain and my son is not baggage. What am I going to do? I'm going to tell Robert about you. Who do you think you are to come into my house with your insults and sly remarks?" Her words were forceful, but only slightly above a whisper.

Veronica turned her face away, drew in a long breath then reeled around. "I don't think. I know who I am. I know what I want. I also know about you, so let's get things sorted. You were a friend to Robert's wife, Julie. You helped Robert when she passed away. Don't be fooled, my dear, that doesn't constitute more than a friendship." Veronica rose to her feet and slid her hand in her pocket. "A real man needs more than friendship."

Shirley glared and thrust her hands on her hips. Anger burned from within. "So, you think you know about real men. What about your husband, I'm sure he must've been a real man, otherwise you wouldn't have married him?" She paused and rubbed her chin. "So, tell me, Veronica, do you blame yourself and wonder why he chose death over you?"

"How dare you! I don't like your tone or what you appear to be insinuating."

"My tone?" Shirley thrust her finger to her chest, with eyebrows raised. "You started with the insults. I was trying to get to know you. I asked about your husband. You fired back and insulted my family. All I know is you had a terrible relationship. Your husband did himself in and now you seem to be after Robert."

Veronica glared. Shirley could feel her racing heart. She was determined to hold her stare. The past would not repeat. She would prove her mother wrong. Being rich did not entitle.

You will not beat me, Lady Penelope Rothchild.

Goosebumps covered her body as she gazed into Veronica's eyes. Her breathing shallow and muscles tense.

My house. My rules. Outstare. Outsmart. Outlast.

The seconds passed slowly. Neither would back down. Dryness burned Shirley's eyes. Unease prickled the back of her neck, clenching her jaw she fought the urge to blink.

I can't fail. I have to do this.

Itchiness engulfed. Veronica continued to stare. Shirley's stinging worsened. Her vision blurred. Breaking point was imminent. Her eyes felt like they had been jabbed with metal filings then doused in lemon juice. Just when it looked like all was lost, Veronica flinched and blinked. She clasped her hands over her mouth. A merciless Shirley continued to stare through her pain. She smiled.

Was that defeat within her quivering lips?

"You know nothing!" Veronica's body shook. Breathless and a little desperate, she brushed tears from her reddened cheeks. "I've been to hell and back."

"We've all experienced pain in our lives, Veronica." Shirley remained unsympathetic, calmly opening and closing her eyes. The burning lingered, but it had been worth it. Standing up to someone with money and defending those she loved was everything she believed in and everything that mattered. Shirley's voice remained expressionless, as if discussing household chores. Hushed, toneless words were all Veronica deserved. Shirley felt sick to her stomach.

"Who do you think you are to question me?" Spit flew from Veronica's mouth. Shirley pulled back, dodging the spray. Edging closer, Veronica stopped and stared clutching at her chest. "I don't need to listen to this." Snatching her bag, she whirled around and swung it over her shoulder. Thundering steps carried her out of the room. The front door slammed.

Shirley thrust her fists in the air. Despite winning that battle, she knew the war was far from over. For now, it was time to celebrate.

"Jai, you can come out of your room. Our guest has gone and Mummy has a surprise for you."

Jai dashed down the hallway. "Yes, Mummy."

"Mummy has something for you, sweetheart. Close your eyes. I'll be right back."

Jai closed his eyes and waited for his mother's return. Soft footsteps approached. His mother sneezed. A clunking noise, things moved on the coffee table. Jai stood with his hands over his eyes, bouncing with anticipation.

"Okay, you can open them." Shirley stood back and watched her son's reaction. Itchiness invaded her nostrils, grabbing a tissue she wiped her nose.

Jai jumped up and down. "Oh wow! That's amazing. Where did you get it?"

"I told you I've been working on something in the laundry."

Jai circled the table with excitement, hands gliding along the carefully-moulded lava channels, over the green terrain. Shirley chuckled, as his tiny fingers gently fluffed at the cotton ball topped trees.

"You made my volcano!"

"See what happens when you do as you're told?"

"Thanks, Mummy! It's amazing! You're amazing!" He raced to his mother and wrapped his arms around her, giving her a hug then dashed back to the table. Leaning over he ran his hand along the mountain to the crater opening. "Will it explode? Mrs Brakenridge said we should make an exploding volcano. There's a prize for the biggest blast."

Shirley laughed as Jai threw his hands in the air imitating the explosion. "Yes, Jai, it will explode. Mummy's got it all ready, a bottle full of red liquid lava and a tissue with some baking soda to drop in after the liquid. Your volcano will definitely explode, but not today."

"Oh, but Mummy."

Shirley raised her eyebrows and stepped over to Jai, reaching down she grabbed him under his chin.

"Jai, do you hear me?

He frowned. "Yes, Mummy, not today."

"Okay, then off you go. Go and play. I'll put this away so it doesn't get damaged."

Shirley lay on her bed, body sinking into the soft mattress, fingers gliding over the threads in her sheets. The tension of earlier was gone. Peace. Though she would invariably have to face Veronica again, she felt pleased with the day's events and empowered by having Veronica concede defeat. Forcing the snooty fat cat to scurry off and lick her wounds was invigorating. The thought of standing up for her beliefs made her proud. She smiled.

Absolute stillness, a tropical scented candle burned at her open window, it reminded her of Robert. Veronica's opinion was irrelevant. His actions spoke louder than Veronica's words. An impromptu visit after dinner proved he cared. Shirley's muscles relaxed as she watched her chest rise and fall. Closing her eyes, she drew in a lungful of air, listening to her breath.

In her quiet contemplation, she considered her plans. Everything was coming together. Jai was ecstatic, in his eyes she was a hero. Next week, he would present his exploding volcano. Robert had proven he cared by calling in for coffee after dinner. For now, she was happy in her decision to keep the Veronica incident to herself. Let the woman stew.

Relaxed, everything was peaceful. Things appeared hopeful. A bright future was just around the corner. Shirley was confident in her goals. No one or nothing would stand in her way.

Hysterical screeching.

Soothing stillness shattered.

Shirley leapt to her feet and raced up the hallway. "Jai!"

CHAPTER THIRTY-ONE

A passing glance. A distressing jolt. Silence. Disbelief. Doubt. Elsie snatched her chest. Gulping breath. Praying above shooting pain, and attempting to ignore the sudden chill. Had she seen correctly? Nausea lashed; her stomach cramped. Hands trembled as she tried to shake off the numbness. A second look. A better view. She stumbled forward. Down the back steps. Bracing hands. Thudding crutches. Shuffling feet. Praying. Hope. Uncertain steps. Uneven ground. Thunder. Lightning. Blinding rain. Her body saturated, eyes squinting. In the distance, was it her?

Not my poor Tinkerbell.

Quickening steps. Unsteady feet. A sense of urgency. Reaching arms. Pounding crutches. Tripping. Falling. Crashing. Elsie's face smashed into the muddy ground. Breathless gasps. Outstretched hands. Realisation. Devastation. A deathly scream.

"Tinkerbell! My poor Tinkerbell!"

Elsie struggled to her knees and crawled forward. She gently scooped Tinkerbell into her arms. Cradled against her chest, she watched, praying for her cat to move. To show any sign of life. Surely, she would move. She had to.

But she didn't.

Tinkerbell lay still. Stroking her fur, Elsie burst into tears. This wasn't supposed to happen, not to her loved and loyal companion. Tinkerbell's friendship was supposed to last a lifetime. Elsie rocked back and forth. What happened to Tinkerbell? How did she get there? Her tiny body was covered in blood. Elsie's shoulders jerked. Her tears hidden within the pelting rain. Fear percolated in her head as she recalled the growling noise. She shook, petrified of looming danger. Her body tortured by the inability to stand.

Time suspended. Both drenched. A moment to breathe. Another excruciating attempt. Straining muscles. Agonising moans. Her pain, heavier than her body. She collapsed to the prickling itchiness of grass.

Uncontrollable sobbing hid her silent prayer. Increasing frustration. Tinkerbell's body protected against her chest. Elsie gave her cat a peck on the head.

Oh, my baby, I love you.

Her head jerked. The doorbell taunted. The deluge continued. Minutes passed. Stuck in the eyewall of the storm. Squalling winds. The earth shaking beneath. More thunder and lightning. Summer storms were potentially deadly. Elsie continued to pray.

The back door slammed.

"Robert!" Elsie gave a frantic wave.

Robert leapt down the back stairs and sprinted to her side. "What's happened?"

"It's Tinkerbell. My poor baby. I think someone's killed her."

Elsie shook her head. Robert saw the cat within her arms. Blood covered Elsie's hands.

"Oh God." Fighting back the urge to vomit, he whipped a hand to his mouth. "Here, let me help you." He reached under her arm.

Elsie's body jerked and rolled to the side as he pulled her towards himself.

"Take Tinkerbell. Take her inside where she'll be safe."

Thunder cracked. Robert jumped as the sky lit up and

he released his grasp.

"I'm not leaving you here."

"But I can't get up, I'm too weak."

"Hold Tinkerbell."

Robert wiped his face and darted behind Elsie, grabbing her under both arms, he lifted her to her feet. Elsie's knees buckled and her body twisted. Robert lunged and wrapped his arms around her tiny waist.

CHAPTER THIRTY-TWO

Resting on his elbows Jai leaned over his bowl of cereal, sniffling persisted. Shirley glared, clenching her jaw. Pushed to her limit, she slammed her mug to the table. Coffee splashed. Jai's head snapped up, his tiny lips quivered. Tears brimmed within his red and puffy eyes.

"Sit up straight. Eat your breakfast. It's over, Jai, it happened. Stop your nonsense." Closed fists hammered the table.

The young boy jumped, dropping his spoon. "I'm sorry, Mummy—"

"Stop!"

"But—"

"But nothing! I told you to stop. I told you to stay out of the laundry. I locked the door. When will you ever listen?"

Jai burst into tears, sobbing uncontrollably. Heaving in air, he coughed and spluttered. "I-I didn't, I didn't mean to—"

"It's done. It's finished."

"My volcano?"

"Shut up and eat! There are more important things than your volcano. It's over." With one final threatening look, Shirley flew from her chair. Grabbing her mug, she launched herself towards the sink.

The young boy flinched. Ducking his head, he picked

130

up his spoon and took another mouthful between sobs. A choking noise, he retched and gagged struggling to suck in air. He gasped and coughed then gasped again. Shirley stood with her back turned, washing her mug under the running water, seemingly oblivious to his struggle as she questioned his behaviour.

She was tired of his antagonistic crying and whining, fed up with his disobedience. Acting out at home, defiant to her instruction. Punishments proved meaningless. Why was he an angel with others and yet the devil around her? Snatching the steel-scouring pad, she scrubbed the coffee stains from her mug. Long threads of metal ate at her fingers and scratched through the discoloured porcelain. Behind her milk and mushed up cornflakes spewed from Jai's mouth and out his nose. Wetness covered his school shirt, flecks of white, and clumps of yellow. His spoon dropped. His bowl smashed to the floor. Shirley whirled around. Her mug shattered at her feet as she raced towards her son. Jai collapsed forward. A dead weight.

Screaming, she snatched under his arms, yanking him from the chair pounding on his back. "Breathe, Jai, breathe!"

His skinny arms flapped within her heaves. His legs dangling as she thrust. No response. Heaviness. Hands slipping. Unable to hold him up, she dropped to the floor. His limp body on top of hers.

"Jai! Jai wake up. Jai!"

A panicked push, she rolled him to his side. Milk and mush seeped from his mouth.

Airway clear. Head back. Nose blocked. Blow.

Come on, Jai. Come on, baby.

Nothing. Blow and again.

Jai's body jerked. He coughed. Endless milk and mush flowed from his mouth. His chest expanding as he gasped for air. Shirley snatched him from the floor shaking him. "Breathe, baby, breathe. Cough it all up."

Tears flowed as she cradled him in her arms. He was

alive. Her precious boy was alive. Tears of joy.

Sorrowful eyes stared up at her. "I'm sorry, Mummy, I'm sorry." He coughed again.

Pulling him to her chest, her voice softened. "Shh. I told you last night, you have to listen. Not another word."

Yapping barks. A droned roar. The neighbours' dogs and the damn school bus. Shirley glanced at her watch. If they didn't get a move on, they'd be late. "Are you okay, baby?" She looked at her watch again and gently rubbed his shoulder.

Jai nodded and sniffed. "Yes, Mummy."

As she struggled up from the floor, Shirley's concerns were interrupted by her ringing phone. She looked to it and dragged Jai to his feet. Clasping her hand around his cheeks, she pulled his face to hers. Vomit lingered on his breath, covered the table and splattered over the floor. "You promised me, Jai, not another word. Go clean yourself up."

"Yes, Mummy."

"What happens in our house, stays in our house."

"Yes, Mummy."

Releasing her hold, Shirley watched Jai stagger towards his room with downcast eyes. She picked up her phone. "Hello... Oh my God, when? Oh my God. I'll be there soon. I'm leaving now." Shirley grabbed her bag from the kitchen bench. "Jai, get a move on. We have to go. Now, Jai, now!"

Bashing and crashing. Jai emerged from his room, tucking a fresh shirt into his shorts. Shirley snatched her keys from the hook and grabbed his backpack from the kitchen bench as he raced down the hallway. Both rushed out the front door.

A morning of chaos and drama, Shirley wiped sweat from her brow as she watched Jai disappear into his classroom. Fear and guilt took hold as she sped down the road. She prayed he would keep his mouth shut and hoped from now on he would behave and do what he was told.

Jai is safe. I'm a good mother. I can deal with anything.

Jai is safe. I'm a good mother. I can deal with anything.

Tyres screeched. Her car door slammed. Shirley dashed along the crooked pathway, through the door and into the darkened lounge room.

"I came as soon as I heard. Oh, my poor dear, are you okay?"

Dropping her handbag, she flung onto the couch and wrapped her arms around Elsie who sat crying, shoulders slumped. "What can I do? Tell me, you name it... anything. Would you like a cuppa? I could make you a nice cup of tea."

Elsie's body trembled beneath Shirley's tightening arms.

"It's so painful to see you like this, if only I could take away your heartache. If only I'd tried harder. I should have searched more. I'm so sorry. I'm so, so sorry, Elsie. Why didn't you call yesterday? Robert should have called yesterday."

Releasing her hold, she frantically raked through her handbag. "Here have some fresh tissues. Cry as much as you need and for as long as you want. Crying is healthy. You need to release all those pent-up feelings. I'm here for you now."

Elsie took the mass of crumbled white softness and wiped her face as Shirley pulled her back into her chest.

"It's my fault. I'm so sorry. I should've looked harder." Her hands clasped around Elsie's wilted body, her chest soaked by raw emotion. Muffled sobs and howling misery arced in waves, broken only by stuttering breaths. Five minutes passed then five more.

Finally, Elsie freed herself from Shirley's embrace, took her hand and stared into her eyes. "Don't be too harsh on yourself, my dear, you tried," she said. "Tinkerbell had a wonderful life. You can't blame yourself."

Shirley bowed her head and covered her eyes with her hands. Elsie brushed her fingers against Shirley's cheek, and Shirley raised her chin. She looked at Elsie. The room fell away as they gazed silently into each other's eyes.

Don't be too harsh on myself. Are you serious? I can't blame myself.

Rising to her feet, Shirley plucked at her blouse as she paced back and forth. Elsie remained seated on the couch. The cat, the blasted cat. Of course, the cat had a wonderful life. A large percentage of Elsie's shopping money was spent on luxurious food items. King prawns and barramundi, Shirley couldn't afford king prawns and barramundi. The blasted cat ate better than most people did.

You miserable old bag. How dare you! I did everything for the damn fluffball fleabag.

Pushing her tongue against the roof of her mouth, Shirley smiled while fighting back the urge to tell Elsie what she really thought. Unappreciated, unnoticed and taken for granted. For years she had gone above and beyond, she'd looked after the evil, murdering lap-monster. Cleaned up its vile poop, washed down vomit and mess, been clawed at, bitten and scratched. She'd had to shove tablets down its hissing, snarling throat. Gagged and sneezed, endured sleepless nights. And for what? Her only reward tortured and mangled birds and mice. Actions spoke louder than words. Restraint and patience were for the weak and undetermined. There would be no more waiting. Shirley knew what she wanted and was steadfast in her plan.

You self-absorbed, cashed-up old trout.

Tilting her head forward, her eyes narrowed and her lips curled upwards. "How about I make you a nice cup of tea."

Elsie nodded. "Thank you, my dear."

In the kitchen the kettle boiled, Shirley coughed and

spat, stirred the tea and returned with a smile. "Here you go, my darling, you've earned this."

Elsie wiggled forward on the couch and took a small sip. "Oh, that's lovely."

CHAPTER THIRTY-THREE

By mid-morning, Shirley had Elsie out of the house. A trip to the shops and a relaxing meal at Elsie's favourite coffee shop would work wonders. Settling into the cushioned booth, Elsie sipped on her strawberry milkshake. Her routine was always the same; first she ordered a strawberry milkshake. Looking over the menu, she would appear undecided, after five minutes of procrastination she would invariably choose the same thing, a club sandwich. Toasted bread filled with sliced poultry, bacon, lettuce, tomato and mayonnaise, cut into quarters and held together with cocktail sticks. With her order taken, came the routine urge to use the bathroom.

"I'll be right back, my dear."

Shirley watched Elsie totter towards the back of the café and out of sight then reached into Elsie's handbag. A quick slide of her hand, Shirley sat upright and took a few gulps of her pineapple juice.

Elsie returned looking relieved just as the waitress delivered their food. Compliments flowed from Shirley's mouth like melted butter over a hot baked potato. Seasoned by a touch of flattery, Elsie relaxed and enjoyed picking at her lunch. The occasional smile and chuckle showed Shirley's plan was coming together.

"Thank you so much, my dear, it was a wonderful

idea to get out of the house." She placed her knife and fork on to her plate.

"My pleasure, Elsie. I just want to see you happy."

Elsie became teary; taking a tissue from her pocket, she wiped her nose. "Without you, I have no one."

"No one?" Shirley leaned closer. "But what about family?"

"Tinkerbell was my family. Without her I have no one." Elsie slumped forward and began to weep. It was the first time she had opened up about her private life.

Shirley reached out and took her hand. "You have me, Elsie, you can count on me."

"Thank you, my dear, I don't know what I would do without you. Your kindness means so much."

"And you mean the world to me, Elsie."

"Thank you, I want to thank you. Let me pay for lunch."

Shirley placed her hand to her mouth. "Oh, you don't have to." It was the first time the old woman had offered to pay for Shirley's meal.

"I insist." Elsie grabbed her handbag and released the clasp, smiling as she reached inside. Her breath quickened, her hands buried deep within the tattered brown leather. Frantic grabbing, panic rose to her face as she reefed her bag from the seat next to her and up-ended its contents over the table.

"My purse, my purse is missing." Trembling hands clutched at her chest. She stood and whirled around, staggered a little to the left and went limp.

Shirley jumped to her feet, snatching Elsie's arms she lowered her to the seat. "Oh, my poor dear, are you all right?"

Elsie puffed and nodded. "But my purse. I need to find my purse."

"You wait there. Let me go. I'll see if I can find it."

Elsie nodded and slumped back into the chair as Shirley dashed from the coffee shop.

By the time Shirley returned Elsie appeared a little calmer. Weaving between the tables, she flapped her hand above her head. "I found it. You must have dropped it under the car."

"Oh, my angel of mercy. I can't thank you enough."

Shirley sat and handed Elsie her purse. The old woman reached over, grabbed her hand and kissed it. "My angel of mercy, my sweet, sweet angel of mercy." Unclasping her purse, she looked inside. Feeble fingers flicked as the woman sighed in relief. "Here take this." Elsie pulled her hand from within her purse. A wad of polymer big pineapples flashed.

"Oh, I couldn't," Shirley said, batting her eyelids before looking down.

Elsie leaned across the table, placed the small stack of fifty-dollar notes in front of Shirley. "I insist."

Dinnertime couldn't come soon enough. Shirley's day had gone from disastrous to delightful. At last, she had money in her pocket. Tonight, she would eat like a queen.

Licking her lips, she marvelled at the Wagyu steak. One inch thick, edges drooping over the side of her plate, and crisscrossed with gridiron marks – the best beef money could buy.

She took her first slice, and the meat gave way between her teeth, like soft caramel. Juices glistened and pooled on her plate. Before her first mouthful was gone, she stuffed another piece into her mouth. Jai sat opposite, stabbing at his sausages.

"Jai, eat your dinner."

The young boy turned his head in disgust. "I can't."

"Why not?"

"It's meat." Pushing the greasy sausages to the side

of his plate, he screwed up his nose and flopped back into his chair.

Shirley shook her head and pointed her knife towards his plate. "You like sausages."

"I don't. Yuck! It's an animal, a poor dead animal." He shoved his plate away and kicked the leg of the table. Shirley glared. His moody silence was like an ungrateful two fingers up to everything she did for him.

"You're not starting this again. Eat or go hungry. It's your choice." Rolling her eyes, Shirley shrugged and continued with her steak. Ridiculous comments would not spoil her feast, besides Wagyu beef had a price tag comparable to some precious metals. One bite followed by another.

Jai remained firm with his refusal to eat. Shirley soldiered on regardless, devouring a warm mix of succulent steak and hot chips saturated in beef juices. Half had gone, and Shirley slowed her pace but would not be defeated. Her eating became bird-like, thin slithers mopped up the final juices. Ignoring Jai, she wiped her mouth with her hand and slumped back into her chair undoing the button of her pants. Satisfaction. She'd had a taste of what others took for granted and understood now how she needed to break the rules in order to realise her dreams. Tonight, she would revise her long-term plans and short-term strategies.

"Off you go. You don't eat, then you go to bed hungry. Hunger is good sauce, tomorrow you'll think twice, young man."

CHAPTER THIRTY-FOUR

Having woken in darkness, Robert lay beneath the warmth of his feather-down quilt listening to the world wake around him. A hint of light. A chorus of birds chirped beyond the slight breeze through his open window. He smiled then yawned and stretched, feeling his muscles tighten from his pointed toes through his muscular legs, along the arch of his back and finally up his arms, to his hands and outstretched fingers above his head.

Today he was looking forward to another date with Veronica, of which he hoped there would be many more. As the sun rose, silence disappeared behind the ever-increasing hum of distant cars. Warmth and stillness replaced the refreshing breeze. Time to rise, close the window, shower and get ready. Sitting on the edge of the bed, his feet gently searched out his slippers, and he stretched again.

***

Stabbing at her soggy Weet-Bix, Veronica released a heavy sigh. The recent conversation she'd had with Amanda ran through her mind. Her brow furrowed and concern overrode her eagerness to spend the day with Robert. What if Amanda spoke to him before she had the chance to set him straight? Everyone had a past, but some things were better received when told by the person they concerned.

THE BELONGING

I'm sure he'll sympathise.

Enthusiasm waned. Dropping her spoon, she stood, picked up her bowl and sauntered to the kitchen sink, kicking the chair on her way. Why did people insist on interfering in matters that were of no concern to them? Anger brewed as she dropped her bowl into the sink and leaned against the bench, squeezing her eyes closed. Her frustration increased as coolness from the laminate crossed her palms. A gentle swipe of her hand to her pounding forehead was no relief. Sucking in her bottom lip, she shook her head. Random sparks of white light flashed behind her tightened eyelids.

Stillness. Silence.

After a few moments, the flashing lights disappeared. Maybe the nausea and headache were from inhaling smoke. Her first attempt to make breakfast had been a dismal failure. A temporary lapse in concentration. A smoke-filled kitchen. Smoke alarms screaming and the charcoal remains of toast tossed into the bin.

Why did Amanda so desperately want to disclose all? *I need to tell him. It has to come from me.*

By the time Veronica arrived at Robert's the day was half over. Still heat and high humidity replaced the freshness of hours past. With a quick apology for her lateness and an explanation of not feeling well they decided an afternoon inside would be better than their plan to go to Maroubra Beach.

"I think it's just the heat." Veronica rubbed her forehead, leaning against the wall she bowed her head forward. Robert stepped closer and gently rubbed her arm.

"How about you sit and relax and I'll make you a nice cup of tea."

The look on his face showed concern. Maybe it would be better to leave her chat for another time, but when was the right time? Inhaling deeply, she released a loud sigh. Robert took her hand within his and led her to the couch. Veronica plonked into the softness as Robert released her hand. She watched him leave the room and slowly looked around worrying how he would perceive her past. The thought of him not accepting her was frightening. The guy was so kind and caring, surely, he would understand.

Nausea swirled and her head continued to pound. She clenched and released her hands, then wiped her sweaty palms over the cushions on the couch. Dread. Silence broken by the clinking of cups and spoons in the kitchen. Shifting on the couch, she clutched at her chest and took a deep breath. Blowing out her cheeks she reassured herself all would be fine. Today, she would talk with Robert.

After their cup of tea, both relaxed into the softness of the couch. Veronica turned to Robert with a twinkle in her eye. Leaning closer she reached up, her palms embracing his warm and bristled cheeks. He smiled and winked. It was time.

"I need to tell you something, Robert." She looked downwards, before she had a chance to see his response. His closeness remained and his smiling face welcomed her return glance. Removing her hands from his cheeks, she wriggled on the couch then touched his leg and looked at him.

"I want you to know everything about me." She paused. A shadow seemed to sweep across his face and she quickly averted her eyes. She began to shake. Robert placed his hands over hers.

"What's wrong?"

"I've been threatened." Drawing in a slow breath she glanced up.

Robert pulled away. Cocking his head, his brow furrowed. "What do you mean, you've been threatened?"

Shifting on the couch, Veronica blinked as his words struck.

"Veronica!" He grabbed her arm. "Tell me, Veronica.

THE BELONGING

What are you talking about, threatened?"

Tears glistened within her eyes as his grip tightened. His voice raised and demanding. Veronica collapsed forward forcing Robert to release his grasp. Bursting into tears, she buried her face within her hands. "I should have kept quiet." Her words were mumbled as she raised her chin. Taking a deep breath, she tucked her hair behind her ears and wiped her eyes. "Women can be so jealous." Shaking her head, she looked at the ceiling.

"Who's threatened you?" Robert jumped to his feet and leaned over Veronica's wilted body. Propped against the arm of the couch, his finger pointed. Veronica flinched.

"Amanda!" She looked away then turned to him.

Robert dropped his arm and frowned. His head tipped to the side. "Amanda?" He repeated, raking his fingers through his hair. Stepping towards her, he looked flushed, as if he had been told all the stars had fallen from the sky. Stopping, he tugged at his collar. "Why?"

Veronica remained seated. Glancing upwards she met his unrelenting stare. Her face reddened as the air around her appeared to heat up. Closing her eyes for a second, she pressed her lips firmly together knowing this might be her last chance to tell her side. Nausea swirled from the pit of her stomach as her nails cut into the palm of her hand.

"She's an interfering, jealous cow." Scarlet heat burned her cheeks and red blotchiness wrapped her neck as she shifted on the couch straightening her back. Her breath hitched a little. "I told her my inner most secrets and now she's threatening to use them against me."

Robert stared motionlessly, his brows lifted and his eyes widened. "She can't do that."

"She said she will. She's jealous."

"Jealous of what?"

"You, me, anyone who appears to be happy. I told her all about my marriage, the abuse and arguments. I shared

143

my feelings of guilt. How I blamed myself for my husband's death and now she's convinced herself that I'm some sort of evil vixen."

"She doesn't know you. Has she lost her mind?"

"She knows about my past. She knows about Henry."

"Henry. Who's Henry?"

"Henry came to therapy for a while. We got along really well, but he decided therapy wasn't for him. Amanda's got it in her head that I drove him away. She's lost the plot. The woman is jealous and will do anything to destroy anyone's happiness."

"That's ridiculous. She can't threaten you. You've told me about your husband. I know you blamed yourself and I've told you, you're not to blame. He controlled his actions, not you. And as for this Henry and me, a man can make his own decisions. I'll decide who I see and I don't take kindly to malicious gossip or threats."

Veronica leaned back into the couch, looked away for a moment, bit her lip and looked up at Robert. "You shouldn't be too hard. She's young and innocent."

"Young, yes. Innocent, no. Innocent doesn't threaten."

"But the poor girl needs help."

"Poor girl, nothing. You don't deserve her threats. I know about your husband. I'm not concerned about Henry. I won't let Amanda get away with this. You leave it to me. I'll set her straight."

Robert dropped to the couch and wrapped his arm around Veronica, pulling her close. And for a moment her mind went completely blank in the best possible way. Gone were her concerns. His words offered hope for a future. She relaxed into his warm embrace.

CHAPTER THIRTY-FIVE

A prickly sting, and icy chills rushed through Shirley's body as she whisked around. Leaves crunched beneath her feet. Her knees buckled and she slammed to the ground, hidden within a fortress of flowering grevilleas brimming with swarming bees. Racing thoughts paralysed. A sudden gasp to catch her breath, she needed to catch her breath. Moisture laden air sucked into her lungs. Still, everything was still and silent. Except for the bees.

Shirley blinked as her eyes adjusted; her vision distorted and blurred. Had someone been watching? Flexed hair follicles had warned. Invading energy had assaulted. Churning within her gut and clammy hands didn't occur without cause. Her body trembled as her mind raced. Were they still watching? Wiping sweat from her brow, she tried to think back. It had been dark when she left. She had kept her headlights off until she was down the road and had turned them off on her return. Had someone seen? Had someone heard her car engine? Was she a suspect?

It had been two days. Two days since Elsie had discovered Tinkerbell's lifeless body. Within that time, she had seen both Elsie and Robert, neither had suggested she had anything to do with the cat's death. But why did she now feel as though she was being watched? Was Robert peering across from the other side of the road, watching and waiting to see if he could find a link between the two?

Clutching her chest, Shirley struggled to regain composure. Tingling ravaged her body. She had to look. She couldn't stay on the ground.

Sweat trickled from her brow as she clambered to her knees. The morning sun always hovered above Robert's house. Looking that way would be a challenge. Trembling hands clutched at the dense bush as she squinted into the blinding light. Nothing, the street was deserted. The blinds in Robert's house appeared closed. Had she imagined everything? Was it guilt for her failure to find and safely return Tinkerbell as she had promised? Or jealousy that Robert had been able to console Elsie before she could?

Staggering to her feet, she brushed leaves and dirt from her body and retreated to the coolness of her house. Concerns vanished over a relaxing breakfast with Jai. A summer storm blew in. Lightning filled the sky. Claps of thunder and torrential rain. Within an hour, it had passed and the suffocating humidity returned. After lunch, Shirley decided to go to the shops. Jai insisted he would be safe at home alone. With a promise he'd not answer the phone and keep the doors locked, she left.

The shopping centre was crowded and the air cool. Time passed too quickly. Shirley glanced at her watch; it was nearing dinnertime. Afraid Jai might have been concerned as to where she was, she made a dash to her car for the quick drive home.

When she opened her front door, Shirley paused at the sound of Jai's voice. He was having a conversation, but with who? Slamming the front door, she hurried to the lounge room. Jai continued talking. Grocery bags battered along the hallway walls.

Shirley lunged into the lounge room. "Robert." She was careful not to sound annoyed.

Robert jumped to his feet. "Shirley, are you okay? You look as though you've seen a ghost."

There was a short pause. Shirley placed her groceries

on the floor. Jai squirmed near her feet, but did not look up. She felt like kicking him to attention. Why had he ignored her instruction and what had they been talking about?

Clearing her throat, she returned her focus to Robert. "Yes, yes, I'm fine. I wasn't expecting you to be here, is all."

"I hope you don't mind."

"No, not at all. How have you been?"

"Not bad. I think I'm starting to cope. Well, at the moment that's how I feel. I'm trying to keep myself busy." Pursing his lips, he placed his hands on his hips. "Returning to work has been positive. Don't get me wrong, I still can't sleep properly and I keep thinking Julie will walk through the front door, like it's a nightmare I'll wake up from, but…" He dropped his hands to his sides and looked at the floor. A slight step forward, he looked up and smiled. "Therapy has been good. I know I have to stop living in the past. I need to move forward. I think I'm starting to have slight glimpses of hope." Tears sparkled on his lashes as he took a deep breath and wiped his hands down his side.

Shirley smiled. "That's great."

Robert nodded, placing his hands in the pockets of his pants. "Yeah, one day at a time." He paused. "Hey, have you noticed anything strange lately?"

She frowned. "Like what?"

"I thought I heard someone lurking about the other morning."

Shirley took a few seconds to think as she looked towards Jai who appeared oblivious of their conversation. Robert reached forward and stroked her arm. Shivering beneath his touch, she raised her chin. His eyes steadied on hers. Her shoulders tensed. Was he trying to lure her into a trap?

"The other morning." She shifted from one foot to the other. "Nope, didn't hear a thing. I've actually joined the local gym and have been going some mornings. I'll have to keep my eye out." She shuddered.

"Please do, I wouldn't want anything to happen to you."

Shirley nodded, but remained silent. Robert's gaze felt intense. Did his slight glimpse of hope include her? His touch was warm and his voice reassuring.

"I bet you get some hearts racing at the gym." Robert winked and smiled, nudging towards her.

Shirley giggled and gave a dismissive wave. Was her mind playing tricks or was Robert making a pass? He stepped closer, gaze unbroken. The prickly sting from her morning returned. Warm breath swept across her face as she held his gaze. Nervousness rose; Robert was deep within her personal space. Her heart raced. It was too much. Jai was only meters away. Robert released his grasp on Shirley's arm as she stepped back and took a deep breath to steady her voice.

"I need to talk with you about Elsie. Did you want to stay for dinner? I could phone Bella Pizza and have one delivered."

Robert stuck his tongue out and released a gagging sound. "Didn't you hear, the Food Authority has closed them down. That's where I got my pizza from the other week when I was sick. Seems I got off lucky, others ended up in hospital with Salmonella poisoning."

Shirley took a step back and folded both arms across her chest. "Oh wow, I hadn't heard."

"Anyway, I think that may have given me the nudge I needed. I'm back to cooking for myself." He looked at her and smiled. "Sausages and mashed potato tonight, it's already prepared so I will have to pass on dinner. What was it you wanted to say about Elsie?"

Shirley leaned over, picked up her groceries and held them in front of her chest. Silence. She looked at him with pursed lips, letting him stew for a moment. Fear crossed Robert's face as he waited for an answer. Jai stood, stretched as he yawned, breaking the silence. Both watched as the boy left the room.

Curiosity must have bit hard, for Robert reached forward and tugged her hand. "Is something wrong?" he asked, pressing his lips together.

Shirley's lashes fluttered, she squeezed her eyes shut, placed her groceries on the floor and turned away.

"Shirley, you have to tell me what's wrong. I'm not leaving until you do."

Spinning around she burst into tears and took a couple steps forward collapsing into his arms. Robert wrapped his arms around her and gently stroked her back. She sobbed as her body shook. Her head rested against his chest for a minute or two.

Robert loosened his grip as Shirley sniffled and wiped her eyes with her hands then looked up at him. "It's probably just me being silly. I didn't realise she had no one." She burst into tears again.

Taking her hands within his, he pulled her to his chest and wrapped his arms around her shoulders. "Oh, come here. You're not being silly. You're kind and caring."

Shirley relaxed into his warmth, inhaling his Old Spice scent. "I'm sorry," she said, wiping a tear from her chin.

"You have nothing to be sorry about. I didn't know either. Come on, there's no need to cry. She has us."

Inhaling his smell, no other thoughts mattered. Shirley had a sense of belonging. Kind and caring, Robert had said. Us, he also said. Not 'Elsie has you and I,' he'd said, 'us.' Did it mean he viewed them as being a team, a package, together? His hug was firm and soothing. Her body relaxed, her mind wishing it would last forever. But it didn't. Within seconds Robert relaxed his grasp and stepped back. The warmth of his body disappeared.

"Elsie will be fine. She's a tough old chook." He looked at his watch. "I don't want to shrug you off, but I have to go. I told Veronica I'd give her a call at six."

Shirley's chin dipped to her chest. Annoyance lodged in her throat. Rejection stung. Jealousy burned. Anger churned. Clenching her hands, she walked Robert to the door and said goodnight.

Leaning against the door she counted to ten trying to ease her agitation.

Inhale. Hold. Exhale. Inhale. Hold. Exhale.

"Jai!" she screamed up the hallway.

CHAPTER THIRTY-SIX

Thumbing at the next page, Elsie's tired hands trembled while uncertainty clouded her mind. Everything appeared so surreal, even the warmth from the morning sun appeared fake and offered no relief. Closing her eyes, she began to pray wanting to believe not all was lost. A moment of silence and quiet reflection, she focused on her breath and sank into the softness of her couch, her body relaxed. After a few minutes, she opened her eyes and allowed her fingers to flick over the tattered pages once more. The flicking stopped. Fingers pushed between the pages as words of wisdom appeared.

Jeremiah 29:11 - For I know the plans I have for you, declares the Lord, plans to prosper you and not to harm you, plans to give hope and a future.

A tear released from the corner of her eye as she read the words. Leaning forward, she moaned as her fingers touched the table. Coolness, and a familiar hardness. As she placed her Bible down, her mind was taken back to countless Sundays, sitting on hard wooden pews listening to the preachings of The Lord. Elsie understood and respected that not everyone believed in God, but many of her earliest memories involved religion. Her parents were especially devout and would read the Bible daily.

In her silence, she longed for the return of happiness and joy, she prayed for a sense of purpose and acceptance.

She raised her hand to the gold chain around her neck. Gazing at her diamond-encrusted cross she felt proud and worthy. For Elsie, the cross was the most important symbol in the world – it represented hope and forgiveness. After a moment, she returned her cross to the safety beneath her blouse, picked up her Bible and searched out another passage.

Psalm 23:4 soothed her soul. Rising to her feet, she returned her Bible to the bookcase and shuffled out to the kitchen. Elsie stopped at her open back door and peered into her backyard. Sunlight danced on her cheeks while sadness overwhelmed her. Without Tinkerbell everything appeared so quiet, lifeless, void of colour.

Elsie gently massaged the dull ache that radiated from within her chest. If only her loving and loyal friend were still alive. When she looked at her watch, her lips rose then quickly fell. Shirley would soon arrive; she always said how she loved Tinkerbell. It was nice to have a carer who identified herself as a 'cat person'.

Elsie would make a pot of tea and when Shirley arrived, they would sit in the lounge room and talk, they would reminisce so their healing could take place.

***

Anger and resentment brewed as the teapot emptied, by the time Shirley took her last sip she felt like screaming. Everything that left Elsie's mouth was about blasted Tinkerbell. Over and over, like a broken record. Stories tediously repetitive. Biting her tongue, Shirley forced a smile, patted dry her scant tears and leaned closer with false interest. She'd come too far to discard her mask. No sacrifice was too great when it came to her ultimate game plan. Double dealing and duplicitous behaviour was a necessity. Her innocent lie about being a cat lover from years past should have died with the blasted cat. All she could do was hope Elsie's grief was short lived, but the woman would not stop.

Shirley bowed her head, forced to endure her façade. Minutes dragged by, one story after another. Her disingenuous laughter had been rehearsed, but it built trust. Patience would see the old woman eating out of her hand, but how many more painstaking stories would Elsie need to tell?

With her loving and loyal companion dead, hope had been destroyed and Elsie aged overnight. Whiskers seemed to spring up on her chin like weeds after a rainy night, the lines on her face deepened, and her eyelids drooped. Gone was the sparkle in her eyes, the enthusiasm in her voice. "I'm just a misery," she would say. "Death is inevitable. What's the point to living?"

In contrast, Shirley's sense of wanting intensified with her ever-increasing fixation about Elsie's fortune. The old woman had no one, and Shirley wondered how much longer Elsie would live. Five years was possible, but then again, her health had deteriorated over recent years.

She smiled as the old woman squinted back grief. Death could come much sooner. Elsie appeared hunched and weak, and dragged her feet more frequently. In the three days since Tinkerbell's death, she had transformed from a woman who dressed with fastidious care to a battered shell old biddy in crumpled clothes – her inner torment reflected in slumped shoulders and bouts of sadness, while trembling hands dabbed at her tear stained face.

Shirley couldn't help but think about her recent Wagyu beef reward. The experience had been truly intoxicating, but all too brief. She knew exactly what she needed to do.

I will have what my heart desires.

Shifting on the lounge, she leaned close and wrapped her arm around Elsie, feeling her thinness she gently patted her back and pulled her close. Strands of cat fur embedded within Elsie's cardigan itched and aggravated, making her sniff.

She turned her face slightly away. "It's going to be okay, I'm here for you. I'm not going anywhere."

Elsie wriggled within her embrace, coughed and cleared her throat. "I keep thinking she will come through the door. I can still feel her nuzzling at my feet. I hear her meow and purr then I realise it's all just in my mind. She's… she's gone. Gone forever." Elsie turned to Shirley with quivering lips, her breath caught in a tiny gasp.

Shirley turned her nose as warm sweetness from Elsie's sugary tea brushed against her cheek.

Heartbreak, acknowledgment, and more tears. Sobbing filled the room. Minutes passed. At last Shirley could feel Elsie relax within the comfort of her silent embrace. Shoulders rising and falling between jagged breath.

The old woman began to chuckle and shake her head. "She was so funny, the way she would do the complete opposite of what I would expect. So curious, she'd wrap herself in clothes and covers, pounce out, chase ghosts and yet she was so loving and lived life by her own rules. Oh, how I loved to watch her. As a kitten she would play for hours. She would make me laugh, she always made me smile." A mirthless smile crossed her face.

Shirley smirked then laughed along as she silently recalled her own memories, in particular the day she took to Tinkerbell with the vacuum. Everything was fine until the suction pipe stuck to her side, the cat snarled and lashed out jumping from her grasp. Howling as if its body had been wedged in a vice, it flew up the stairs. The scratches on Shirley's arms took weeks to heal. The blasted cat did more than purr and meow. It also scratched and bit, hissed and left mess. In recent years it coughed up vile hairballs. Reminders of Tinkerbell were everywhere; in the air, in bedding, in the carpet and embedded within clothes.

THE BELONGING

Elsie thrust her hands forward and slapped her thighs interrupting Shirley's memories and forcing her to release her grasp. Shocked by Elsie's lashing out, she stood and stretched trying to deflect what she feared would follow. The old woman remained seated. Shaking her head, she uncrossed her ankles and leaned forward placing her elbows on her thighs.

"I have nothing. I have no one. What's the point to living?" Elsie burst into tears again.

Shirley glared and turned her back. Crossing her arms, she rolled her eyes skyward and released a faint huff.

What about me? I'm no stick of rhubarb. Pick me, you old bat. I'll happily take what you have.

Elsie's attitude to life reflected that of her Aunt Valda just prior to her death. Aunt Valda was a great artist, extremely skilled in watercolour and oil paintings. She was also a particular snob about unimportant things. One would dare not say less than, it was always less in quantity and fewer in numbers.

Her Aunt, a widow, lived a fugal life, and when she passed, left her estate near Bushy Park to a local charity. An action Shirley's father claimed he would never forgive. "Family, family should come first, not strangers who don't care," he would say. "Did she not believe we loved her? Did she not think her money would make our lives more tolerable?" he would question.

Unfortunately, Aunt Valda left no written explanation for her actions and so his questions were left unanswered and their struggles continued while strangers enjoyed her millions. Life would have been so different.

Taking a few calming breaths, Shirley regained her focus on the present, walked to the table, took another tissue from the tissue box and handed it to Elsie. "There, there, it's going to be all right. I know what it's like to feel abandoned, as if you have no belonging in the world, but I'm here for you. I care about you." Flopping onto the couch, she wrapped her arm around the old woman's shoulder. She wanted to believe in her words.

Elsie sniffed and looked with mournful eyes. Reaching across, she tapped Shirley's arm. "Thank you, my dear, I really don't know what I would do without you." Leaning in close, she wiped her puffy eyes.

"And I don't know what I'd do without you. You're like the mother I never had." Furrowing her brow and tilting her head slightly to the side, she was sure to mirror the old woman as she pressed her hands to her cheeks and let out a harsh breath. Her eyes downcast, and her voice soft and a little strained.

Elsie smiled and her eyes lit up momentarily. "Oh, Shirley, that means the world to me. I know it must have been hard losing your parents at such a young age."

Shirley nodded, but remained silent as she embraced Elsie. Holding her tight, she contemplated her next move as she nestled closer. "It was hard. Life is hard. I struggle every day. Being a single parent. Feeling I have no support, no one to turn to in times of need. Worrying about finances keeps me awake at night. I worry Jai will consider me a failure. When I was younger, I always thought I would belong to a loving family and be financially secure by forty. Look at me, the only family I have is Jai…"

Releasing her grasp, she pulled away, cupping her face within her hands she began to weep. Elsie leaned closer and handed her a tissue from the mound she had accumulated on her lap.

"It's going to be okay, my dear, please don't cry." Elsie paused and leaned back on the couch as if searching out answers, while Shirley remained slumped forward and sobbing. "Is it money you need? I can give you money. I want to help you as you have helped me."

Blood rushed through Shirley's head. At last, the

opening she had been waiting for. On the verge of tears, she tried desperately to hide her enthusiasm, to keep her face and words straight. "Oh, I couldn't." Lifting her head slowly, she turned to Elsie. "I can't ask you for money, it wouldn't be right."

Elsie shook her head and placed a reassuring hand on Shirley's arm. "But you aren't asking. I'm offering. I want to help."

Shirley turned away and shook her head then turned back with teary eyes. "I couldn't. I'd feel so embarrassed. I'm sure I'll be fine. I can battle through. Jai will understand. He knows he can't go on every school excursion. We like the simple things, vegemite and baked beans."

Warmth wrapped around her shaking hands as Elsie reached for them. She bit her lip and turned towards the old woman who appeared to be struggling for breath.

"A young boy can't miss valuable experiences. You can't live on vegemite and baked beans. I'll hear no more."

Elsie released her hold. Grabbing the arm of the couch, she groaned and rose to her feet. "I'll be right back."

Lifting her chin, Shirley wiped her eyes and watched the old woman leave the room, convinced her plan and patience were beginning to pay off. Fist punching the air, she hoped her reward would be generous... and then she wondered if the old woman had a secret stash.

***

Elsie clung to the cupboard door, taking a moment to catch her laboured breath. Climbing the stairs to her bedroom was exhausting. She looked over her shoulder and listened, brow creased. Maybe she should have closed the door behind her. Silence. She was sure Shirley would remain seated downstairs.

Opening the cupboard, she was greeted by a pile

of mixed blankets stacked on top of three old suitcases. Removing the blankets was easy, retrieving the larger blue suitcase a little more difficult. It was wedged between the cupboard wall beside two smaller brown cases. After considerable moaning and straining and nearly toppling over, it was free. Steading herself with her crutches, she dragged it along the floor and heaved it onto her bed. Unbuckling the leather strap that secured around the middle was challenging with her arthritic fingers, but with two flicks the metal catches popped and the case was open. She paused and listened, her eyes watering as she stared down at its contents – nine old shoeboxes wedged tightly together. A noise. Possible footsteps. She froze.

"Shirley, is that you?" She peered into the darkened hallway.

No answer.

Somewhere in the distance a dog barked. Leaning against the suitcase, she held her breath. Silence. Stillness. The dog stopped barking.

Probably my imagination.

After a short while, she reached into the case, retrieved a box and opened the lid. Inside, thousands of dollars in fifty-dollar notes. She took a handful and counted, placed one pile on the bed and returned the rest to the shoebox. Another noise. A sense of urgency. Elsie snatched the money from her bed and put it into her cardigan pocket. She shoved the shoebox into the suitcase, sealed it, and dragged it back across the floor. Pausing for a moment, she looked towards the door. Still, silence. Her self of calm returned only when everything was packed away and the cupboard door closed.

***

Slow shuffling and the accompanying tapping of crutches signalled Elsie's imminent return. Shirley resumed her slumped position on the couch and waited with baited breath. Finally, the frail woman appeared, hunched over and relying heavily on her crutches, she took a moment to catch her breath.

"Please, I want you to have this." She stepped closer and put her hand in her pocket. Shirley raised her chin and wiped her eyes, her stomach flipped and fluttered as she battled to contain her joy. Excitement gripped her as Elsie waved a handful of fifty-dollar notes. Her eyes widened and with a swoop of her arm, she flung her hand to her mouth and burst into tears.

"Oh, Elsie that's too much. I couldn't accept."

"Yes, you can." The old woman stomped her foot. "I want you to. I insist."

"But I've always believed I should be independent. Struggling makes me feel so ashamed. I'm a failure, a failure is what I am."

"You're not a failure and you shouldn't feel ashamed."

Shirley raised her hand slowly then jerked it back, shaking her head. "If I take it, it has to be on one condition. I promise to pay you back."

"No, no not at all. It's free. Gratis. I wouldn't make a left-handed offer. A thousand dollars means nothing to me, but it would make things far more comfortable for you."

Slowly extending her arm, Shirley's hand wrapped around the money as she lowered her head appearing defeated. Inhaling the rich polymer smell was empowering.

Yes! At last.

Leaping from the lounge, she wrapped her arms around the old woman, thinking of all the ways she would celebrate. Closing her eyes, she imagined her future, preparing for great wealth and Elsie's mansion she would one day inherit, if only she played her cards right. She visualised the wild and extravagant parties she would host with her newfound circle of friends.

Elsie loved to feel needed, Shirley could tell by the look on her face. Nothing would change the fact Tinkerbell was dead, but her death left a void Shirley was more than happy to fill.

CHAPTER THIRTY-SEVEN

Robert's brow creased, his body stiffened, and heat crept into his cheeks. Had he seen correctly? Jai sat on the floor playing with his toy cars, and as the boy had leant forward, Robert caught a glimpse of a purple-black stain poking from under the sleeve of his t-shirt.

The boy straightened. It was gone. Was it a bruise? Swallowing a lump at the back of his throat, Robert recalled Shirley's chat about recent bed-wetting. If it was a bruise, was it the result of an accident or had something far more sinister caused his injury? The thought of Jai being bullied angered him. He knew Jai had been picked on before. At school they called him Moose. Jai had the biggest set of ears on him you'd ever seen. But that was no reason to be bullied, he couldn't help his physical features. The boy was weak and defenceless, as timid as a petrified cat when around strangers, a loner with few friends.

Earlier in the morning they'd had a chat about school. Jai hadn't mentioned anything about being bullied.

Robert wiped a stray tear and glanced at his watch. Confronting the boy could be embarrassing and would go against Shirley's wishes. She would be home within the hour. He would wait and raise his concerns with her.

***

Distant thunder. The skies darkened as another storm approached. Wiping her brow, Shirley pressed her foot on the accelerator. Stifling summer winds delivered suffocating humidity. Opening Elsie's front door had felt like entering an oven. She dropped her window and sighed. Slight relief from the sweltering temperatures inside. Loose strands of hair whipped across her face. Sweat covered her body. Driving with your windows down offered freedom, there was nothing like catching a breeze with your hand outside the car window. It had been six months since the air conditioner in her car screeched, clunked and finally stopped working. Shimmering heat bounced off the road in front. Behind, innocent bystanders coughed and spluttered. Clouds of blue smoke poured from her exhaust pervading through the streets delivering the putrid stench of burning oil. Excitement swirled within as she felt the bulge of folded notes within her pocket. Music pumped loudly from her car stereo as she bounced around in her seat.

"A little ray of sunshine has come into the world. A little ray of sunshine in the shape of an old girl."

Tapping her steering wheel, she laughed and thought about the feast she would soon devour. She felt rich. Empowered. Overjoyed. She glanced down and forced her hand into her pocket, plucking at the banknotes. Thrilled by her windfall, she inhaled the polymer scent of fifty-dollar notes, fanning them passed her nostrils. Tomorrow she would hit the town and spend up big. Tonight, would be a reserved event; she would ask Robert to stay. Hopefully he would accept her invitation and share in a meal with a nice bottle of wine. He would see her soft and generous side.

Yanking on her steering wheel, she swerved to the left and thudded into the driveway of the local grocery store. There was a sense of urgency to her actions, she jumped from her car, shoved the money back into her pocket and dashed across the smouldering asphalt. At last she was inside the air-conditioned relief. Sweat chilled, Shirley shuddered as she weaved her way up and down the aisles. Grabbing everything that took her fancy created spontaneous joy. With grocery bags full she dashed back to her car. Within minutes she would be home.

When she opened the front door, she could hear Jai and Robert talking and laughing together. She smiled, gently closed the door and tiptoed up the hallway. Peeking around the corner she was delighted to find the pair sitting on the floor surrounded by toys.

"Hey, sorry I'm so late." She stepped into the room.

Jai remained silent, still focused on his toys. Robert looked at her and smiled. "It's okay we've just been playing."

As she walked towards them, she gently kicked stray cars that had made their way out of the lounge area then went into the kitchen with her groceries. "Hello, Jai. I hope you've been behaving."

Jai looked up. "Yes, Mummy."

"Well, I think you should give Robert a break from playing on the floor and go wash up for dinner."

Rolling his eyes, the young boy mumbled under his breath and walked out of the room.

Robert stood, looked over his shoulder and walked into the kitchen opposite Shirley who was taking groceries out of shopping bags. "Psst, Shirley."

Her unpacking stopped.

"I had a word to Jai," he said, his voice only loud enough for her to hear. He paused and looked over his shoulder. Water ran in the bathroom. Robert turned back to Shirley. "The other week you mentioned he'd been wetting the bed. You were worried about him being bullied."

Shirley frowned, glancing down the hallway. The bathroom light was still on and the sound of running water continued. Spinning around she stared at Robert with her fists clenched and body rigid. "I asked if you would keep that to yourself."

"I did. I just asked him about school."

Shirley relaxed her hands. "And?"

"He said it was good, we spoke about his grades and he said he got a great mark for the volcano assignment."

"And?"

"And nothing." Robert thrust his hands to his side. "He seemed happy, so I left it there. I told you I wouldn't say anything and I meant it, but…"

The toilet flushed. Both turned their attention to the hallway and the high-pitched screech of tennis shoes.

Jai rushed into the kitchen and stood next to his mother with his hands on his hips. "I'm hungry," he said, wiping his hands down the front of his shirt.

"Well dinner will be soon, young man, and patience is a virtue. Why don't you go and watch some television so Robert and I can have a talk?"

Without a word of resistance Jai walked off and flopped to the couch. The faint sound of cartoons buzzed in the background.

Shirley recommenced unpacking the groceries. "Would you like to stay for dinner, Robert?"

"Thanks, that would be nice." He paused and leaned close, his voice softened. "I still want to talk to you about Jai."

Shirley's brow furrowed as she looked beyond Robert. Jai sat oblivious. "What now?" she whispered.

Robert glanced over his shoulder then turned to her. "I'll tell you later, I wouldn't want him to hear. How was Elsie today?"

Shirley snatched the bottle of milk from the bag. She didn't like to be left hanging. What else did Robert want to say about her son? "I'm afraid she wasn't too good. I worry about her so much. I worry she has no family." With milk in hand she waited for his response.

Robert leaned against the bench and shook his head. "I worry about her too. It's so sad, so many old and lonely people. I hope I don't end up that way."

Shirley snickered as she walked to the fridge with the milk. "You will never be old and lonely. A strapping young man like you, when you're ready you'll find love."

Shirley closed the fridge and returned to the groceries, removing a chilled bottle of white wine and gesturing to Robert.

He nodded and chuckled as he nudged her arm. "Oh, you're too kind."

Shirley poured the wine and handed him a glass. "I'm just being honest. So how about a toast to happiness and finding love." She raised her glass.

"I'll drink to that." Robert picked up his glass and took a mouthful.

Shirley finished unpacking the groceries, all the while wondering what Robert wanted to talk about. Had Jai disclosed more than Robert had let on?

She reached over the bench and gently grasped Robert's hand. "I hope you like oysters."

Straightening his stance, he slid his hand out from under hers and cleared his throat. "I love oysters."

"I thought you did." She smiled. "I want to show you how much I appreciate you. They say the way to a man's heart is through his stomach."

Robert blushed and looked down, drawing his chin towards his chest before turning his attention to Jai. Annoyed by his response and determined to rid them of distraction, Shirley placed her glass on the bench and stepped into the lounge room. "Jai, I think you should have a shower before dinner."

The young boy shook his head and sighed. Shirley

fixed on him with a stony stare.

"Yes, Mummy."

Mission accomplished. Without another word Jai left the room and headed up the hallway to the bathroom.

Shirley strolled over to the kitchen sink. "Now, where were we... the way to a man's heart. What about steak, how do you like it cooked? I was thinking of making a nice medium to rare fillet steak with garlic mash, carrots and beans."

Robert's eyes widened. "Oh wow, you are going all out. Maybe the way to a man's heart is through his stomach." He laughed.

Shirley giggled and raised her eyebrows. "You never know."

Their playful banter continued while Shirley prepared dinner. With Robert around Shirley felt complete. The three were like any happy family. Robert was strong and protective. She admired his caring nature, appreciated his kindness and respected his loyalty. They had been through so much together, shared so many amazing memories. Intense emotions rushed through her body as she looked at him. How much longer would she be able to deny her cravings? He was the answer to all her prayers. When he was away, she worried about him, each time she saw him she was thrilled. Would they one day look into each other's eyes as lovers? Setting the table, she reassured herself that everything took time. Some things were worth the wait.

Shirley set the oven timer; dinner would take about thirty minutes. Taking a seat on the stool next to Robert, she couldn't stop the frown, and her voice trembled. On the verge of tears, she tried desperately to keep her words straight. Robert edged close and wrapped his arm around her waist as she described Elsie's deteriorating state.

"Today I found her floundering on the floor,

she'd stumbled, hit her head and was unable to get up." Collapsing forward Shirley's cheek brushed against the hairs on Robert's arm, skin to skin contact, a guilty pleasure that fuelled desires. Closing her eyes, she inhaled his Old Spice scent. Shirley moaned as she melted into Robert's warmth. Moments of silence, a melancholic landscape, both lost for answers. One glass of wine became two. Would the old woman's frailty precede death or would she overcome her despair? Jai dashed down the hallway as the oven timer went off. Wiping her eyes Shirley slid from Robert's arms and silenced the buzzer.

"Dinner's ready!"

Pleased with her game plan, Shirley opened the oven. Baked macaroni and cheese would keep Jai satisfied and prevent a repeat performance of the 'sausages are meat from a dead animal' episode.

Placing the plates down she sat at the head of the table. Robert sat to her left tucking his napkin into the collar of his shirt. Jai sat opposite Robert and to her right. Shirley smiled as she watched her son copy Robert's actions.

"Be careful, that just came out of the oven, Jai."

The young boy stabbed at the cheesy crust with his spoon. Steam released. Jai prodded and blew while Shirley and Robert devoured their oysters. Shirley collected Robert's plate, quickly stood and went into the kitchen. Seconds later she returned with two steaming plates. The heavenly smell of garlic fried in butter followed.

Robert looked at the mound of food and smiled as he picked up his cutlery. "Oh wow, this looks and smells delicious."

Shirley raised her eyebrows and giggled. "The way to a man's heart."

Slicing into her tender steak, she looked at Jai and

was taken back to her childhood family dinners, she smiled remembering the excitement she felt anxiously waiting for her father to arrive home from work. Chatting, laughing and joking as she helped her mother in the kitchen. Sitting at the table and sharing a meal was a symbolic demonstration of family unity, stability, love and respect. But those times were long ago. Things took a drastic change when she began to voice her point of view.

Time had passed so quickly. Cheerful conversations were replaced by differing opinions that turned peaceful meals into a battleground. Shirley's memories were tinged with bitterness, she could no longer recall the last time she ate with her parents. Looking around the table she hoped Jai never experienced the resentment she held towards her parents. Warmth radiated from within as she wiped a tear from the corner of her eye.

She hesitated briefly then leaned back in her chair staring at Robert.

"You could do better."

"Sorry." Robert looked up and placed his cutlery on his plate.

"You could do better."

"Better than what?"

"Better than Veronica."

Robert laughed. "I thought you said you wanted me to be happy."

"I did. I do."

"Then what's this all about."

"She's wrong for you." Shirley shook her head and rolled her eyes. "She's a manipulator."

Ripping the napkin from his collar Robert wiped his mouth. "Oh, come on now, that's a bit harsh."

"Maybe." Shirley shrugged, she believed Robert

was acting pig-headed, but scoring points in winning an argument was not going to help. Picking up her cutlery she scraped up the last of her mashed potatoes. "I'm sorry."

Robert remained silent and stared at his food. Shaking his head, he tucked his napkin back into his collar. "I'm sorry too, but I have to disagree with you."

Shirley bit the inside of her lip. Tolerance was vital, but not easy. She smiled and nodded as Robert took his last mouthful. Reaching across the table she gently touched his hand. "It's not my intention to hurt you, I just care."

Robert returned her smile and handed her his plate. "I know you do and I care about you. How about we just change the subject. I was thinking Elsie might like another cat. Maybe we could get her a kitten."

"No!" Shirley snapped and dropped the plates to the table.

Robert reeled back, eyes wide. "Whoa... I guess you've spoken to her about it then?"

"Well no, not directly, but she did say she'd never be able to replace Tinkerbell. I think she needs some time just to come to terms with losing her."

"Fair enough. Oh, one more question, is there something wrong with your toilet in the laundry?"

Shirley squirmed on her chair. "No, why would you think that?"

"The other day I noticed the door was locked. Jai jumped up and told me I couldn't go in there and if I did, there would be big trouble."

Shirley laughed loudly as she kicked Jai under the table. Her face reddened. "That's ridiculous. Why would you say such a thing, Jai?"

A fleeting look of trepidation passed over Jai's face as he looked down at his plate and shrugged. "I don't know."

Robert looked towards Jai then back at Shirley, who stood, fumbling for the plates.

"I must've locked it out of habit. I'd been making the volcano to surprise Jai and so I had it locked," she said, walking to the sink. "You know what boys are like, snooping. It's hard to keep a secret."

Robert chuckled. "I guess it is and Jai has a great imagination."

"He certainly does." Shirley turned on the tap and looked at her watch.

"Well, young man it's past your bedtime so how about you go and brush your teeth and get ready for bed."

Jai looked at her meekly, and without another word said goodnight and hobbled up the hallway.

Robert rose too, thanked Shirley for the meal, and with a kiss to her cheek he, too, said goodnight.

Shirley grinned as she washed the dishes, she was pleased with the evening, and couldn't wait for a shopping spree tomorrow. Only one more job remained. She grabbed her keys and headed down the hallway. When Robert returned the laundry door would be open. Sliding the key into the lock she paused, heat rose to her face and her stomach flipped.

Robert didn't tell me about Jai. What was he going to ask?

CHAPTER THIRTY-EIGHT

"Look at me! Look at me!" Jai flew down the centre of the road, his tiny arm waving and legs pumping furiously. "Look at me! I'm flying."

Shirley dashed from her garden. "Slow down! Slow down!" Flapping her arms, she ran along the side of the road as he sped past. "Jai, you're going to hurt yourself. Slow down!"

But the young boy ignored his mother. He didn't care. At last he was free. Autonomy was within his fingertips. Power surged through his legs and feet. On his shiny new blue bike, he could do anything. Up the road he swerved widely and paused for a moment catching his breath. At the bottom of the road his mother waved, the black and white sleeves in her top resembling a chequered racing flag. He glanced over his shoulder, the coast was clear and his body was charged with energy. Surely, he would go much faster downhill.

"Houston to control, prepare for lift off in three, two, one!"

He pushed down on his pedals as hard as he could. With every metre his speed increased. Aided by a strong tailwind, he hurtled down the steep incline. The hill felt like a ramp; he wanted to soar like an eagle. In a burst of courage, he released one hand. Concentration, his heart racing. An unforeseen wobble. Snatching his handlebars, he stabilised. Determination and persistence pushed through doubt and nerves. He clenched his jaw. A second attempt. Steady. A deep breath. He released one hand, quickly followed by the other. Pedalling paused. Arms stretched outwards like the wings on a plane. In that moment nothing else mattered. Hot wind buffeted his face, his smile widened. Scorching heat streamed over his body, and all sounds muted within his enthusiasm. His mother had promised a surprise and she had delivered. Additional courage stirred from within.

I could do this with my eyes closed.

He shut his eyes. Blackened silence. Everything appeared in slow motion. Peace. His body relaxed. Lost in a trance. An unexpected bump. A sudden dip. Tranquillity shattered.

Jai's eyes shot open, his tiny hands grabbed for the handlebars. Squinting into the blinding sun all he saw was the flash of a silver car. He jammed on his emergency brake and swerved to the left. But it was too late. His bike slammed into the front guard, and he shot forward, his body somersaulted over the bonnet and he tumbled along the roadway.

Disbelief, shock then excruciating pain. He dared not move. Burning heat, his skin felt like it was roasting on the cracking asphalt. Lying on his back he worried about his bike. Had he scratched the paint? Would the frame be bent?

Screams.

Jai moaned and turned his head slightly. A distant figure raced towards him. Bare feet pounded the pavement, flashes of black and white. His worst fears realised. Not only had he ignored his mother, she had seen the accident and she was terrifying when mad. Taking a deep, shaky breath he closed his eyes and waited for the onslaught.

"Mummy's coming, don't move. Oh my god, Mummy's coming."

He could hear her approaching. Within seconds Shirley swooped down next to her son. "Oh my God... Are you okay? Are you okay? Open your eyes. Talk to Mummy, are you okay?"

Jai groaned and opened his eyes to his mother's gentle touch.

"Where's your pain? Tell me what hurts? Can you move?"

The questions stopped. The engine to the silver car whirled to life, its driver slowly edged forward. Tinted windows made seeing the driver impossible. Shirley leapt to her feet. The car squealed. Waving her hands like they were on fire, she made a frantic dash.

"Get back here! You hit my son. Get back here!"

The engine roared and tyres spun creating a small cloud of burning rubber. Within seconds the powerful sports car was gone. Jai struggled to his feet and hobbled to his bike. It didn't look good, the front tyre rim was mangled metal. Jai burst into tears as Shirley raced down the hill to his side.

"Where's your pain?" She checked for injuries. Numerous cuts and scrapes covered the young boy's body. The worst was a gash to his right knee. Besides that, he was lucky, he could stand and walk albeit with a limp. In time he would heal. Gathering his bike Shirley wrapped her arm around Jai's waist and they returned home along the grassy nature strip.

With her son showered, patched and fed, Shirley helped Jai to bed reassuring him his bike was fixable. Closing his bedroom door, she sighed, cupping her face within her hands she burst into tears. Imagining a life without Jai was like imagining a life without sunshine. Wiping her tears, she thanked the angels for looking over them and promised to be a better mother.

The next thing to do was to assess her injuries. Running barefoot along the fiery road had felt like storming across a bed of hot coals. Her feet were blistered and sore.

Sitting on the side of the bath, she closed her eyes reliving the distressing event, each flashing memory appeared worse than the previous. She needed to relax, to think of happier times. She undressed and sank into the water with a sigh.

A half-hour soaking in the cool water and a lathering of moisturiser worked wonders. Stepping onto the cool tiles was no longer painful. Gazing into the mirror she smiled at her new look, only one thing was missing. Her new diamond earrings. She was about to put them in when Jai had called from the road. She picked up the jewellery box from the vanity and opened the lid. She froze. Nausea swirled. One of her new earrings was missing.

***

It had been a long day for Robert, but he was pleased with his achievements. He'd finally managed to apply the first coat of dusty pink to Elsie's lounge room. A thumping headache, most likely from inhaling paint fumes and the disappointment from Shirley's failure to help could not dampen his delight. At last he had managed to lift Elsie's spirits and the old woman had talked about things other than her loss of Tinkerbell.

Sinking into the softness of his couch he popped some pills and closed his eyes. Within minutes he was asleep.

Screeching tyres. Robert's eyes snapped open, heart pounding as he jumped to his feet, tripped and landed face down on the floor.

Where am I?

The sound appeared close, but he was unsure if he'd

been dreaming. Darkness. Had there been an accident? Wiping his face, he opened his eyes. Shadows swirled at his feet. Fear gripped his trembling body. His head throbbed and vision blurred. He must have passed out on the couch, forgotten to turn on the air conditioner. Straining into the darkness, he raised his arm and squinted at his watch. Almost midnight. Scrambling to his feet he stumbled forward kicking something on the floor.

"Ouch!"

Intuition told him something was wrong outside, uneasiness swirled as he wiped the sweat from his brow. The room was sweltering hot.

Disorientated he staggered to the front door with outstretched arms guiding him along the hallway wall. Stillness greeted him as he opened his front door. Peering out, all was quiet. He stepped onto his verandah and looked up and down the street. No strange cars, no accident, just silence broken by the overwhelming buzzing of restless cicadas and crickets.

All of a sudden, in the shadows the glimpse of a darkened figure. Did they crouch into the dimness of Shirley's front garden? Was it a prowler? His sighting had been brief. The figure appeared slim, too fine to be that of a man. Was he hallucinating? He stood there for a while, just watching and staring as if in a trance. The only thing he could hear was the sound of his own breathing. Just over a week ago he'd had a similar experience, a visitation from Julie. Was she now urging him to leave his house? Cautiously, he took a step forward, his eyes scanning as his mind questioned. Was this real?

"Julie." His voice slightly louder than a whisper as he edged towards the road. He paused, tightening his hand around his front fence, staring into the darkness and nothing else. He had to know what it was. Feeling the pulse beating through his veins, he cautiously stepped forward. On the road he began to shiver, his body covered by a throng of goose bumps. Movement. The bushes rustled. Robert jolted as the hairs on the back of his neck stood up. Steadying his breath, he took two small steps forward.

"Julie."

"Robert." A soft reply. Something moved in the shadows.

Robert's eyebrows shot up and he instinctively jumped backwards. "Julie, is that you?" He began to cry, not believing she could be real.

"It's me, Robert."

The figure emerged from the darkness. Stumbling backwards with one hand over his mouth, Robert's face drained of all colour. Hollowness. His stomach twisted and his eyes widened. Too stunned to move he jammed his hands in his pockets. Hands hidden clenched into fists as he watched her move closer. He shook his head. "Shirley!"

"Robert."

Every muscle quivered as she stepped closer. "What are you doing? It's after midnight, and what happened to your hair?"

Shirley stepped on to the road and twirled around as if she were modelling a new outfit. "I thought I deserved a make-over, my hairdresser said she'd surprise me. Do you like it?"

Robert shook his head as she puffed at her shoulder length hair. "You look like Julie." Inhaling sharply, he turned away in an attempt to hide his shock.

Shirley's smile vanished within the abruptness of his words and she ducked her head, there was no denying it. She did look like Julie.

Robert turned and glared while the muscles in his clenched jaw twitched. His statement may have sounded harsh and appeared to make Shirley feel awkward, but he didn't care. Her actions felt like a betrayal and he wanted answers. "What the heck are you doing? And why didn't you come to help me at Elsie's like you promised?"

Shirley threw her hands to her mouth and stared. Tears formed within her eyes, she stepped closer and grabbed Robert's arm. "Oh, my goodness, I'm so sorry. I totally forgot. I went shopping in the morning. I bought Jai a new bike. Long story short, he got hit by a car."

"Are you kidding? Why didn't you call? Is he all right?" Breaking free from her hold, Robert shifted from one foot to the other.

"He's fine. Bruised with some cuts and grazes, but he'll bounce back."

"Why didn't you call and what are you doing out here?"

"I'm sorry. I didn't think. My focus was on him. And now my focus is on finding my new diamond earring, I must have dropped it in my panic."

"And the car horns I just heard, the screeching tyres, what were they?"

"Fools, that's what they were. I was looking along the gutter."

"Are you serious? Couldn't it wait till tomorrow? I'm sorry Shirley, but you're crazy and I'm going to bed."

Robert stormed back across the road.

"So, do you like my haircut?"

Stepping onto his verandah he ignored her question. He couldn't believe she would do such a thing. Wanting to have a make-over was one thing, but to have her hair styled the same way as Julie…

Nausea churned in his gut as he closed his front door.

CHAPTER THIRTY-NINE

Tugging at his shirt collar, Robert eyed the sky nervously. It had been overcast since he'd woken. The air was heavy, almost suffocating. Black storm clouds had overrun the earlier greyness that had been tinged with streaks of fiery red. Tossing his cigarette to the ground, he coughed and wheezed as a gust of hot humid air swept across his face. A quick stomp and it was out. It was just before seven and the world was eerily quiet. The sharp, fresh aroma of rain filled the air. Another thunderstorm was approaching. A distant flash. A heavenly war would soon unleash. Robert dashed inside and slammed his back door.

Flopping on to his couch, he struggled with his feelings of disillusionment. His cigarette had done nothing to ease his agitation. Wiping beads of perspiration from his forehead, he couldn't help but think about the previous night. Recalling that hot flush of recognition, that moment he believed Julie had returned, only to realise it was Shirley flaunting a copycat hairstyle.

How could she?

Sick, that's how he felt, sick to his stomach. And betrayed. In his mind, her actions were grossly insensitive, hurtful and careless. A violation of trust and friendship.

A bolt of lightning and a crack of thunder, Robert's eyebrows snapped together, and he jolted in his seat as his house shook.

THE BELONGING

Why would she?

She knew how he longed for Julie. She'd listened when he'd spoken about his heartache, his sense of deep yearning. He'd told her how he still searched for Julie even though intellectually he knew it was impossible for her to return. Torrential rain pelted against his windows. Robert squirmed on his couch and closed his eyes, agonising over what he should do.

Had Shirley stopped caring, stopped listening? Did she not realise how having her hair cut would impact his feelings? A plethora of thoughts raced through his mind. Images of Julie. Flashes of Shirley. Like a blinding slide show, their faces blazed behind his tightening eyelids, overlapping and blending, faster and faster. Robert thrust his hands to his face.

"Stop!" His eyes flew open.

The images were gone.

Clasping his hands behind his neck, he shook his head and stared towards the ceiling.

What had she been thinking?

If Shirley had wanted a change, she could have had her hair coloured. Raking his fingers through his own hair he contemplated his next move. Hammering rain obscured his view out the window. More lightning and thunder. His lights flickered while outside the wind howled and branches were sent flying.

Should he tear across the street and demand answers?

His breath quickened as he clenched and unclenched his hands. Robert wasn't a violent man, but never in his life had he felt so much resentment. He tried to swallow his anger. If he confronted Shirley in a rage, he could lose the one person who had stood beside him. Closing his eyes, he attempted to steady his thoughts, concentrating on Julie and the love he felt for her. Julie was more than a haircut. She was a person, a complete person. She was his gorgeous woman who radiated love, kissed him passionately, held him close, and reassured him when he was uncertain.

It's just a haircut.

Drumming his fingers on his thighs he held his breath for a few moments then exhaled loudly. Tears filled his eyes as he bowed his head, listening to the wind and rain.

I'm not an angry person.

But resentment clouded his thoughts; pent-up energy prepared him for battle. Nothing could calm his mind. What Shirley had done was sick.

Whatever was important in our friendship is now meaningless.

"Damn you!" He snatched his ashtray from the coffee table and hurled it across the room. Cigarette butts and ash were sent flying. An explosive bang. The ashtray shattered against the wall. Hundreds of glittering fragments scattered over the floor.

Robert stared, expressionless, at the large hole in his wall then looked to the shattered crystal. Shocked by the sheer force in which he had propelled the ashtray, he burst into tears. Was this destruction a reflection of his future? What was the point if he couldn't trust? His childhood in a succession of foster homes had him unable to trust or rely on anyone. Julie had been the only person he had dared open up to and now Shirley was trying to steal her, impersonate her with a copy-cat appearance.

How would he ever face her again?

***

Bandaging someone's hand can be tricky if you've never been shown how and especially if you don't have a proper dressing. Bandaging your own hand in the same circumstances is even more of a challenge. By the time Robert applied the mix match of duct tape and tissues to his hand he looked as though he were ready to have a bout with

THE BELONGING

Mike Tyson, but that was the least of his problems. He was running late for work.

For now, the rain had stopped and as Robert sped out his driveway, he had no time to glance across the street, which was fine by him. Seeing Shirley was the last thing he wanted. At least Elsie and Veronica appreciated his actions and showed respect. Maybe it was time to reassess where he directed his concerns.

He arrived at Elsie's at five past nine. With any luck his lateness would go unnoticed. Perspiration trickled down Robert's cheeks as he heaved in a deep breath. Wiping his face, he could feel a slight sting to his eyes. Fumbling for his keys he leant against the wall at Elsie's front door. Sliding his key into the lock, he bit his lip and pushed the door open. All was quiet. Inside the temperature was much cooler and the air laced with the chemical stench of fresh paint.

"Elsie?" He called out softly in case she was sleeping.

The house remained silent.

Creeping down the hallway and into the dining and lounge area he found everything just as he'd left it. Large canvas sheets covered almost all the furniture that had been piled into the centre. Long strips of blue painters' tape ran along the skirting boards, the doors, and window casings. The room popped with vibrant pink. It was a vast improvement from the dreary peeling taupe wallpaper he'd scraped away yesterday. Robert smiled. Another coat was all that was needed. With a couple of quick pulls, he opened the curtains and inspected his painting skills more closely.

Not too bad.

Tackling one wall at a time, Robert cut in with his brush then used his roller to apply the final coat. A thump interrupted his quiet. Footsteps from upstairs. Glancing around the room he hoped Elsie would be pleased with his efforts. Tapping crutches announced her approach. By the time she appeared in the doorway, he was back up his ladder painting the trims in a gloss white.

"Oh my, what a wonderful job." The old woman grinned as she stepped around the mass of covered furniture. "It's beautiful. Oh, Robert, it's just so beautiful."

Robert smiled. "Thank you, I'm so pleased you like it." Cutting in around the final window casing, he let his brush glide against the timber trim then glanced over his shoulder. He froze. For a brief moment he thought he saw tears in Elsie's eyes, but she turned.

Surely, she's not crying.

His chest tightened as he watched her dip her head. Elsie took a tissue from her pocket, wiped her face then returned his smile.

"Like it? I love it." Clinging to her crutches, Elsie cast her eyes around the room once more. "I need to pay you for it."

"You'll do no such thing." Robert pointed his paintbrush towards her.

"But—"

"But nothing. I don't need your money. Seeing your face light up and hearing your appreciation is all I need." Climbing from his ladder, he wiped the sweat from his brow then dipped his paintbrush into the can of gloss white. "Let me finish up and I'll grab us a cold drink, unless you would like to paint the final bit."

"Me?" Elsie laughed as she held up a trembling hand. "I'm afraid I would ruin it. This heat is wreaking havoc on my weakened body."

Within minutes the painting was complete and brushes washed. Strolling into the kitchen Robert heard the kettle click. Elsie swung around on her chair, her eyebrows went up and she knocked her crutches to the floor. "Oh, Robert, what happened to your hand? I didn't see it before."

"Just an accident before work, nothing to worry

about," he said, wanting to hide his wrapped hand.

"Here, let me take a look. Sit, sit."

Robert took the seat next to Elsie and offered his hand across the table. He squeezed his eyes shut, leaned back in his chair and held his breath as best as he could.

Real men don't cry.

Seconds seemed like hours. Elsie slowly and carefully picked at the tape and peeled the tissue from his wound. Robert opened his eyes as she released her grasp, but her work was far from over. Adjusting her glasses, she leaned forward and nodded towards his hand. "Now let's get this nice and clean."

A slight sting followed by gentle coolness. Elsie dabbed a soft wash cloth into a bowl of water and swiped gently around the wound. Robert watched her face harden beneath her concentration and marvelled at the tenderness of her touch. She squinted as she leaned closer then turned to him. "That looks better."

A quick glimpse of shimmery grey. Robert tilted his head and tried to take another look, but Elsie pushed herself from the table and hobbled out of the room. Did tears cloud within Elsie's steel-blue eyes or had it merely been reflected light?

"Are you okay, Elsie?" he called out, leaning towards the doorway.

"Yes, just grabbing a bandage."

Moments later Elsie staggered back into the kitchen. Seeing the woman's pale complexion and unsteadiness, Robert jumped from his chair. With a guiding hand he helped her to her seat.

"I think you need to sit and rest. You need a drink."

Elsie wiped her clammy forehead. "Oh, this heat."

"Let me get a damp cloth, you need to cool down."

Robert raced from the room and returned with a damp face cloth. Folding it over he urged Elsie to lean slightly forward and placed it on the back of her neck.

"Oh, that's nice, but what about your hand? I was supposed to be looking after you."

"Never mind my hand." Robert passed the woman a glass of water. "Here. Drink this, you need to cool down and get yourself hydrated before you pass out."

Elsie looked up beyond the rim of her glass. "I do feel a little dizzy. Let me rest for a while and then I'll tend to your hand."

Robert nodded and sat quietly watching Elsie sip the cool water. Colour returned to her face, and Robert offered his hand for bandaging before Elsie retreated upstairs.

By the time Elsie reappeared all the paint was dry and Robert had the lounge and dining area back in order. Hours of silence had allowed him to be productive, but it had also afforded him the time to dwell once again on the events of the previous night. Revitalised by her nap, Elsie sat on the couch eating a sandwich he'd prepared while admiring the freshness of her surrounds.

"Are you okay, Robert? You seem a little distracted."

Robert rose from the couch and walked to the dining table with his hands on his hips. He paused then spun to face Elsie. "Distracted, you could call it distracted. I've been sitting here thinking and I can't believe it. I just can't believe it."

Elsie returned her sandwich to her plate. "What can't you believe?"

"*Her.*"

"Who?"

Stepping closer he threw his hands in the air. "Shirley, of course she's up to it again."

"What do you mean? What's the poor dear done now?"

"She's cut her hair. I can't believe she had the audacity

THE BELONGING

to cut her hair, surely she knows how that would make me feel."

"Why would it worry you, if she cut her hair?"

"Why? Why? Because she looks like my Julie." He turned and huffed then stomped back to the dining table shaking his head.

"Oh, Robert, I think you are letting your frustration with the world get the better of you. Shirley's a kind soul. She would never intentionally hurt anyone. I'm sure she didn't have it cut to upset you."

Robert scoffed and eyed her with scepticism.

"Why are you being so harsh with her? The poor girl was probably hot."

"I'm not being harsh. I'm just starting to see things a little differently."

Elsie shook her head, hesitating with her response. Shifting on the couch she placed her sandwich to the side then focussed her gaze. "Death does that to us, Robert. I'd imagine you've been seeing things differently for the past seven months. Losing a loved one changes our views. You have to learn how to be by yourself. You are forced to examine feelings and confront emotions."

"Confront." He shook his head and thrust his hands to his hips. "I don't feel like I can confront anything. What's there to confront?"

"So, it's easier to run away, to be angry." She paused and raised her eyebrows all the while maintaining eye contact. "Running away from your feelings is a race you'll never win. You have to make peace with your past. You have to let go of your anger and focus on what you have, not what you don't have."

"But I have nothing. Julie was the light of my life."

"And Julie will always be the light of your life, but you have *you*." Elsie shifted on the couch, gave a half smile. "I want you to do something for me. I want you to touch your own hand."

For a moment Robert stared blankly, then he did as she asked.

"See," she said.

"See what?"

"You exist, and you existing is proof you have every right to be here and to be happy. You must have faith. Beyond this anger and heartbreak there is hope. You must believe this, Robert, things will get easier."

Robert crossed his arms over his chest thinking over what she said, wishing he could believe her. He leaned against the table. "Have you ever lost a loved one, I mean besides your parents?"

Elsie's brow furrowed as she bit her lip attempting to fight back her tears. "Yes, yes I have."

"What happened?"

Turning away Elsie released a loud sigh and shook her head. Robert stood quietly, but after a few moments she returned his gaze.

"I didn't lose him through death. I lost him through my own stupidity. I was young and naive. My parents disapproved and took a firm stance demanding I end the relationship. I did. Rather than fighting for love, I let it go. And that was it, one of the biggest regrets in my life. I grieved. I cried. I was angry, angry at the world and everything in it. I put up walls and never let anyone get close. It was easier to be alone, but loneliness devours hope, it devours time. So many wasted years, so many regrets. If only I could go back and change things, how different my life would have been." She shook her head. "I always wondered how my life would have turned out if I'd had the courage to stand up for what I believed, if I'd fought for what I wanted. I'm plagued by so many questions. What ever happened to those I lost?"

Releasing another sigh, Elsie's shoulders dropped and she bowed her head. For a moment Robert stood staring, wondering.

What right did a parent have, to forbid their child of love?

Robert pushed himself from the table, he sat beside Elsie and placed his hand gently upon her arm. "You loved him, didn't you? You truly loved him."

"Oh yes, I was in love, deeply in love. My heart broke the day I said goodbye to William." Elsie sniffed as she retrieved a tissue from a pocket.

"William, was that his name?"

Elsie nodded slowly, "Yes, William Honeysett, my dear Bill. He was my love, the love of my life. I guess I'll never know what happened to him." She bowed her head and began to weep.

Robert edged closer and gently placed his arm around her shoulders. He'd never seen Elsie this upset before. Of course, she'd been upset about losing Tinkerbell, but this was different. The woman was heartbroken, her shoulders rose and fell beneath his gentle clasp.

Her eyes flickered as she stared towards him, her lips quivering as she spoke. "Maybe I deserve to be alone. I didn't fight for what I believed. I harboured resentment and withdrew. With my bitterness intact, I created a new identity, for I was the person who had been wronged and my grudge against the world was proof that I'd suffered." She paused and shifted on the couch, picking up her glass of water she took a sip then stared into Robert's eyes. "People think I'm stupid, they think I don't hear because I keep to myself. I know they call me the cranky cripple. Words can be hurtful, but nothing hurts more than regret." She returned her glass to the table.

Shame dropped Robert's shoulders, heat flushed his face as he swallowed back guilt. Did Elsie know he'd used similar words to describe her? Before he had a chance to respond she cleared her throat and continued.

"We can't change the past, Robert, and we can't go

back. My days are numbered. I know I will die with regrets and unanswered questions and there is nothing I can do about it. So many countless dreams unfulfilled. Why didn't I have the courage to stand up for myself? Why did I care about the opinions of others? Why did I hold onto my bitterness? Why did I worry so much? Why didn't I express my feelings?" She shook her head again. Robert maintained his silence, with downcast eyes he watched Elsie's feeble hands slap her thighs. Short jagged gasps escaped the old woman's lips. For a moment both remained still. Elsie stared as if gathering her thoughts then straightened a little and took a staggered breath. "Why, why, why, so many whys. So many friendships gone. Friendships I allowed to slip away. I should have appreciated the little things. I should have given myself permission to be happy, to laugh, have fun and to act foolish. I've wasted countless years, Robert, years that will never return. I don't want you to follow the same path. I don't want you to be the old man who in years to come looks through hollow eyes regretting his past." She gently patted his arm. "Forgive, accept, and look to the future with love and hope in your heart. Please, Robert. It's never too late, you must never give up hope."

Tears brimmed within Robert's eyes as he listened to her words. Was Elsie simply offering advice or was she trying to prepare him for her approaching death?

CHAPTER FORTY

My dearest Julie,

I so wish you were here. I wish I could talk with you. I need to talk with you. Can you hear me? Can you see me? I'm looking. I'm listening. Please, please send me a sign that you're okay. Please send me a sign you have not deserted me. I feel so alone. I so wish I could see you. I long to hear you. At night I lie in silence. It's a silence I despise. To think back to when we were together, how I longed for a peaceful night's sleep. You always fell asleep so quickly. I would lie next to you listening to your snuffled breath. Snuffled breath that would take on a life of its own. Blowing puffs would wisp across my face, some nights I thought I was sleeping with a shuddering wind turbine. I would throw my pillow over my ears trying to mute your puffs and snorts. I would gently tap you and urge you to roll over. And now I would do anything to have it all back.

I hate this stillness. I reach out and can no longer feel you. Oh, my dearest Julie, nothing compares to this torturous silence. Please, please send me a sign. I need to talk, but I have no one. You were my strength. Oh, my dearest Julie, I feel so alone. You were the one person I could talk to. You made me feel better, lessened my concerns. I really don't know what to do without you.

I'm worried about Elsie, I admire her honesty, but I fear her health is declining. I don't think I could handle another funeral. I also worry about Shirley. I don't know what to do about her and the way I feel. You probably know she cut her hair. For now, I'm going to bite my tongue about that, but there's something else. I have a niggling feeling that won't go away. Something doesn't seem right. What should I do? If I say something, she could take offence. Maybe I'm wrong, I could lose her friendship. I thought about saying something to Elsie, but I can't be assured of her silence.

Please show me a sign, I'm begging you. It's been seven months and one week without you. I feel I'm losing it. Is there any sense in writing? I find myself questioning so many things. The only thing for certain my dearest Julie, is my love for you. Until we meet again...

Love always and forever,
Robert

CHAPTER FORTY-ONE

Only one thing was worse than coming home to an empty house and that was sitting in its silence. Minutes dragged into hours and so when the telephone rang Robert pounced from the couch, thankful for the distraction.

"Hello," he said, brushing crumbs from his shirt.

"Robert." The voice sounded breathless and strained.

"Elsie, is that you? Is everything okay?"

"Yes, dear. I just wanted to check and see how your hand was."

Robert looked at his bandaged hand and smiled. "It's fine, thank you, Elsie."

"I also wanted to talk about your painting."

"Don't tell me you want to change the colour." He laughed.

"No dear, but I'd really like to pay you for your efforts."

"Elsie, your payment was your thank you. I wouldn't feel right in accepting your money, besides even if I wanted to take it, if my employer found out I'd get the sack."

The phone line went silent. Robert placed his ear firmly against the receiver. "Elsie? Elsie, are you there?"

"Yes, dear." She paused as if catching her breath. "Oh no. I hope, I hope Shirley doesn't get the sack."

"Why would Shirley get the sack?" Placing his hand

to his forehead, Robert's mind wandered and again the line was silent. He listened. Faint breathing. "Elsie?"

"Oh dear, I think I may have done something wrong."

"Why would you think that?" Shifting from one foot to the other, Robert feared her response.

"I gave Shirley some money."

"You gave Shirley money?"

"Only a thousand dollars. The poor girl was upset. I couldn't bear to see her upset. She needed to buy food and pay bills. I wanted to help."

"A thousand dollars." Robert squeezed his phone tightly.

One thousand dollars. One thousand reasons to buy diamond earrings.

Robert struggled to swallow as his throat tightened. Biting back bile, he fought the urge to vomit. Bitterness soured his tongue. Taking a deep breath, he steadied his voice. "I'm sure everything will be fine, Elsie. Thank you again for your offer and your concern, it was very kind."

"Thank you, Robert. I should go now, good night."

"Good night, Elsie."

Robert hung up the phone and stormed towards his front window. He glared across the street then glanced at his watch.

How could she? How dare she?

It was time to confront Shirley.

***

Shirley stuffed the fifty-dollar notes back into her pocket. "I didn't ask for it. She gave it to me. What else is the old woman going to do with all her money? She has a fortune." Crossing her arms, she looked away as Robert shook his head and rubbed the back of his neck.

"It doesn't matter how much money someone has or doesn't have. You had no right to take it. Why are you acting like this?"

"Acting like what?" Shirley shrugged, her focus on the floor.

"You won't even look at me."

Cocking her head, she glared at Robert and shoved her hands in her pockets. "There, I'm looking at you now." Her eyes wide and staring.

"And now you're being ridiculous."

"Me. I'm being ridiculous. What about you?" Her faced reddened. "Why are you acting so righteous? Why do you consider Veronica so much more than me?" Returning his glare, she stomped her foot.

Robert took a step back and pointed to his chest. "I'm not acting righteous." He dropped his hands to his side. "What's this about, Shirley? Why are you deflecting? I asked about the money you took from Elsie and now you're talking about Veronica."

"That's right, I'm changing the subject. I'm talking about the real issue, how you treat me and consider me less than Veronica. You put her on a pedestal. You look at me as though I belong in the gutter."

"No, I don't."

"Yes, you do, Robert. Yes. You. Do." Shirley turned and flopped on her couch, burying her face in her hands.

Robert stood silent, confused by her responses.

Shirley's head jerked and she stared up at him. Tears filled her eyes; her body shook and her words trembled. "We've known each other for years, Robert, yet do you really know me? You don't. You don't know the struggles I've endured. I never really knew my parents. I can relate to you. I understand you. Unlike Veronica who treats you like a toy, someone she can play with."

Her words struck a chord; Robert walked over and gently placed his hand on her shoulder. "I didn't know about your parents. I'm sorry if that's the impression I gave you. I didn't mean to upset you. Talk to me, Shirley. Tell me your story," he said as he sat next to her.

Shirley looked at him then burst into tears. "My parents are dead. I have no family except Jai. I love him with all my heart. I would do anything for him. I would die for him and yet sometimes I…" She began wailing and turned away.

Robert moved closer and gently rubbed her back. Shirley trembled beneath his touch and fiddled with her earrings. Slowly, she turned towards him. "Sometimes, sometimes I despise him. I have no life. I struggle from week to week, every day I worry how I'll make ends meet. I want to provide him with what my parents were unable to offer me, so while you may be offended that I accepted Elsie's money you must believe me when I tell you, I didn't ask for it. I'm not the type of person who accepts handouts. I believe hard work creates good luck. Family is the most important thing in the world, family and love, that feeling of belonging. That's what I want, that's what I strive for, a happy family filled with love."

Robert remained silent while she spoke, his hand gently rubbing her back. Shirley knew these values were important to Robert. She'd witnessed his devastation when he lost Julie. Julie had confided in Shirley, she'd spoken about Robert longing to feel a part of a loving family, how he had never felt he belonged anywhere throughout his childhood.

Shirley placed her hand on Robert's knee, her voice softened. "Veronica is not like us. I know you won't like me saying this, but she's hiding something. I know it. I feel it. She isn't like you and me. For us, family is the most important thing. Veronica may think she's better because of the clothes she wears, but fashions come and go. Love and family is forever," she said, leaning closer.

Robert wrapped his arm around her. "Yes, family and love should be forever and I'm sorry I upset you, Shirley. I was just shocked when Elsie told me she gave you the money."

"I didn't ask for it, Robert. You have to believe me."

Taking her chin within his hand, he turned her face to his and looked her in the eyes. "I do, I do believe you, Shirley."

"Thank you, Robert." She kissed his cheek. Robert released his hold and leaned to the side creating a slight distance between them.

"Sorry." She blushed.

Robert gave a half smile. "That's okay. Just know I'm here for you. I'm here for both you and Jai. Veronica has no bearing on our friendship."

Shirley nodded and wiped her reddened eyes as Robert rose from the couch. "Well it's past my bedtime. Good night, Shirley."

CHAPTER FORTY-TWO

It had been another long and sweltering day. For Robert, it was one of the hottest summers in living memory. Resting against the back of his house he stared toward the dark storm clouds hovering over the horizon. Straightening his body, he closed his eyes and stood still, listening to the sound of the wind in the trees, the rustling of leaves. Coolness touched the warmth of his body. The hairs on his arms flattening in waves as he held them outstretched. Relief, at last some relief from the shocking humidity. For a moment he thought about his conversation with Shirley, although his greater concerns were for Elsie. The old woman had so many regrets. Witnessing her heartache had been painful and she'd forced him to question.

Do I really want to be the old man with hollow eyes?
Opening his eyes, he took a deep drag on his cigarette.
It's never too late, you must never give up hope.

He threw his butt to the ground. The woman was frustrating. She was doing the exact thing she was telling him not to do. If a person had a question, then why would they not try to find an answer? Especially if they thought their days were numbered. Surely, some of those long-lost friends were still alive. And what about William Honeysett, wasn't he worth finding?

Elsie cared, her words touched and inspired. Surely, Elsie Graham deserved to be more than just an old woman

196

with hollow eyes. Robert's gaze shifted to a tiny sparrow nesting in the eucalyptus tree in the far-right corner of his yard. For a few moments he watched the tiny creature duck and bob, pecking at twigs and grass. The tiny bird had more confidence than Elsie. Spreading its wings, it took to the sky and disappeared over his neighbour's fence. If a tiny bird could find twigs and sticks for comfort then surely Robert was capable of tracking down long-lost friends.

Elsie deserved happiness and was worthy of the answers to her lingering questions. Glancing at his watch he knew time was of the essence. In three hours, he would be on his date with Veronica. A few days earlier she had been upset and he'd learned of the threats made by Amanda. In three hours, he wanted to not only be able to put Veronica's mind to rest, but also have some clues as to the whereabouts of those with whom Elsie had lost contact.

***

Grasping the piece of paper in his hand Robert thundered to the front door. A rush of multiple knocks, he paused for a moment then began pounding with a closed fist. Within seconds the door flew open.

"Robert!"

"Hello, Amanda, I need a word," he said, glaring.

"Is everything okay?"

"It will be, after our little chat."

"Little chat?" The young woman stiffened then looked beyond Robert into the street. "What do you want to chat about?"

"You." Anger swelled in his chest as he pushed his finger towards her face. "You need to mind your own business."

Robert barged into her hallway and spun around.

A blush spread from Amanda's neck to her face as she

stumbled back against the wall. "Sorry?"

"Let's not play games. Veronica told me everything."

"Did she tell you—"

"Stop! I said everything, including your threat. I know about her husband and what he did. I know about Henry. So, you need to stop. I won't let you threaten people. Veronica is distraught about your confrontation."

"But I—"

"But nothing. It stops here. Do you hear me?"

Robert knew from the look in her eyes that the young woman was trying to justify her actions. Snapping forward, he grabbed her arm and pulled her close. "I don't care. You hear me? I don't care what you think. You stay out of my life and I'll stay out of yours."

Releasing her, he turned and stormed off.

**

The traffic lights turned red. Robert gripped the steering wheel and stared into space. Veronica sat next to him.

"Hey what's wrong?" she said, waving her hand in front of his face. "You appear a little distracted."

"Sorry, I was thinking about Shirley and something she said."

Veronica pushed herself back in her seat and chuckled. "Ha! That woman, she's got all the charm of a dead cobra. I believe she has it in for me. The way she looks, what she says when you aren't around." She paused and rolled her eyes. "I don't trust her." She smiled at him and gently placed her hand on his leg.

Robert looked towards her, at her hand then back to her face.

"I'm sorry, Robert, I shouldn't have said anything."

Robert shrugged. "It's okay, I don't think she's

pleased with me at the moment. I don't know. Something's changed. Maybe it's me. I'm not going to let people push me around."

Tightening his grip around the steering wheel, he straightened and breathed deep. Silence, he held his breath for a moment then glanced towards Veronica. "While we're talking about snakes, I've dealt with Amanda."

"You what?"

"She won't be hissing anymore." Robert cleared his throat. "Veronica, I'm sick of people interfering in my life. I'm not going to take it. This world is changing and I'm changing too. No more Mr Nice Guy. People are either with me or against me. I don't need negativity. I deserve peace and happiness and I'm going to get it one way or the other."

Veronica calmly rubbed his thigh and winked. "Well I'm happy to oblige."

Instant warmth rushed through Robert's body and his arms tingled. A quick glance at her naked ring finger told him she was ready to move forward. Although he wanted to take things slow, he could no longer ignore the way she made him feel. A shiver took hold as he gently clasped his hand around hers.

Arriving at the restaurant, Robert jumped from the car and dashed around to open Veronica's door. Taking her by the hand, he allowed his fingers to intertwine. Veronica's hands were much smaller than his and they were cool, but her soothing touch unravelled the knots within his stomach.

They chose a table against the wall surrounded by few people. There they would be able to talk openly without interruption. Sitting to Veronica's right, Robert turned and gazed into her eyes, a natural smile, instant warmth stretched throughout his body and he leaned closer. Was he falling for her or just falling for the ideal of love?

Veronica's eyes were mesmerising, golden and

captivating, her lips appeared soft and moist, Robert wondered what they would feel like to kiss. Over the course of dinner, he fell into her words as she opened up about her abusive husband. Veronica was like a scared and wounded bird, exhausted and trapped by her past, unable to fly. Robert struggled to understand the depth of her distress.

"You're not alone. I want you to know that I'm here for you," he said.

Veronica nodded. "I know. It's just that we felt like strangers. Arguments appeared endless. He wouldn't talk. It was as if I didn't know him anymore. Couples don't get married to live separate lives, do they?"

"Well no, I wanted to share my life with Julie. We enjoyed sharing experiences and growing together. I guess some people have different opinions. Maybe some people would feel smothered. I felt loved, wanted and appreciated. We belonged together."

Veronica placed her cutlery to her plate and bit her lip. "Exactly. I felt rejected, I know it sounds cliché, but we became ships passing in the night. Before we married, we spoke about having a family. After marriage he changed his mind. We drifted apart. He said he wanted to do things with his mates. He wouldn't answer my phone calls. Towards the end, he wouldn't come home. When I asked him why and where he'd been, he would tell me we weren't joined at the hip and accuse me of nagging. I should have seen the signs. Why didn't I see the signs?" Veronica pressed a trembling hand to her mouth.

"You can't feel guilty."

"But I do."

"Listen to me," Robert said calmly but firmly. "You need to listen to me. You're a gorgeous woman, Veronica. None of this is your fault and I'm here for you. If you need a shoulder to cry on, if you want to sound off or if you want to just get out and do something, I'm here for you." Robert paused and gazed into her eyes; his heart hammered and heat surged to his face.

He wondered about her, was spending time together the right thing? They were both dealing with grief. Was moving forward together the right thing? The giddy feeling in his stomach, the warmth inside he experienced, did she feel the same? Or would expressing his feelings be viewed as overstepping the mark with someone who was vulnerable?

I have to tell her. I have to tell her how I feel.

Veronica pulled a handkerchief from her purse and wiped her eyes and nose.

Robert took her hand in his. "He can't hurt you any more, there's no reason for you to feel guilt. You were a victim and now you are a survivor."

Veronica started crying and looked down. "I feel so ashamed."

"You have nothing to feel ashamed about."

Shifting his chair, Robert wrapped his arm around her and pulled her close. "How about we finish here and go for a walk along the pier?"

Veronica nodded and sniffed. "That would be lovely, I could do with some fresh air."

Robert called for the waiter and paid the bill. Taking Veronica by the hand he led her to the front door. Outside it was dark. Together they strolled along the water's edge watching the sky ignite with distant streaks of lightning. A cool breeze. The gentle sounds of water lapping against the pier.

Couples walked hand in hand, a few people sat fishing with their legs dangling over the edge while further along a group of people stood talking. Robert tugged Veronica's hand and guided her down some stairs that were used for smaller boats. It was private and dimly lit. There no chance of interruption. The moment seemed right, his stomach fluttered with the overwhelming urge to pull her close.

Squeezing her hand gently, he hoped he was doing the right thing, she turned towards him. In the shadows her face was so near he could smell the sweet strawberries she'd just eaten. Raising his hands, he held her face and gazed into her eyes, looked at her lips then returned his gaze to her eyes. He smiled and she smiled back.

Then he kissed her, gently at first. He kissed her like he wanted to be kissed and Veronica kissed him back. Soft and moist, she pulled him close and moaned. Their tongues met, their kiss more intense, her hands grabbing at his shirt and her mouth on top of his, demanding more. They moved together, melting into the emotion.

Thunder rumbled above. Robert softened his hold and shifted, a weak gasped escaped Veronica's lips.

"Forgive me," he said.

"There's nothing to forgive, Robert."

Robert stepped back, creating a little distance and placed his hand to his chest. "You are gorgeous, Veronica, and your eyes, I could just sink into them. They are like the warmth of golden sand, but I shouldn't have kissed you. I'm not sorry that I did, and it was wonderful, but we need to sort through our grief before we can move forward."

Veronica gave a half smile and gently placed her hand against the bristles of his cheek. "Well, I guess I know what I have to look forward to."

Together they walked back along the pier to Robert's car. The drive home was silent. Pulling up at Veronica's house Robert jumped out and dashed around to open her door. Holding her hand, he walked her to her front door.

Robert kissed her cheek. "Goodnight, Veronica, and thank you for a delightful evening."

Robert found it impossible to sleep that night. Alone

in the darkness of his lounge room, he recalled events of the day. His body jerked. Intense heat tore through his insides as his thoughts turned to Amanda. Frantically he tugged at the collar of his pyjama shirt, gasping for air.

Oh my God. What was I thinking?

Amanda hadn't deserved his attack. It was impossible not to feel guilt for his actions and pity towards the defenceless young girl. Robert shook his head in disgust and shifted on his couch.

You don't protect a person by attacking another.

Nervous energy rose as he dissected every second of their brief encounter. Emotions bundled inside like a ball of knotted twine. Abuse was never acceptable. Violence solved nothing. Robert bowed his head in shame. The poor girl would have been terrified.

I could be charged.

Robert's mind demanded he re-examine his actions as he fought back the urge to vomit. His body trembled and his stomach continued to twist and burn. He'd never done anything like that before. Regret bit hard as his inner critic appeared, insisting on answers. Robert rubbed his face like he was trying to rub away the memory. He tried to think about something else, but that only made him focus more.

Why? Why did I do it?

Had he gone overboard in protecting Veronica because he had failed in protecting Julie? There was no way to explain what happened, nor was there any excuse. Robert closed his eyes, inhaled a shallow breath. Struggled for another. He vowed to never again raise a hand in anger.

CHAPTER FORTY-THREE

Time passed at an amazing rate when Jai went to visit Robert. Everything appeared simpler to a child. When Jai was around, Robert had time to breathe and block out his adult concerns. Focus was on fun, new experiences and challenges. Hours were spent completing puzzles, playing board games, riding bikes and reading books. Jai was complex and unpredictable, despite being only seven years old he spoke words of wisdom beyond his years. His simplistic ideas and beliefs as to how life worked were refreshing, and one of the only things capable of grounding Robert within his tormented existence.

Robert's colourful front garden was filled with marigolds and pansies, and was transformed into an amazing imaginary city. Small shrubs and bushes became mountain ranges. Stacks of stones and pebbles formed buildings. Compressed soil created racetracks and roads. Toy cars and trucks would zoom over bridges made from sticks. Fresh air and sunshine, laughter and conversation beat sitting inside a stagnant room and dwelling on the unfathomable riddles of life. Digging in the soil, getting dirty and creating things delivered happiness. From mud pies to building scarecrows, from planting seedlings to watering and weeding, picking and tasting. Robert looked forward to the time they spent together and dreamed of one day having a loving family of his own.

It was normal for Shirley to accompany her son across the road, but today the young boy had wandered across alone.

"Hey mate, how are you? Where's your mum?" Robert asked, looking over the boy's shoulder. "I haven't seen her for a couple of days, is she mad with me?"

Jai shrugged. "I don't know. She says she's busy. She's working on something. Something big." The young boy threw his arms wide.

"Big, like what?"

"I don't know. She says we won't have to worry soon."

"Worry?"

Jai shrugged. "Can we play now?"

"Of course, we can. Let me grab my hat."

In the garden Robert chatted with Jai and watched him play, his thoughts drifting in and out of their conversation.

What's Shirley planning? What's Veronica doing? I hope Elsie's okay.

But Jai's words soon interrupted his thoughts, Robert swung around and stared towards the boy. "What did you say?"

The boy cowered and turned away. "Nothing."

"Yes, you did. You said your mum was on the phone."

"No, I didn't."

"I heard you, Jai."

"No, no you didn't. I didn't tell."

"It's okay, Jai, you're not in trouble."

"But I didn't tell."

"Okay." Robert nodded as he looked towards the seemingly terrified boy. "It's okay, you didn't tell."

Throwing his head back, Jai's shoulders jerked

as he began to gasp for air and shake uncontrollably. Tears streamed down his face and his stomach heaved. "Mummy's… Mummy's going to be so mad. Please don't tell her."

"It's okay. I can see you're upset, but we'll work it out. I won't say a word." Robert remained calm and gently rubbed the boy's back. "I promise. You trust me, right?"

A sobbing Jai turned and nodded.

"Come on mate, come here." Robert hugged him, hoping Jai knew how much the boy meant to him. Jai didn't move. After a few seconds he returned Robert's hug and snuggled against his chest. Robert squeezed a little tighter; he wanted the boy to feel safe.

Wiping his eyes, Jai gazed up from under Robert's chin. "I don't want Mummy to be mad," he whispered.

Robert gave him a reassuring wink and smiled. "She won't be mad. I won't tell her. Now come on, how about you take some deep breaths and blow them out through your mouth like a dragon."

Jai turned, trying to catch his breath and began to smile then giggled. "A dragon?"

"Well I'm a dragon, but I'm a hungry dragon. Are you a hungry dragon?"

Jai sniffed, wiped his teary face against Robert's shirt and nodded.

"How about these two hungry dragons go and get something to eat." Releasing his hold, Jai latched onto Robert's fingers with his small hand. Together they strolled inside.

By the time they finished their dragon treats, Jai was calm and they returned to the warmth of the sun. Not another word was said.

"Do you think butterflies remember their life as a caterpillar?" Jai asked.

"I don't know."

"I bet it bugs them."

The young boy giggled and Robert laughed. He wondered if Jai missed the presence of a father just as he had when he was growing up. He watched as Jai stabbed his stick into the dirt. The stabbing stopped, Jai's face scrunched.

"I wish I had a pet."

"What type of pet would you want?"

Jai jumped to his feet and stretched his hands above his head. "A tall giraffe so it could look over the fence."

Robert laughed at the boy standing on his toes. "I don't think you could have a giraffe," he said, tossing a toy car between his hands, "maybe something smaller, like a tortoise."

"A tortoise, what would I do with a tortoise?"

Robert shrugged. "You could look after it. Feed it. I don't think you would take it for a walk though."

Both laughed as Robert mimicked the actions of taking a tortoise for a walk.

"What about a lion?" Jai roared jumping up and down, hands out in front, fingers bent to claws.

"Maybe a cat," Robert said. "A lion is a bit dangerous."

Jai dropped his bottom lip and lowered his head, crossing his arms over his chest. Laughter and happiness vanished. "I can't have a cat. Mummy's allergic to cats." He paused and kicked at the dirt. "Anyway, she said I can't have a pet. I wish I could, but I'm not allowed."

Robert rubbed Jai's shoulder. "Maybe you'll have one when you get a bit older."

"I hope so. I really wish I had a pet."

The sound of a car horn beeping interrupted their discussion. A trail of blue smoke followed Shirley's car into her driveway. The engine clunked then stopped. Shirley leapt out, waving her hands and coughing. "Hey there, sorry I'm late I got held up at the store," she yelled, before reaching inside and pulling out a handful of bags. "Come on, Jai, Robert has things to do. Thanks, Robert, I really appreciate you looking after Jai."

Robert leaned against his front fence and waved. "No worries, my pleasure."

Dropping his stick, Jai picked up his cars and waved goodbye as he dashed across the road before disappearing inside his house with his mother.

Robert glanced at his watch then raced inside to the paperwork he'd gathered. His information, albeit limited, was a start.

His search would soon begin.

***

Perspiration clung to Robert's forehead as he nervously climbed the steps towards the front door. Was he doing the right thing? Would she accuse him of interfering? Taking a deep breath, he wiped his sweaty palms down the leg of his pants, adjusted his tie, pushed the doorbell and took a step back.

Darn thing sounds like a sick frog.

He chuckled then focused. In that moment nothing else mattered. He was there for her. Cars driving by, children playing cricket in the front yard of the house next door, the yapping dog that had set off barking when he approached… everything disappeared into obscurity as he stared through the oval-shaped frosted glass housed within the red timber door. It was as if the universe paused. Heart pounding. Blood rushing. Hands twitching. Robert closed his eyes and bowed his head.

Please God.

Nothing. Nothing, but the beat of his heart and the churning within. Opening his eyes, he took a small step forward, cupped his hands around his face and peered through the translucent window. Shapes and shadows, possibly a long hallway with a tall side stand to the left. Dark floors with a light hall runner, but no movement. Time stood still. Time created distance. Time, the great divider. People say time heals, but over time things could be destroyed. Surely, she was worth his time. What good was time if your life was void of friends and family? What was it then, but marking time? Marking time for what? Death?

He'd been standing under the scorching sun for over five minutes, but what was five minutes in a lifetime. Pushing the doorbell once more, he straightened his stance and checked his reflection within the glass. Heat penetrated his shirt, sweat encased his body, but he continued to wait. He was doing it for her. Closing his eyes, he bowed his head and made a steeple of his fingers.

Please God.

The silence continued. Robert remained still. Sometimes people took a while to answer the doorbell, especially if they were elderly.

What was that?

Robert's eyes sprang open, his breath quickened. A noise, it was definitely a noise from inside. And then a silhouette, someone entered the hallway from the right. A slow-moving shadow, wobbly and hunched. The sound of shuffled footsteps. Robert raked his fingers through his hair, straightened his tie and smooth down his shirt. The doorknob rattled and finally, the door opened. Querying eyes squinted below a ridge of bushy brows. An older gentleman with a touch of distinction puffed, trying to gather his breath. Was he the man Elsie had described? Decades had passed. Thinning grey hair could have replaced his once dark locks. Shuffling footsteps could have replaced a once youthful strut.

"Can I help you, young man?" the old man asked. His voice gravelly and strained.

Robert smiled and stepped forward all the while thinking about the raspy guttural tones of Christian Bale's infamous *Batman* performance in, *The Dark Knight*. The voice similarity was astounding.

"Hello sir, are you William?"

The old man nodded. "Yes."

Oh my God!

Robert's eyes widened. "Oh, my goodness, you're William."

"Yes, I am William."

Robert whisked forward with his right hand extended. A stale muskiness seeped from the old man's grey suit. William stared, dubious, then slowly raised his trembling hand. His hand was cold and fingers crooked; knuckles larger than normal while his grip lacked strength. Robert was sure to be gentle. Time, time made the once young and confidant grow old and uncertain.

After a couple of shakes, Robert released his hand and stepped back. "You must forgive me. I'm just so happy to have found you."

The old man looked him up and down then rubbed his whiskered chin. "And you are?"

"Oh, yes. I'm Robert. Oh wow! I'm so sorry, where are my manners."

The old man stared as if he were inspecting every part of Robert's face. "Have I won the lottery or something?"

Robert shook his head. "Please forgive me and let me introduce myself properly. My name is Robert Jackson. I look after Elsie Graham. Elsie and I were talking and well, you came up in conversation. I wanted to surprise her, so I decided to track you down and...." Robert paused and stepped back yet again. Taking a deep breath, he thrust his hands forward palm side up. "Here you are."

Wrinkles gathered as the old man scrunched his face. Robert could not help but notice the sad and pensive look on his face. The old man's face twitched as if he were biting the inside of his lip.

Robert stood silent.

The old man rubbed his whiskered face once more. "Who's Elsie Graham?"

"Elsie Graham from your adolescent years. You were nineteen. She was sixteen."

The old man shook his head and stared blankly.

"Surely you remember, Elsie."

"Nope. I think you have the wrong William, young man."

Robert's heart sank. How could he have the wrong William? Stepping back, he looked at the number of the house. Spinning around he glanced at the street sign. The address was correct.

"Young man, I think you're looking for William Honeysett."

Robert spun around and leaned forward. "Yes, that's right. William Honeysett. Is William Honeysett here?"

The old man bowed his head then looked up with saddened eyes. "I'm afraid he's gone."

"Gone? What do you mean gone? When will he be back?"

"Young man, William Honeysett has gone to be with the angels. I'm afraid you're about one month too late."

Robert stared, transfixed by the old man's words. How could William be dead when he'd just found out about him being alive?

William's gone. I'm too late. How can he be gone?

Why is this happening? Why are the angels stealing all the good people?

High-pitched ringing filled Robert's ears as he struggled for air. Heat, unbearable heat and dizziness. Robert squinted. Everything became clouded and dim. The old man's voice distorted muffles. Robert lurched forward. Then there was silence. Blackness.

Gentle nudging. Robert felt gentle nudging to his side and firm coolness on his back. Placing his hand to his nose, he inhaled through his mouth trying to shut out the musty smell of aging wood and the stench of rotting fish. Harsh scratchiness rubbed against his cheek as he turned his head slowly opening his eyes. He was inside. The room dark, dusty and more than a little run down.

Where am I?

Another nudge from behind followed by a deep throaty rumble. The stench of rotting fish returned.

"Welcome back, young man."

Robert rubbed his face and looked over his head in the direction of the voice. William sat watching.

"Oh, I'm so sorry… I don't know what happened."

"Shock, my boy, I should have asked you inside before I told you about William."

Rubbing his hands over his face Robert recalled their brief encounter. "So, William passed away?"

"I'm afraid so."

"But this is his house and you are William?"

"Yes, I am. I'm William Douglas. I live across the road." He nodded. "William and I were friends for over thirty years. Ever since my wife and I moved in."

"And William. Was William married? Did he have a

family?"

The old man shook his head. "Nope. Never married, no family."

Propping himself onto his elbows Robert was nudged again. He turned. A ginger cat stared and purred. "And the cat?"

The old man chuckled. "She was his. William loved his cats, he would spoil them and talk to them as if they were human." He paused and chuckled again. "I think this one is about the fourth Missy G. I always asked why he didn't change names when he changed cats. William would just shrug and tell me the real Missy G stole his heart, then vanished. Having a cat with the same name reminded him of his love for her and a time he never wanted to forget."

"Miss Graham!" Robert exclaimed.

William gazed up at the ceiling with a raised eyebrow as Robert climbed from the floor and sat on a chair next to him.

"Ah, yes, Graham that could be her. Elizabeth, no. Ella, no. Elsie, yes Elsie Graham. That's her, the young woman who stole William's heart. He never got over her." William paused and placed his hands on his lap. "Always wondered, but never had the guts to look. Worried how he'd feel if he found her with a new love and family. But he always carried her photo."

Robert sat upright and hooked his feet around the chair legs. "You've got a photo?"

"I do."

Pushing himself to his feet, William shuffled out of the room. He returned moments later. "Here it is, William always carried it in his wallet."

Robert took the old black and white photo, edges

tattered and worn with age. Flipping it over he read the faint and scratchy words. "Love always and forever, your Missy G."

"I can't believe I was so close, if only I'd come last month."

"Time gets away from us all, my boy. Live while you can, before you know it, you'll be old just like me."

Time passed by quickly. When Robert eventually glanced at his watch, he'd spent over three hours listening to stories and looking at old photos. William had been a talented carpenter. His friend described him as a true gentleman, respectful of others, loyal and caring. In retirement he'd diverted his talents to building model ships. What started out as a hobby became a passion. Some days he would work on his ships from sunrise to sunset and even late into the night. The largest in his collection was a replica of *The Victory*.

Robert stood in awe as he studied the masterpiece and listened about its creation. Total construction took twelve months. Resting above a timber wine rack, the ship was nearly as tall as it was wide. From bow to stern, it was the span of Robert's arms. A magnificent creation with perfectly stitched sails and hundreds of tiny strings meticulously tied and knotted for rigging. The hull and decking constructed from tiny slivers of polished timber. Complete with little lifeboats, canons, ladders, lanterns and internal stairs. It was easy to understand why William had viewed it as one of his finest creations.

"It's amazing. You know I've always loved models. I've made a few of my own, but nothing as spectacular as this. Thank you so much for letting me into the life of

William Honeysett. I feel like I know him so well and although I wish my timing could've been earlier, I'll be proud to go back to Elsie and reassure her of the wonderful life lived by the fine young man she met and fell in love with all those years ago."

"You're always welcome back, Robert, and Elsie too."

"I'm sure she'll be thrilled by your invitation. Thank you, William." Robert headed for the door and paused to shake William's hand. "I'll give you a call later."

The old man nodded. "I look forward to hearing from you. Bye, Robert."

CHAPTER FORTY-FOUR

Robert entered the room with a heavy heart. The moment he'd been dreading had arrived. From the corner of his eye, he watched Elsie sip her cup of tea and read the newspaper. The old woman appeared relaxed on the couch, but how would she handle hearing about what he'd discovered? Had he done the right thing?

Clearing his throat, he rubbed the back of his neck and straightened his tie. Elsie looked up from the newspaper. Robert picked up his cup and looked away, taking a sip of his black coffee to try and soothe his dry mouth.

Suffocation.

An invisible wall descended, the air appeared thick, pain and tightness filled his chest, Robert struggled for air and his hands began to tremble.

I have to tell her, she deserves to know, but the shock could kill her.

Gulping down the last of his coffee, he could no longer stand still. "I might go and have a quick smoke," he said.

"Okay dear." Elsie's focus remained on the newspaper.

Outside, sweat began to bead on Robert's forehead as he paced back and forth. The very act of watching someone who was oblivious to imminent pain made him nauseous, his heart pounding, his hands shaking as he took a deep drag of his cigarette.

Oh God, how will she handle another loss? Am I

doing the right thing? Maybe I should leave the past in the past. What good is it to stir old emotions?

Flicking his butt to the ground, he raked his fingers through his hair and recommenced his pacing. Only a few clouds hovered above, the sun was warm and the humidity much lower than previous days. Stopping near the back steps he looked skyward and placed his hand above his forehead watching the clouds drift within the tepid breeze.

Everyone deserves the truth. The truth will set you free. We can deal with what's known. I have to tell her. She deserves to know.

Taking a deep breath, Robert made his way into the lounge room. "I need to tell you something," he said, his voice shaky and uncertain as he stood in front of the couch.

Elsie looked up from the newspaper as Robert dropped next to her, his stomach knotting up when she turned towards him. Raising an eyebrow, he studied Elsie's face. Deep ravines carved their way across her forehead as she folded her paper and dropped it to the floor. He froze. Nerves danced within his throat. Rapid pounding consumed his temples as he chewed on his bottom lip. If only he had looked for William a few months ago. Elsie frowned at his hesitation. Robert sensed she knew something bad was coming.

He took her hand in his. "I'm so sorry Elsie."

Elsie remained silent, releasing her hand, she turned away tugging at her cardigan. Robert's heart ached for the woman, he wanted to wrap his arms around her and tell her it would be all right, but it wasn't all right. It would never be all right.

Swinging around she stared. "What's happened?"

"I'm… I'm so sorry to be the bearer of bad news. It's about William."

Elsie seemed to wilt at his words and her shoulders slumped. Silence lingered. Robert sat wondering what he should do. He watched the gentle rise and fall of her shoulders. Finally, she turned towards him, clenching the bridge of her nose. "He's gone, hasn't he?" she whispered.

Robert nodded. "I'm afraid so."

Elsie straightened herself and sniffed. "He'd probably forgotten me anyway." She picked lint from her cardigan.

Robert shook his head. "I'm so sorry, Elsie, but you're wrong. He never forgot you."

Elsie stopped her picking and placed a trembling hand to her lips. "He never forgot?"

"No, he never forgot you, Elsie."

She bit her lip. A shiver took hold. Inhaling a shallow breath, she clutched her chest and struggled for another.

Robert placed his hand in his pocket and handed Elsie a photo. "It's you, isn't it?"

Elsie's eyes widened, the old black and white photo trembled in her hand. "He never forgot," she whispered a second time. Her eyes searched Robert's for a moment then returned to the photo. "It's me. He never forgot. It's me." Her voice was brittle while her gaze was intense. Robert sat silent.

Elsie cradled the photo within her hand the same way he cradled photos of Julie. Closing her eyes, her shoulders slumped as her head swayed. Was she praying for William's return as he had prayed for Julie's? Was she telling William she loved him and wished things could have been so different?

Opening her eyes, she looked at Robert with glistening eyes. "I feel hot, I need some air." The old woman plucked at her cardigan and snatched for her crutches. Pulling herself forward, she released a loud moan and took a few staggered steps. Robert remained seated hoping she would be okay.

Suddenly, Elsie stumbled and her body lurched forward. Crutches flung into the air and slammed to the floor, Elsie fell headlong against the wall. Robert leapt from the couch and sprinted to her side. Throwing the crutches off her crumpled body, he kneeled next the sobbing woman. Bottled up emotions spilled to the floor.

"Are you okay? Stay still. Does it hurt? Let me help you to the couch."

Robert ran his hands over her frail body, her face was grey and gaunt, her eyes red and puffy, and her nose watered. Draping his arm around her tiny waist he helped her to her feet and allowed her to steady herself.

"Let me help you to the couch. I'm so sorry, I should have asked before I went looking for William."

The old woman shuffled between Robert's guiding arms. Raising her tearstained gazed, she looked into his eyes. "It's not your fault."

Robert shook his head. "I never meant to hurt you."

"And I should have found the courage to look long ago, but I was afraid of what I'd find." She paused and took a breath. "This will be my regret. I wasted so many years thinking and wondering when I should've acted."

Robert eased Elsie to the couch and she slumped back burying her face within her hands. "I have something else, Elsie."

Elsie lifted her chin. "What?"

"Wait there, I'll be right back." Robert jumped to his feet and dashed from the room.

Moments later he returned.

"Oh, my goodness. Oh, my goodness." The corners of her lip rose, Elsie reached forward and stared with outstretched hands. A pair of blue eyes blinked back. Robert knelt beside the couch and passed her the purring bundle. It stared, then blinked, and then opened its eyes wide. Elsie reached up and gently stroked its head. The cat's paws pushed in and out against her lap.

"Oh my, where did you find her?"

"She belonged to William. She needed a new home. I

thought you'd be perfect."

Leaning forward, Elsie kissed the top of the cat's head, it turned and rubbed its face against her cheek. Elsie smiled. Robert stroked his hand along its back. Pouncing to the floor the cat wandered for a moment then began rubbing its body against his legs.

"William had a cat. She's beautiful. What's her name?" Elsie said.

"Missy G."

The old woman burst into tears. The cat stopped and stared towards her. Without warning, it leapt to her lap. Elsie wrapped her arms around the purring joy and it lay still, resting against her trembling body.

"He never forgot. All these years I thought I didn't matter. I imagined him with a new love and a family. All this time, all this wasted time." She paused and shook her head while stroking the cat, her hand tickling under its chin. The cat stretched its neck and squirmed then rolled over. Fur whisked into the air as Elsie gently stroked its belly. She paused. The cat squirmed again and nudged her hand with its nose. Elsie's fingers gently caressed, the cat relaxed its body and purred.

"I did matter. He was thinking of me. I was thinking of him and he was thinking of me. Thank you so much Robert, thank you for the answers to my life-long questions."

CHAPTER FORTY-FIVE

Shirley slapped her hand over her mouth then threw her arms around Robert, nuzzling into his chest. "The poor woman, she must be devastated."

Robert stood still, his hands hovering gently around her waist. He wanted to reassure Shirley that everything would be fine, yet he still found it difficult to look at the woman who so closely resembled his wife. Warm hands gently stroked his back making him squirm beneath her touch, he flinched and her warmth was gone.

"Yes, the news of William's death came as a shock, but—"

"But nothing." Shirley lurched back and glared. "I didn't even know about William." She thrust a pointed finger towards Robert's face. "Why did she tell you?"

"What do you mean, why did she tell me? We were talking. William came up in conversation. I thought it would be nice to track him down. I'm simply telling you what happened. Why is there an issue? We both want what's best for Elsie, don't we?"

"I didn't say there's an issue. Of course, I want what's best for, Elsie. I need to see her. I have to make sure she's all right."

"I'll come with you."

"You've done enough, Robert. Besides she'd probably feel more comfortable talking to me, we've known each other for years. Women can relate better to other women and our emotions, we're wired differently to men."

Robert placed his hands on his hips and rolled his eyes.

Shirley shook her head. "That came out the wrong way. Surely, you know what I mean."

Robert shrugged as he thought about Julie. She'd enjoyed her girl-time, catching up on gossip, talking about books and movies and life in general with girlfriends, it was a time when the girls caught up and men were generally unwelcome. Maybe Elsie would benefit from a visit from Shirley alone.

"Okay," he said. "But you promise to call me if you need."

"Of course, I will."

***

Letting herself inside, Shirley found Elsie sitting on the couch. "Oh my god, where did that come from?"

The old woman looked up and laughed. "Isn't she beautiful?"

"Where did it come from?"

"Robert found her."

"What?" Clapping her hands loudly, Shirley hurried towards Elsie. The cat flew from the couch and dashed out of the room and up the stairs. "Oh my, it's a bit flighty. We'll talk about it later, but tell me, how are you? Robert came over. He told me about William. I came as soon as I heard."

Dropping to the couch, Shirley reached for Elsie's hand. "I'm so sorry for your loss, I never knew and I can only imagine how heartbroken you are. Robert told me he died from a stroke. I hope he didn't die alone. I would hate to die alone. That's one of my worst fears." Shirley stood and began to pace. "Its moments like these that I'm reminded how important it is to have one's affairs in order. What would happen to Jai, if something happened to me? I need to do something, see a solicitor, get my affairs in order."

"Oh, Shirley you have nothing to worry about."

Shirley spun and faced Elsie. "But I could have an accident. Accidents happen, a car hit Jai the other day. What would happen if it had been me, if I'd been permanently disabled or killed?" She paused shaking her head. "I need to go to a solicitor. I need to sort out my affairs. Set up a will, an enduring power of attorney. I need to think about who could be Jai's guardian." Dropping to the couch, she rocked back and forth. "I don't even know a good solicitor."

"Calm down, you need to calm down, Shirley."

"Do you have a will, Elsie, do you have your affairs in order? What would happen if something happened to you? Who would act in your interests? I couldn't bear to think of you in a helpless situation, it's too awful to imagine."

Elsie turned ghostly white and smoothed down her skirt. "I never thought about it. I've only ever needed home care. I don't have any family. Maybe I should speak with my solicitor too."

"Is he good? Do you think he could help me?"

"Oh yes, he's lovely. Maybe we could go together, if you like?"

"Would you mind?" Shirley asked.

"Of course not, dear. What you've said has made me think. I should deal with these issues while I can. I need to protect my future."

"Of course, you do. We both need to. I'd be happy to take you to your solicitor, to give you peace of mind. And I'd be more than happy to be your enduring power of attorney to ensure your welfare is protected and your wishes are respected. I'd hate the thought of you getting sick and me not being able to speak up and tell people what you want."

"You'd do that for me?" Elsie placed her hand on Shirley's thigh and Shirley placed her hand over the top.

"Of course, I would, Elsie. I'd do whatever it takes to make sure you have peace of mind. You mean so much to me."

"Thank you, Shirley. You really are my angel of mercy."

CHAPTER FORTY-SIX

Loud music pumped from within Robert's house as Veronica poured two glasses of wine. Relaxing on the couch, she smiled. Robert had been surprised when she'd arrived with a gift and he was more than eager to show her what they looked like.

"I'll be right back," he said dashing into his bedroom. "Prepare yourself for a show you're never likely to forget."

In the bedroom Robert stripped and threw on his new briefs. Studying his reflection in the mirror, nerves began to build. The red satin boxers fit perfectly, his muscles toned and body tanned, but would he have the courage to parade in front of Veronica? He'd danced for Julie, but would Veronica encourage his playfulness or find his near-naked body inappropriate?

Opening his door, he slowly stepped out. Absorbing her gaze, his eyes lit up. Veronica took a small sip of her wine and edged forward on the couch placing her glass on the table.

It's now or never.

Taking a deep breath, he relaxed allowing his body to sway with the music all the while trying to gauge Veronica's reaction. Licking her lips, she appeared impressed. She rubbed her hands together, leaned forward, eyebrows raised. Robert took off strutting towards her. Pausing within reaching distance, he placed his hands on his hips, one leg out, and the other foot ready to pivot. Chest and arm muscles flexed smoothly.

"I love them, they're perfect and oh my god, your body. Look at those pecs, you're like a real-life Adonis," she said with excitement.

Robert smiled and flexed his biceps. Running his thumbs behind the elastic waistband, he winked before turning and strolling around the room. Veronica lunged. Snatching fingers failed to make contact. With his back turned, Veronica unclasped the top button in her blouse.

A knock at the door.

Robert froze.

More knocking.

Robert's eyes darted around the room. Veronica's hand shot to her mouth. Robert raced to turn the stereo off. Veronica laughed as she watched him sprint to his bedroom.

"Hang on, I'll be there in a minute," he yelled.

Within seconds he reappeared wearing a t-shirt. Fingers fumbled as he struggled to button his jeans in his dash along the hallway to the front door. Greeted by a warm burst of air and a familiar face, Robert stepped back.

"Hey, Robert, I've got some great news." Shirley barged past.

Veronica rolled her eyes as Shirley entered the lounge room. "Hello, Shirley," she said, straightening on the couch.

"Veronica." Shirley turned towards Robert. "Maybe I could have a quick word with you out the front."

Robert nodded. "I'll be back soon, Veronica."

Veronica clenched her teeth and cursed under her breath. All was silent. Pushing herself from the couch she edged closer to the hallway and peeked around the corner. The hallway was empty and the front door closed.

By the time Robert returned she was back to sitting on the couch, but within seconds she leapt to her feet. Hands flew to her side. "I can't believe her. I just can't believe her."

"What?" Robert stiffened at her tone and placed the envelope he was holding onto the coffee table. "She had some information about work."

"There's always a reason, Robert. A cup of sugar. Jai wants to play. She needs a man's strength. Does she ever leave you alone?"

"Of course she does, but it was about work. I finish my relieving soon. I have to look at my options."

"Well I best leave you with your paperwork, please don't get up on my account. I'll let myself out and maybe we can catch up when you have things sorted."

Robert stared blankly as Veronica snatched her handbag before storming down his hallway. The front door slammed.

What the heck.

***

Veronica raked her hand through her handbag searching for her keys, unaware she was being watched. Pushing her remote, the door clicked and she reached for the handle. A warm hand snapped around her arm and she spun to meet Shirley's glare.

"Don't worry, Miss Botox, Queensland is calling us and soon Robert will be nothing more than a distant memory."

Stumbling back, Veronica's body fell against the side of her car as she tried to free herself from Shirley's grasp. "What are you talking about?"

"Robert's moving. Oh no… he didn't tell you, did he?" She laughed.

"Let go of me, I don't answer to you."

Shirley released her grip and Veronica flung her door open. Stepping back Shirley smiled as she watched Veronica speed off down the road.

***

A disturbing phone call left Robert fuming, attempting to distract his thoughts he wandered outside to the garden. A combination of sweltering heat, high humidity and above-average rain resulted in large unwanted weeds. There was enough to keep him busy for hours. One full bucket followed another. Hearing voices and car doors, he looked up from behind his front fence. Across the street a strange car was parked in Shirley's driveway. Shirley was leaning into the passenger window of a car. Jai sat on the seat of his bike next to the driver window. Both appeared happy. He smiled when he heard them laugh. After a few moments the car's engine started and it reversed out the driveway. It was a typical scene, Shirley and Jai yelled from their front gate while those in the car waved and with a toot of the car horn, Jai took off chasing the car on his bike.

But it wasn't the scene that left Robert shocked, more so what he had heard Jai yell. Seizing the moment, he dashed across the street and grabbed Shirley's arm and she spun around.

"I just saw Jai. I heard him yell. He was yelling goodbye then he followed the car on his bike."

Shirley squirmed within his grasp. "Ouch, Robert, you're hurting me. What's wrong with you." She glared at him as she pulled free of his grasp.

He stepped closer and waved his finger towards her face. "What's wrong with me? What's wrong with you?"

Shirley took a step back. "What are you talking about?"

"You told me your parents were dead."

"And?"

"Then why did Jai just yell out, 'bye Poppy'?"

228

THE BELONGING

"Oh, Robert, I'm not even going to respond to that." Turning away Shirley flicked her hair and brushed past as she walked to her front gate.

"And why did you tell Veronica about Queensland?" He lunged and grabbed her arm again. "She phoned me and said you ambushed her when she left. Why did you tell Veronica we were moving to Queensland?"

Shirley remained silent. Releasing his hand Robert stared as she scratched the back of her head.

"What are you talking about? I never said anything. She probably snooped and heard our conversation." She dropped her face to her hands, turned her back and bowed her head. Her shoulders jerking between her sobs. "I can't believe you'd think that. After all I've done for you. A bit of fancy fluff flaunts in and you believe her over me. Can't you see what she's doing? She's trying to turn us against each other."

"Why would she do that? Tell me, why?" Robert snapped, throwing his hands to the side.

"She's jealous of our connection?"

A child squealed. Robert looked over his shoulder. Jai peddled down the street towards them.

"Hey, Robert." The young boy waved when he was in front of the neighbours' house. Shirley ignored Robert and pointed towards her driveway. "Come on, my little champion, you can come inside and play now. How about I find some batteries for the remote-control car Charles and Poppy were kind enough to buy you." Turning she glared towards Robert.

Jai cheered, as he swerved past. "Hi, Robert. Bye, Robert, I'm going to play with my new car."

Robert stood motionless. His heart sank as they disappeared inside. What had he done? Had Shirley said something to Veronica, or had Veronica overheard? Worse than that was his allegation of her lying about her parents.

It was utterly understandable for Shirley to have walked away, but would she accept his confusion? Would she be able to appreciate how innocent words had created a false impression? His conclusion had been harsh. Had his words cut too deep?

A simple misunderstanding, that's what it was. I'm sure she'll understand.

Staring at the cracking driveway, Robert thought about his next step.

CHAPTER FORTY-SEVEN

Shirley strolled into the kitchen carrying a freshly-baked banana and walnut cake. Dirty dishes lined the sink, Elsie sat staring towards the back door, oblivious.

"Good morning, Elsie, how are you today?" she said, dropping her backpack to the floor.

The old woman turned. "I'm sorry, I didn't hear you come in." She looked to the black backpack on the floor. "Oh my, that's a big bag for work."

Shirley laughed. "It's new. I joined a gym for a trial, but have worked out it's a bit expensive so I thought I'd just buy a bag and carry around some sports shoes. If I have some spare time this afternoon, I'll take a long walk around Fleming Reserve."

"Good for you. I'm glad you're looking after yourself."

Shirley smiled. "I am, Elsie. I'm looking to the future. It's hard with everything that's happening, but I'm trying to remain positive. Anyway, how are you?"

"I'm above the earth, so that's a good start." She chuckled. "Did you see my lovely lounge and dining area? Robert painted it." She pointed towards the door.

"No, I must admit I didn't notice it the other day. I was more concerned about you, when I heard about William. Let me take a look." Clearing a bench space, Shirley carefully placed the cake down then left Elsie to sip her tea.

"Oh my, that's beautiful." She yelled from the other room. "You know, I'm going to miss Robert so much."

"Miss him?" Elsie straightened on her chair and leaned towards the door. "Why would you miss him?"

Returning to the kitchen, Shirley held her hand to her mouth. "It's nothing."

"But why would you miss him? Doesn't he live across the road from you?"

"Yes, and please forget I said anything."

"How can I forget? What's going on?"

Shirley shook her head, then dropped to the chair next to Elsie. "It's really not my place to say. He's going to kill me for opening my mouth. Seems I can't do anything right," she said with a sigh. "Yesterday afternoon he stormed over to my house, assaulted me then accused me of being a liar."

Elsie coughed and spluttered on her mouthful of tea. "He what?"

"He grabbed my arm so hard he left bruises." Rolling up her sleeve Shirley revealed a purple blotched hand impression.

Elsie gasped. "Oh, my goodness. What's gotten into him?"

Shirley began to sob. "It's so hard seeing his world fall apart. Maybe a move will do him good. Queensland is beautiful."

"Queensland? He's moving to Queensland?" Elsie dropped her cup to the saucer, tea splashed to the table. The old woman snatched a tissue from her cardigan pocket and frantically dabbed at her mess.

"Oh please, Elsie, promise me you won't tell him, I'm just so upset."

Elsie reached across the table and patted Shirley's hand. "I won't tell him, but I can't help worrying about him, and you too. Look at your arm."

"It will heal, I just hope…" She paused and looked

towards the old woman. "Thank you, Elsie, thank you. I don't know what I'd do without you."

Elsie smiled, scrunching up the tea-soaked tissue. "And I don't know what I'd do without you, Shirley, you've been by my side for so many years. Your sweetness brightens my day."

Pushing the chair from behind her, Shirley rose to her feet. "Talking about sweetness, how about I cut you a slice of cake. I baked it this morning, it's your favourite, isn't it?"

Elsie nodded and smiled. "Shirley Jones, you spoil me."

Shirley's lips curved upward, a rare flash of crooked teeth as she sauntered to the kitchen bench. Retrieving a knife from the drawer, she paused tapping it against the palm of her hand then cut an extra-large slice for the old woman. Placing the plates on the table, she sat next to the old woman and took a small bite, her head dropped and her fingers gently poked at a fallen walnut.

Elsie returned her cake to her plate. "Come now, Shirley, things can't be that bad."

Shirley raised her downcast eyes and shrugged slightly. "I was just thinking about Robert. He's been so angry lately. Everything I do appears to be wrong. I cut my hair because I was hot and he hates me. I confided in him about my fears of having no one and then next minute he's accusing me of lying. I love him, Elsie, yet—"

"Shh!"

"But if he leaves, I'll have no one." Picking up her plate, Shirley dragged her feet to the sink then turned with teary eyes and leaned against the bench. "I feel like I'm drowning. I should feel secure by my age. I should have a house. Yet, I'm worried about being evicted. I'm going to end up on Struggle Street, in the gutter."

Elsie straightened on her chair and retrieved yet another tissue from her cardigan pocket. "There, there." She waved the tissue. "That's not going to happen. Everything is going to work out fine, you just have to have some faith, the good Lord will guide and protect you."

Tucking a lock of hair behind her ear, Shirley stepped towards the old woman, took the tissue and wiped her eyes then looked down at her feet. "The Good Lord... I feel like I've been abandoned."

"God is with you, Shirley, He will not leave you or forsake you. The Bible teaches us that God not only offers us encouragement when we're in a difficult pit, but He actually enters into the pit with us to see us through."

"Then why do I feel so sad?" Shirley picked at her nails.

"Because you care. You're a sensitive soul and often sensitive people feel too much and feel too deep. But being sensitive is a beautiful quality, it's one of the reasons I admire you."

Pinching the bridge of her nose, Shirley pushed her chest out and shoulders back. Her eyebrows furrowed and her voice hardened. "Maybe I should care less and act more, I can't leave my life in the hands of a book." Pausing for a moment she could smell the old woman's sweet tea as she leaned forward and her voice softened. "I know you have your beliefs, but I need to act, I need to look after my son. I worry about him, Elsie. It's like I said the other day, what happens to Jai, if something were to happen to me? How can I protect those I love when I have my hands tied? I'd be devastated if you were struck down and I had no way to help."

Elsie nodded, but it took a moment for her to find her words. "I know, my dear, we spoke about my solicitor. How about I make an appointment, we could go next week when you take me to the bank?"

Releasing a loud sigh, Shirley rubbed her temples then turned towards the bench. With her palms flat against the cool surface, she bowed her head and smiled.

Yes, at last she's listening.

She went and crouched next to the old woman and reached for her hand. "Thank you, Elsie. You don't know how much that would mean. I think if I sorted everything out, I might feel like I could breathe again."

The old woman tapped her hand. "Good, then its sorted. Next week we will go to my solicitor. We will get our affairs in order."

Shirley's afternoon had dragged like a pair of Elsie's bloomers with no elastic. She'd finally been able to convince the old woman to venture outside. As Elsie sat enjoying yet another cup of tea in the cool of her shaded backyard, Shirley got to work with housekeeping. After all her years of cleaning for Elsie she'd never toughened to the task of cleaning the old woman's toilet. Shirley gagged and held her breath as she scrubbed the surfaces with bleach. Finally, the bathroom was done and so she ventured into Elsie's bedroom. The forefront of her mind consumed by thoughts of a possible secret stash of cash and the appointment with Elsie's solicitor. Shirley looked out a rear window and saw Elsie relaxing in the garden. She smiled then glanced at her watch. She needed to get a move on, Jai was expecting her to be home in an hour and there was still so much she needed to do. Picking up the cat from the bed she hurled it across the room and got to work.

Elsie jumped and stumbled backwards as she spotted Shirley coming down the stairs. "Oh, Shirley, you frightened me," she said, clutching her chest. "I thought you had finished for the day."

"I was… I am… I mean… oh, Elsie, I'm sorry for frightening you," Shirley said, swinging her backpack over her shoulder. "I was about to leave when I realised, I hadn't washed down your shower. I wouldn't want you to slip."

"Thank you, my dear."

"Well, I had better run. Don't want to keep Jai waiting."

CHAPTER FORTY-EIGHT

By the time Shirley arrived home, all she could think about was Elsie's money and her house on the hill.

I'm going to be rich. I'm going to live in the mansion.

Clasping her hands behind her head, she paced around her kitchen struggling to comprehend the enormity of the changes she would soon experience.

I won't have to work. I won't have to cook. I'll get a cleaner.

A heady rush of power, a flush of warmth. Sunlight streamed into the kitchen window. Twirling into her lounge room, she spun around like a ballerina. Arms relaxed and outstretched. Fingers pointing and her skirt lifting with flair. Dizziness, she slowed her movement and gripped the back of the couch glancing at all her belongings.

No more second-hand furniture. Everything's going to be new, and a new car. Oh my God, a Merecedes Benz.

Rambunctious laughter reverberated through the house. Swinging her arms wildly she bounced on her toes then punched the air. Tingling warmth filled her body as she clapped her hands. Thoughts surged through her mind.

I have to get prepared. I need to get organised.

Snatching her keys, she dashed towards the front door.

Mounds of mess and garbage, cardboard boxes and

black plastic bags. A floor carpeted with disarray. Jai gasped as he opened the front door. Staggering on trembling legs, he steadied himself and wove between obstacles. A gust of warm air, a large black plastic bag flew from the kitchen and thudded into the lounge.

"Mummy?" With his hand to his mouth, he slowly stepped forward and peeked into the kitchen. Like a rabbit forcing its way into a burrow, all Jai could see was his mother's rear end as she kneeled on the floor with her upper body crammed into the corner cupboard. The young boy stood still, grinding his teeth as his eyes darted, and finally he edged closer.

"Mummy. What's happened? Is everything okay?"

Shirley jumped and smashed her head into the shelf. "Ouch!" She retreated with her hand rubbing her head. Turning around she met Jai's curious stare. "Yes, baby, everything's okay. Mummy's just having a clean out. Why don't you go to your room?"

With his homework finished, Jai wandered down the hallway. In the kitchen, his mother slapped food onto plates. All the boxes and bags were now neatly stacked near their front door.

His mother turned. "Up to the table, young man. We've got to eat and go out."

"Out?"

"Yes, Jai, and I'll have no carry on."

"Where are we going?"

"I have to go to Elsie's, she phoned earlier."

"Can I stay with Robert?"

'No."

"But Mum—"

"But nothing Jai. Sit. Eat your dinner and do as I say."

Jai whacked both hands against the table and sat down. Shirley sat next to him and scoffed into her food. Within minutes her spaghetti was gone. Jai was barely halfway through.

"Come on. I'm not putting up with your nonsense. You've got five minutes."

Increasing his pace, tomato sauce flung to his chin as he sucked on the noodles. Shirley whipped away his plate and threw it onto the sink.

The drive to Elsie's was brief. Jai sat in the rear seat watching as the streetlights came on. Shirley glanced between her speedo and the rear-view mirror, all the while wondering what Elsie wanted to say.

Why couldn't she tell me on the phone? Jai had better be good.

"I'm warning you, Jai, you'd better be on your best behaviour. If she offers you a biscuit, you take just one and say thank you. I want Elsie to see what a nice boy you are. And keep your mouth shut. You sit still, you smile and you keep your mouth shut. Do you hear me?"

"Yes, Mummy."

Elsie greeted them at her front door looking anxious. "Hello Shirley, and hello young man." She ran her trembling hand over Jai's head. "Why don't you come in."

Shirley nudged Jai's shoulder. "Come on, straight ahead and into the lounge." The young boy walked ahead.

Shirley closed the door and gently touched Elsie's shoulder. "Is everything all right, Elsie?"

"Yes, dear, I've just been thinking about the solicitor."

Shirley's heart sank; had the old woman changed her mind?

"Come on in, let's have a cup of tea." Elsie turned and shuffled up the hallway. Entering the lounge room, they found Jai sitting on the floor.

"You've got a cat. Oh, wow, you've got a cat."

Stretching out his hand, he watched as Missy G wandered beneath the dining table. Gently flicking his fingers, the cat waved its tail and wandered closer, sniffing and head butting his hand. Jai reached forward and scooped it from the floor, cuddling it to his chest.

"Wait here. Mummy needs to talk with Elsie."

With the kettle full and turned on, Elsie and Shirley sat at the kitchen table. The old woman tapped her fingers then rubbed her nose.

"I've been thinking about the solicitors and what I should do. I worry about you, Shirley. I worry that you have no family, no support. I want to give you peace of mind. I want to show you how much I appreciate everything you've done for me and for that reason I believe I might include you in my will."

Shirley's hand flew to her mouth; she couldn't believe what she was hearing. She leaned close, her voice hovered above a whisper. "But what about Robert, he's already mad with me because I accepted your money."

"Never mind Robert, he need not know. It will be our secret."

"Oh, Elsie." Shirley jumped to her feet, wrapped her arms around the old woman's shoulders and burst into tears. "And I'll look after you. All I've ever wanted was to look after you."

"I know, my dear, you've been looking after me for years."

THE BELONGING

"And I will continue to do so. People don't have to be of the same blood for one to consider them as family. Thank you, Elsie, thank you so much. I don't know what to say." Releasing her hold, she straightened and fiddled with her earring. "How about I make that cup of tea you wanted?"

The old woman leaned back on her chair and smiled. "That would be lovely, dear. Maybe we could have it in the lounge with some biscuits."

All three sat on the couch while Elsie sipped on her tea. "Are you sure you didn't want one?" she asked.

"No thank you, Elsie, we just finished dinner. Water is fine."

"Would you like a biscuit, young man?"

"Yes, please." Reaching across his mother, Jai thrust his hand into the biscuit tin grabbing a handful. Shirley slid her arm around his waist and pushed her finger into his ribs, the young boy flinched and dropped all, but one.

"Oops, only one." He smiled, then his face scrunched as his mother released another sharp jab from behind. "Thank you, Mrs Graham."

The old woman chuckled. "Oh, such lovely manners."

"I try my best. It's hard raising a child with so many bad influences in the world, so much violence."

"Yes, the world is changing and sometimes I question if it's for the better. I think I'm lucky to have lived in the era that I did. The future is a worry, if I were to die tomorrow—"

"Oh please, Elsie, no more talk like that."

"I'm sorry, dear, it's just that some days I'm surprised when I open my eyes and feel the air in my lungs."

Two cups of tea later Elsie was still babbling about her health concerns. Jai had moved to the floor and was playing with the cat and all Shirley could think about was the solicitor's appointment next week. Elsie had promised to keep their arrangement secret, and Robert only had five more shifts before his relief work finished.

Soon the old woman will have no one but me.

Glancing at her watch, Shirley stood and stretched. "We should be going. It's getting late and Jai has school tomorrow."

Jai jumped to his feet. Elsie stood and with the aid of her crutches she followed them down the hallway to her front door.

Driving home Shirley's lips curved with selfish greed. Looking out the window she couldn't ignore the one obstacle that remained.

Robert has to go.

CHAPTER FORTY-NINE

A knock at the door had Robert jumping from his bed and dashing down the hallway wearing his new red-satin boxer shorts. It was early; the previous night had been muggy with not a whisper of breeze and he'd hoped Veronica was coming to visit. Last night their phone conversation had been cut short, she was just about to tell him something when she said she had to go as a friend had unexpectedly shown up. It wasn't the first time she'd shut down a conversation and Robert was becoming increasingly frustrated.

Taking things slowly had been agreed. Veronica was wonderful, but so often she would cut important discussions short. Maybe she was scared. Maybe it was a red flag. He'd fallen asleep waiting to hear back and as he flung the door open, he hoped she had answers.

"Hey, Robert, how are you this morning?" Shirley said, barging past.

Robert rolled his eyes as he shut the door and followed in her wake. "I'm good, but what's wrong? Is everything okay?"

"Everything is brilliant. I've been thinking about Queensland," she said, dropping to his couch.

Robert stood hands clasped together forming a fig leaf in front of his boxers hoping he was in no way exposing himself. "Oh, so you're going to move?"

"Well, the thing is, Robert…" She paused. "I was thinking about it, and I think you should come too. It would be a fresh start for us all."

"Us all?" Robert met Shirley's gaze and rubbed his forehead.

"Yes. You, Jai and me… don't you think it's a wonderful idea?"

She leaned back, with her arms stretched over the top of the couch, and she smiled.

Suddenly, the air within his lounge room felt hot, almost suffocating. Robert grabbed the remote from the coffee table and turned the air conditioner on.

Stepping closer, he folded his arms across his chest. "No." He shook his head. "I don't think it's a wonderful idea. I'm sorry, Shirley, but you're not in my plans. I said I was thinking of moving so I could have a fresh start. I didn't mean I wanted to move with you and Jai. I like you but—"

"But what, Robert?" Shirley snapped. Her smile crumbled as quickly as it had appeared. Leaping to her feet, she drew her eyebrows together, and pushed her bottom lip forward. Taking a deep breath, she exhaled loudly and stepped closer. "I'm in love with you, Robert!" She thrust her arms wide. "I'm in love with you."

Silence.

Robert felt sick to his stomach. He lowered his head. Closing his eyes, he pinched the bridge of his nose then ran his fingers down the side of his mouth. These were the words he feared. Rubbing his fingers gently across his lips, he looked up and stared directly into her eyes. "No, Shirley, you don't love me. You're in love with an ideal. You want something I can't give."

He turned to walk away, and Shirley grabbed his arm, spinning Robert back to face her.

"Yes, you can. I believe in you. Look how far you've

come." Tears flowed from her eyes. "You think you can't love, but you can. I've seen the way you love. I'm telling you, Veronica is no good. We… we work so well together. You and I—"

Robert snatched his arm away. "Shirley, stop! You have to stop. You're wrong and you need to leave Veronica out of this. I'm sick of you deflecting and putting other people down thinking it will make you look better. It doesn't, Shirley, it shows me how jealous, ugly and ignorant you are. And as for you seeing the way I love… You saw my love for Julie. You…" He pointed towards her. "You aren't Julie."

Shirley stood defiant. Hands on hips, she glared at him.

Robert returned her glare. "Look at you," he said, flicking his hands towards her. "You cut your hair, but it's just hair. You look like Julie, but you'll never *be* her. I don't love you, Shirley."

"You're confused, Robert, I know you love me. I can tell by the way you look at me, the way you touch me."

"People can touch, Shirley. I touch you in friendship to show my affection and appreciation. People touch to show compassion, to express support and admiration and love. Just because I touched… are you serious? That doesn't mean I'm in love with you. There is a huge difference between loving someone and being in love."

"But if we moved, we could try and with time—"

"No, Shirley, no." Robert raised his hand in a stop gesture. "I'm not moving with you. I'm never going to fall in love with you. And I want you to leave."

"But, Robert—"

"Stop! I said you have to stop, and I meant it. Otherwise we'll both say something we regret."

Shirley remained still, clenching her hands and

pressing her thumbs into her palms. Primitive sounds of bewilderment replaced her pleading words. Finally, she looked away.

Robert took her arm, forcing her to face him. Her face flushed and eyes narrowed. He stared unblinkingly.

Shirley raised an eyebrow. "I'll tell Jai you aren't taking him to the cricket on Saturday then."

"Are you serious?" Robert yelled, throwing his hands in the air. "Stop trying to manipulate my words. Your child's not a pawn. This has nothing to do with Jai. We were talking about me. I know what's best for me. I don't need your permission to do anything in my life. If I want to move to Queensland, I will. I have the transfer papers and I'm going to Queensland, alone."

Shirley huffed. "Move then. Go by yourself. Do what you like and I'll decide who my child sees."

"You don't get it!" Stepping closer, Robert watched Shirley's face closely. Unblinking eyes, dull and empty, the woman rubbed her finger gently along her lip then crossed her arms over her chest.

Robert's voice softened as he leaned closer. "You see here's the thing, here's what any good parent would do, they'd put their child's best interests above their own immature reactions."

Shirley jerked her head and turned away. "Whatever!"

A typical reaction, Robert had expected as much from her, to play the boy off as a controlled hostage. Clenching his jaw, he tried not to say anything he would later regret. "Leave, Shirley, I want you to leave. Now!"

Throwing her hands up, she stormed out of his house slamming the door behind her.

Robert breathed a sigh of relief and collapsed onto the

couch. He hoped she finally got the message. It hadn't been his intention to upset her, but he needed to set her straight once and for all. They were friends. There would be nothing more than friendship between them. And as friends, they should respect each other's decisions.

***

Within an hour of leaving Robert's house Shirley had arrived at Elsie's and let herself in. The old woman had given her a set of house keys and it wasn't the first time Shirley had used them. Hearing nothing, she crept upstairs. Elsie was asleep on her bed with Missy G curled next to her.

Darn fleabag.

Closing Elsie's door, she strolled around the remaining bedrooms upstairs and stepped out the layout imagining how she would place furniture. Everything was coming together. Glowing arrogance sparkled in her eyes, her chest puffed out and she smiled as she ran her finger along the banister rail. Good fortune had fallen, but luck favoured the well-prepared and Shirley was masterful. It had been her suggestion that Elsie have a morning nap. Shirley had said it would be a delight to have lunch together and the woman had fallen for it, hook, line and sinker. Shirley's grandmother had always told her, 'you can't catch a fish without the three Ps; a pond, practice, and patience'. It was a memorable quote.

It's time to catch my fish.

She chuckled as she made her way downstairs recalling her efforts. For years she had been slowly weaving into Elsie's life. It was a long-term game with the expectation of generous rewards. Strategies had been honed and revised. Patience was paramount. Determination kept her focused. But when Julie died a better option appeared. The waiting time would be less. Robert was perfect, he was devastated and weak and so she wove herself into his life. She was his support and his shoulder to cry on. His interests became her interests.

But it wasn't meant to be.

Earlier on she had realised she had no way of getting her hands on his fortune. Robert was far too tight and his view on money was the opposite to hers. Elsie would be her fish. Forced leave from her employer created interference. Robert bounced from blessing to obstacle. He was a speed bump who required squashing.

The circumstances required drastic action. Distractions were crucial. Elsie had to believe she was attracted to Robert. Robert had to believe it was more than a crush. Slowly but surely, she had forced her way into his life. She attempted to control his actions, interrupt his relationship with Veronica. Styling her hair the same as Julie had been a work of genius. She knew she would remind Robert of what he'd lost. And now he had made his intentions clear – he would transfer to Queensland. Her one and only obstacle would move nearly one thousand kilometres away.

A change of scenery would do him wonders. What happened to Veronica was of no concern. Soon Shirley would have it all. Elsie would have no one but her.

Flopping onto the couch she flicked her fingers counting down the days that remained on her leave. Next week she would return as Elsie's sole carer and soon after Robert would be gone. The poor old woman would be out of options. Failing health would force her to surrender to Shirley's offer. The woman would feel indebted. What better way to show appreciation than to leave Shirley as sole beneficiary? Elsie's mansion would become Shirley's pond.

I'll make her think it's her idea.

Releasing a snicker, she pushed herself to her feet and danced over to the mirror on the wall. Gazing at her reflection, she was pleased with what she saw. Stepping closer to the mirror, she waved her finger as if it were a wand and spoke in hushed tones.

"I'm going to catch you, you old biddy. I know it'll take a little more time, but I'm going to catch you, oh yes I am," she said, her eyes widening, her breath fogging the mirror. She chuckled, staring at her reflection.

I'm a genius.

Releasing a ragged breath, she straightened her stance, her eyes furrowed and she pouted as if deep in thought.

"I want to look after you, Elsie. You're like a mother to me," she said, her head slightly tilted to the side and hand gently resting on her chest. "It's a sense of necessity, an emotional obligation. Family looks after family and both Jai and I consider you family."

Wicked laughter echoed, Shirley's grin widened as the thought of being showered in wealth and riches left her giddy. Leaning forward she braced herself against the wall on either side of the mirror before kissing her reflection. Raising her chin, her lips curled in triumph and she took a quick bow.

"Are you okay, dear?"

Shirley jumped and spun around. Elsie stood at the top of the stairs. Reaching around, she slid her fingers across the lipstick kiss. Heat rose to her cheeks and her face-flushed red. Had Elsie seen and heard?

"Oh, Elsie, I'm so happy to see you," she said, glancing over her shoulder to make sure her lipstick kiss was gone. "I was just practicing some lines from a play I'm rehearsing with Jai."

Elsie laughed and she slowly descended the stairs. "Well you certainly appeared dramatic. What's the play called?"

Shirley ran across the room and dashed up the stairs.

Oh bugger. What's the play?

"Here let me help you, you look a little frail," she said

grabbing the old woman's arm.

Elsie stiffened and pulled her arm free. "I can do it."

"Of course, you can, Elsie, of course you can."

"Here." Elsie thrust her crutches at Shirley then continued slowly down the stairs. Moaning and groaning and gripping the handrail with each cautious step. Missy G dashed past. Watching from behind, Shirley's hand jabbed forward within centimetres of Elsie's back. Surface swell emerged below narrowing eyes, the corners of her mouth curved. A silent chuckle.

Don't fall now, I wouldn't want an accident before the solicitors.

Elsie paused, her fingertips whitened as she grabbed the rail and turned towards Shirley. "Are you okay, dear?"

"Yes, Elsie. I'm good, just making sure you're safe."

The old woman nodded. "Thank you, dear. I thought I heard you stumble."

"No, no I didn't stumble. It was probably the clinking of your crutches."

Turning back, Elsie continued down the stairs and into the lounge room.

Relaxing on the couch she was promptly joined by Missy G who pounced to her lap. The old woman chuckled and ran her hand down its back. "Isn't she lovely, so affectionate." Fur flew into the air as Elsie continued to stroke her purring companion.

"Oh yes, she's nice… real nice." Covering her nose, Shirley sneezed.

"Oh, bless you, my dear. Now what did you say the play was called?"

"I'm not sure of the name. Jai's teacher Mrs Brakenridge wrote it."

"Oh lovely. I don't mind a good play, although I haven't seen one in years."

"I'd love to take you to the theatre, Elsie, if that's what you enjoy."

"Maybe I could go to Jai's play?"

"Oh, that would've been lovely, but unfortunately the tickets are sold out. I'll tell you what, I'll ask if there's any way I could get a ticket for you. In the meantime, how about I make you a nice cup of tea."

"Thank you, my dear, a cup of tea before our luncheon sounds lovely, and maybe you will be in luck with the ticket. I'll say a prayer tonight."

In the kitchen Shirley rifled through her handbag and removed a little white bottle. Snorting on her nasal spray, she blew her nose and popped some antihistamines. It was time to get Elsie off the couch and away from the blasted cat. The kettle boiled, and Shirley poured the cups of tea. Turning towards the bench she picked up an old plate and studied it for damage, a slight crack. *This will do.*

Releasing her hands, the plate fell to the floor and shattered, Shirley dropped to the chair. Cupping her face with her hands she burst into tears. Loud wailing released. Slight gaps between her fingers provided space to see. Moments for gasping breath allowed time to hear. Thudding steps and staggered clicking. Within seconds the old woman was in sight, puffing and clutching her chest. A warm hand wrapped around Shirley's shoulder. Stale breath washed over her.

Oh God, she's been eating garlic.

Shirley turned her head away, but kept her hands covering her face. Her shoulders rose and fell between sobs.

"Oh, my dear, what's happened?"

"Oh, Elsie, I can't do anything right. I've made such a horrible mess. Robert hates me."

"Robert doesn't hate you."

"He does. I told him I love him. He told me he's leaving. I'll have no one. How foolish of me to think we could be a happy family."

"You're not foolish, my dear. And you won't be alone.

You'll have Jai. You'll have me. You'll always have me."

Shirley looked up with sad eyes and sniffed. "I do have you, don't I?" She gave a half smile, wiped her eyes and took the old woman's hands within hers. "You are my family. You're like the mother I never had. Jai would love to have a nanny like you, I know he would, he'd just love to feel a part of a happy family."

Elsie chuckled and smiled. "That's so sweet."

Shirley studied the old woman's face. What better way to draw her in than to boost her ego and pull at her heartstrings? How could anyone reject the love of an innocent child?

"Come on now, wipe those tears and let me clean up this mess," Elsie said.

"Oh no, you can't do that. I wouldn't dare let you bend over, not in your state." Shirley got to her feet, wiped the tears from her eyes and insisted Elsie sit and drink her tea. "I think we'll stay here, let's leave the cat sleep. With the way I'm thinking, I'd probably trip over it, sit on it or worse."

"You'll be fine, my dear, we'll work things out together."

"That would be nice, Elsie, that would be so nice. Thank you so much, I don't know what I'd do without you."

"And I don't know what I would do without you, Shirley."

CHAPTER FIFTY

"It's in the past," Veronica said over the sound of cars speeding by. "It's not my fault... what's done is done. As you say, the past is the past. Can't change it... Can we?"

Robert stared, refusing to believe what he'd heard. Overwhelmed by the urge to vomit he gasped.

What the heck did she say?

Instant chills. His hands shaking. Heart breaking. Had he heard correctly? The world disappeared. Shallow breaths. Blurred vision. His hands gripped the steering wheel. Blasting car horns. Cars sped by. His car swerved. Tyres screeched.

"Robert!" Veronica screamed, grabbing the steering wheel. "What are you doing? You're going to kill us." She snatched at her seatbelt and braced for impact. "Pull over! Pull over!"

The car veered sideways. Gravel crunched. Stones flew. Dust encircled. Robert slammed on the brakes. They came to a skidding halt. Echoes of her words played over in his mind. Her voice fading within his numbness. He couldn't look at her. His hands strangled the steering wheel as he attempted to smother her voice. It had to be a mistake. It couldn't be true.

"Turn off the car! Turn off the car!" Veronica slapped his arm. "Oh my god! What were you thinking?"

With a trembling hand Robert killed the engine. Still,

253

he couldn't bear to look at her. His eyes wide and staring. Her words received in altering tones of shrieks and muffles. A moment of silence, that's all he needed. But she wouldn't shut up. Why did she have to open her mouth? Robert's head snapped up. A tirade of curses exploded. Pounding thuds. His fists repeatedly smashed into the steering wheel. He stopped. His fists ached. He could taste blood. He turned towards her, face reddened. Tears streamed from his eyes. Echoes of anger released in huffed breath.

How could she be so cruel?

He glared. Amanda had been right. Veronica was a manipulator. Nostrils flared and jaw clenched, teeth grinding. Revulsion formed a hard lump in his throat. "It's your fault. She's dead because of you!" Spit laced words flew from his mouth.

Crack!

Veronica's head slammed against the passenger window as she flung back attempting to shield her face. Tears streamed from her eyes as she shook.

"What are you talking about? It wasn't my fault. You're crazy. You could've killed us!"

Robert's breath quickened as he leaned closer, fingers pointing. "Us? I could have killed *us*. It's your fault. You lied." He ripped off his seatbelt and slapped his steering wheel. "Get out! Get out of my car!"

"What? Why am I a liar?" Clutching her chest, Veronica dodged his rage.

"You never told me. Why didn't you tell me?"

"Tell you what?"

"What really happened when your husband died. Is that why you latched onto me? You felt sorry for me?"

"How dare—"

"Get out!" Robert thrust his fist in the air, narrowly missing her face.

Veronica snatched at her seat buckle and reefed at

the door release. The door flung open and she jumped out. Spinning around, she stared with fierce intensity. "How dare you. I never lied. I thought you knew."

Her words meant nothing. Robert had the truth. But did he have all the answers?

He'd heard enough. Robert turned the ignition back on, and put his foot to the floor. The engine roared. Tyres spun. Gravel and rocks shot out. He took off. The passenger door flew shut as he hit the bitumen. Car horns blasted. His car fishtailed back into the speeding traffic.

Veronica was left coughing, covered in dust.

CHAPTER FIFTY-ONE

"You jerk!" Veronica swung her handbag over her shoulder and kicked the gravel as she clutched her thumping chest. Her hands shook. Her eyes darted. Nausea swirled deep within her stomach. What was she to do? He'd left her stranded. Endangered. Cars roared by. Hundreds of strange cars. Spinning around she became desperate, desperate for an escape, desperate for air. Snatching the lace neckline in her blouse, her imagination ran wild.

Grasping, her fingers fumbled and her hand yanked. Rejection ripped at her heart as she clawed for breath. Instincts told her to get out of there, but how? Scrambled thoughts. A nail snapped.

I can't breathe. I can't breathe. Oh my god, I'm going to be picked up and raped. Picked up and murdered. Oh my god, I can't breathe.

The fabric ripped. A ragged gulp. Lungs expanding. Hands released as she scanned her surrounds. A single woman had no place on a busy highway.

No exit. No escape.

Fear peaked; her heart pounded. A gust of wind, Veronica's skirt whooshed up around her waist. Her hands flapped trying to tame the wild fabric. Bright pink knickers flashed for all to see. Hot air snatched, car horns blasted and dust danced within her gasping mouth. Another gust, this time her skirt flew up over her head. More blasting horns. Yanking at the fabric she reeled it together like fishing net, her fist clenched around the catch of the day. Frozen fury burned from within as she kicked the ground and flicked her hair from her eyes. More dust and dirt filled her mouth.

How dare he!

Stepping as far from the road as possible, she attempted to formulate an escape. Closing her eyes, she tried to work out what would be her quickest resolve. Phoning a taxi would be useless from a highway, hitchhiking too dangerous, climbing the outer barrier impossible. She was fuming.

How dare he. How dare he!

Cursing beneath her breath she set off. Pounding the pavement, her eyes scanned as she dodged rocks that could send her to her knees. Walking towards the traffic was the safest option. Urgency set in. She took off with great pace. Her racing heart matched her thumping footsteps.

It was just after noon, the sun harassed with uncontrollable savagery. Reflecting heat thrust from the smouldering tar. Within minutes her clothes clung to her with sweat, her fierce momentum impossible to maintain.

Fifteen minutes later, the high humidity coupled with blistering heat left her mouth void of moisture. Sweat stung her eyes. Veronica's steps became staggered. She inwardly cursed herself for telling Robert her secret. Kinks and curls turned into a frizzy mess. Fatigue set in. Veronica stumbled, and her heels ached. Stilettos were never intended for hiking.

Pounding toes and aching ankles forced her to slow yet again. Beads of sweat clung to her skin. Furtive stomping became a hot and sticky wavered trudge. Exhaustion. Finally, and nearly forty minutes after she entered the highway, out hobbled a grimacing and extremely reddened Veronica.

Collapsing to the grass she threw off her stilettos. Sweat encased her body. Heat-cramps strangled her legs.

Painful blisters covered her heels. Foraging within her handbag she snatched her phone and called a taxi.

Why did I tell him?

CHAPTER FIFTY-TWO

Robert swerved into his driveway and slammed on the brakes. Tyres screeched. His car skidded to a stop. The smell of burning rubber filled the air. Anger boiled from within as he stormed up the pathway to his house. Everything was in tatters. Existing in a world full of lies and deceit where happiness teased and living resulted in pain was nothing more than cruel. Veronica was a liar, a bold-faced liar.

How could she have done this?

He threw his keys on to the entry table then dropped to his couch. Thoughts raced and anger grew. Kicking his legs forward, he sent a pile of papers from the coffee table to the floor. The mess didn't matter. His life was in ruins.

How could I have been so stupid?

Clenching his teeth, Robert sucked in lungfuls of air. Quiet anger coursed through his veins, and so he sat in stillness. After a few minutes he exhaled, pressing his hand to his chest he wondered what he should do. Staring towards the bookcase, his gaze found rest on a photo of Julie. He edged forward on the couch, pausing for a moment he rested his elbows on his knees. A quick gasp and a ragged sigh.

Thoughts drifted to happier times. A contradiction of emotions raced through him. Tears seeped while a smile arose. Closing his eyes, he could almost hear her cheeky giggle. Behind his eyelids played a time of love, they were strolling along the beach holding hands. Cool waves lapped at their feet. Seagulls circled within the gentle sea breeze. Sun warmed the body while love radiated and soothed the soul. If only he could return to happiness, how he longed to be with her, in a place where he belonged.

Loud and obnoxious ringing interrupted his thoughts. Robert's eyes sprung open. A moment of silence followed by more ringing. Someone was at his front door; an unexpected visitor demanded his attention. If it were Veronica, he would slam the door shut.

Robert flung the door open. "If you think—" The words caught in his throat. It wasn't Veronica. Robert's face flushed.

"Uh. Hello. Sorry. I thought you were someone else."

Two elderly gentlemen stood before him, one thin and the other fat. Both were wearing grey suits. Robert bit his lip and rolled his eyes.

Oh geez, what do we have here, Laurel and Hardy?

"Good afternoon sir," said the thinner of the two, as he removed his hat. "My name is George and this is my friend Joseph. I do apologise if we've interrupted your afternoon. Our fellow parishioners are walking the streets asking our neighbours one simple question. Do you believe in the good Lord?"

Robert tapped his foot as George spoke, when the old man was finished, he chuckled. "The good Lord, is that what you call him? Let's just say circumstances have made me question many things." Glancing between the two, he stepped back wrapping his hand around the door in an effort to close the conversation. "I don't mean to sound rude, but I'm busy at the moment."

"We understand and again I apologise for the interruption, may the good Lord guide you in your decisions and may almighty God bless you and grant you a life full of peace, love and happiness."

Robert scoffed. "And miracles."

Joseph nodded.

"All of us have needed a miracle in the past, need one now, or will need one in the future. God's desire is for you to prosper. Believe in Him, pray to Him and His word will produce a miracle."

The man smiled then placed his hat on his head, both bid Robert farewell and he watched his curious visitors until they disappeared out his driveway before closing his door.

If God was so great why would He allow people to suffer? Flopping to his couch he shook his head and chuckled. *Georgie Porgie pudding and pie, I fear to find belonging I may need to die.*

Stretching along the couch, he rested his head on its arm and yanked at the blanket on the floor, pulling it over his body. Focusing on the stillness, he closed his eyes. At last he would be able to sleep. Or so he thought. Within minutes he was sitting upright, clutching the blanket to his chest. The blasted ringing had returned. Storming down the hallway, he flung the door open. This time he held his tongue.

Oh Geez, this is all I need.

"Hi Robert, I just thought I would come over to see you were okay. I need to apologise about yesterday. I wanted to let you know that I'm happy for you. Moving to Queensland will do you wonders. I hope we can remain friends." Shirley paused and smiled, twirling a finger through her hair. "Jai is staying at a friend's place tonight. I thought you might like to grab a pizza and we could watch a movie together."

"Not tonight Shirley, I'm not in any mood."

"Why? What's wrong?"

"Veronica and I had words."

"I told you she was a good for nothing—"

"Shirley!" Robert snapped cutting her off. "I don't need this. I want to be alone."

He closed the door.

"Why don't I do your shift tomorrow? Take the day

off. I'll look after Elsie," she yelled from the other side.

Robert reefed the door back open and looked towards her with blank eyes. "No thanks. I need to see Elsie. I'm thinking of making some changes. I want to have the chance to say goodbye." He slammed the door.

"What changes? Are you okay? Robert!"

Ignoring her words, he returned to his couch.

CHAPTER FIFTY-THREE

My dearest Julie,

Seven and a half months is too long to be without you. When will I stop crying? I don't know if I can do this any more. My heart aches, my mind has too many questions. What have I done? I'm such a fool. I'm so alone. I miss you so much. Without you, there is no me. I yearn to be with you, to feel as though I belong. All I want is to belong. I don't know how much more I can take. It should be getting easier and yet things are becoming more difficult. Veronica deceived me. Trust is gone. Love is gone. Without you, life has no meaning. I'm overwhelmed by sadness, and devoid of all hope. Life is no longer worth living, I'm not needed, and my living makes no difference. My absence would not result in grief or anguish.

Would I miss the beauty of a glowing sunrise or the warmth of the morning sun, maybe? In death would I crave the delicate mouthful of freshly brewed coffee, possibly? There are so many questions for which I have no answers. In death, would we reunite or would I be banished to a place where darkness surrounds? I don't know, but how can I live in a world in which I don't belong, where every day I am delivered sadness and pain. I know people say time heals all wounds, I have given time. Nothing has improved. You *were my madly, deeply, greatly. You were my belonging, my gorgeous woman who I loved with every sense of my being. My dearest sweet Julie, I'll love you and miss you until we meet again...*

Love always and forever,
Robert

Tears welled in Robert's eyes as he kissed and folded the letter. Placing it in an envelope, he stacked in on top of the others he had addressed to Julie and shut the desk drawer. Closing his eyes, he made a promise to himself.

I'll wait twenty-four hours and won't do anything drastic in that time.

CHAPTER FIFTY-FOUR

Robert's mood was darker than the cloud-covered morning sky. Another storm was approaching. He'd woken from a dream in which Julie had been hiding and had just returned home. Devastated by reality, his heart had broken all over again. Echoes of grief surrounded him as he burst into tears. Thrashing around on the bed, thudding filled his ears as he kicked his mattress and threw his covers to the floor.

Another day of living. Another day of misery.

Rising from his bed he wiped his eyes, turned on the radio and climbed into the shower. Steam filled the room as warm water trickled down his back. Inescapable sadness clung tight. He sucked in staggered breaths, his head pounding as he leaned against the cool tiled wall. Finally, he dropped to his knees and slammed his hands to the floor. He wept. On the radio the morning news finished. Julie's funeral song started to play. Robert leapt from the shower and ripped the power cord from the socket.

Will this pain ever end?

His drive to work slipped by as memories invaded. Was his time on Earth to be nothing more than painful events, mindless monotony and internalised emotions? Compounding his feeling of suffocation was the extreme humidity. Darkening skies, the storm would soon hit.

Let this day be over. Let me sleep and never wake up.

Clenching his hands, Robert kicked stones in his path as he staggered towards Elsie's front door. Four hours of broken sleep and fifteen messages left on his mobile phone from Veronica had done nothing to improve his state of mind. He was fuming and wanted nothing to do with the woman. Arriving at Elsie's, he was in no mood for confrontation. All night he'd been struggling to absorb what Veronica had revealed.

What a fool! I'm such a fool.

Elsie greeted him at the door with a list of chores.

Just give me the list and leave me in peace.

With Elsie relaxing on the couch alongside Missy G, Robert began cleaning the kitchen. All the while his mind was consumed by thoughts, his anger growing. He'd had enough. Dropping to the chair he slumped forward with his face buried in his palms. The world was unjust and everything was upside down. Silence descended and anger seethed from within.

"Are you done with everything?" Elsie yelled from the lounge.

Robert bolted upright, leapt to his feet and slammed his chair to the floor. "No, I'm not!" Storming over to the cupboards, he recommenced his tasks. Dishes and cutlery clattered, cupboards slammed. Elsie shuffled in with the aid of her forearm crutches and stood at the kitchen bench watching, her mouth fell open. Blood drained from her face, her eyes wide and staring. Robert appeared oblivious to her presence.

"What's wrong?" she asked.

Glancing over his shoulder, Robert rolled his eyes and turned away. His hands tightened into fists and he punched the kitchen bench. Elsie jumped and clutched her chest.

"Robert, you need to calm down and tell me what's wrong?"

Robert turned and stepped towards her; his breaths

quickened. Elsie flinched and stumbled back. Robert loomed closer rubbing his forehead. Elsie shifted from one foot to the other, shoulders tense, and knuckles whitened as she gripped her crutches. Robert stopped. Frozen, he stared at Elsie's watery eyes, they were locked on him. Her face paled, her body trembled, and crutches extended as if providing a shield of protection. He let out a harsh breath and shook his head as he dropped his hands to his side.

"I'm so sorry. I didn't mean to scare you," he said, raking his fingers through his hair. He stepped back. Elsie released her grasp and relaxed her stance.

"Why don't you sit and tell me what's wrong?"

Elsie shuffled to the table and collapsed on the chair. She remained silent, staring at the strain on Robert's face. Finally, he followed her suggestion and took a seat.

Silence lingered.

Robert bit his lip as his shoulders sagged. "I was stupid to believe I would find love." His voice began sharp, but then he cracked on the verge of tears. "In the forty-eight years of my life I've never belonged anywhere except with Julie. Why would I think things would change?" He paused. Burying his head within his hands, he began to weep.

Elsie remained silent.

Finally, after a few moments Robert looked up. Tears slid down his cheeks and he wiped them away with the back of his hand. "I dared to love her and she betrayed me."

"Who? Veronica?"

"Yes, Veronica. She's nothing more than a horrible, cruel, vixen."

Elsie's eyes widened as she leaned back on her chair. "How did she betray you?"

"She lied. She's been lying all along, it's her fault Julie died."

Robert rested his elbows on the table, his breaths quickened and eyes darted. Deep lines formed between

Elsie's eyebrows as her head tilted to the side. A clap of thunder shook the house. The old woman jumped and snatched her chest. Outside it began to pour. Strong winds howled.

"How, Robert, what happened? How did she betray you?"

"She had an argument with her husband. She threatened to leave him. Claimed she wanted more than he could offer."

"But what's that got to do with Julie?"

"It was because of that witch, her vile destructive words forced him to kill."

Another crack of thunder, the sky lit up. Jagged bolts cut through.

Elsie jumped again. "I thought you said Julie died in a car accident?"

"An accident… No, I knew it was no accident. I just knew." Robert paused; his jaw clenched as he waved his finger in the air. "I knew there was more to it. I hounded the police for answers and no one would tell me," he said, shaking his head. "And now I know. I know the truth. It was no accident. It was a rejected man's suicide mission."

His voice turned soft almost brittle. Elsie sat silently watching as tears streamed down his cheeks. Robert crumpled forward and propped his chin on his hand. "He told her he wouldn't live without her. He said he'd never speak to her again. He threatened he'd take others with him, that others would feel pain and she would remember always. And she did nothing. Nothing!"

Robert reddened as he tugged at his shirt and pulled his collar. Sweat covered his brow. Snatching at the knot in his tie, a panicked look took hold as he struggled for air.

"I thought I found love. To think that I defended her." He slammed his fists on the table, then collapsed back in his chair and began to sob. "I believed I had a chance at happiness. What a fool I must have looked, threatening Amanda to mind her own business when she was simply trying to let me know the truth. I was played by a vile, selfish woman."

Elsie searched her pocket for a tissue and placed it onto the table next to his hand. "What about Shirley? She's lovely. Shirley cares for you."

Robert sniffed, wiped his nose then rose to his feet tossing the tissue to the table. "Julie cared."

"But Julie's gone. Shirley is here." The old woman's voice soft and gentle.

"You don't have to remind me. I know Julie's gone. I'm reminded every day. I feel her pain every day. No one understands."

Drawing in a long breath, he got to his feet and began to pace.

"Oh Robert, you have that so wrong. People do understand. People want to help. Shirley wants to help. I see the way you are together. You laugh and joke. She makes you smile. I see the love she has for you."

Robert stopped his pacing and stared towards Elsie. "Remember how you said we were birds, you said you were a canary hopping and fluttering around. Me, you said I was an eagle. Well Julie was my swan. We were supposed to mate for life. And let me tell you about Shirley, I've worked her out. Shirley's a seagull. She swoops in, makes a lot of commotion, takes your food, covers you in garbage then flies away. All her squawking about other people is simply a distraction from her ultimate goal. I see it in her eyes, the way they light up when money is the topic of conversation. She doesn't want me. She wants my money. I saw it when we went to the solicitor about Julie's will. Her eyes lit up when she found out how much money I'd inherited, that's when her focus and affection turned towards me." He tried to control his anger. "A seagull. She's nothing more than a scavenger seagull hovering for a free meal."

He stopped and stared towards Elsie, his cheeks pulsating above his clenched jaw. "Poor Jai, he hops and flutters around his mother because she's his provider. She uses him to gain sympathy. The poor single mother with no family. But I know better."

He glared, nodding. "She has a family. She has a mother and a father. Bet you didn't know that! So why does she want us to believe she has no one? I'll tell you why, because she knows we will relate to the feeling of loneliness. That heavy feeling in the pit of your stomach." Robert thrust his hands to his chest. "The heaviness that crushes your heart and rips at your soul, like walking on a lonely path with no direction and no one beside us to help us escape the darkness. And if it's all a lie then ask yourself why, why doesn't she talk to her family? To have an issue with one family member is plausible, but with all family members? Who's the common denominator? Shirley, that's who. But why? Has she cast them aside because they know the truth behind her actions? Does she fear their existence because they may speak out?"

Elsie stared blankly and placed her hand to her mouth.

Robert nodded again. "That's right," he said. "I heard it straight from Jai, from the innocence of a boy and as soon as the words slipped out, he made me promise to keep it a secret. I even confronted her about it and still she lied." Robert stomped his foot before slamming his fist on the table. "All this time she's been lying! Don't you see how every situation is about her? Every problem is someone else's. She's been preying on our sensibilities and emotional sensitivity, praising us for being wonderful while behind our backs she's deceitful. Sometimes it takes a while, but the truth does come out. The manipulation, the hidden agenda, it's a long game, but the truth does come out."

Robert rubbed his shoulder then pointed towards

Elsie. "I know about all the money you gave her, it's got nothing to do with me and you can do whatever you like with your money. But ask yourself why you gave it to her, what story did she spin? Unable to pay her rent, no food for Jai. Do you know she went out and bought new clothes and diamond earrings, took herself out for some pampering, sat back and guzzled down expensive wine with your money? I bet she never told you that."

Elsie's face paled as she leaned back on her chair and shook her head trying to hide her shock behind her hand.

Robert dropped his finger and stood with his hands on his hips for a second before he recommenced his pacing. "Don't you see how she swooped in when she realised you had no one. She did the same with me. Veronica was an obstacle, that's why she was jealous. But she knew she could sink her claws into you. I've heard the way she speaks to you, trying to shake your confidence, attempting to make you feel reliant on her."

Robert stopped, turned towards Elsie while clearing his throat. "I bet..." He paused and waved his finger. "I bet she had something to do with Tinkerbell, I wouldn't put it past her."

Elsie slammed her hand on the table. "Stop, you have to stop this at once! I'm not a fool. I don't believe you. How can you say such cruel things? I know you're hurting, but Shirley is lovely, to accuse her of such loathsome acts... I don't believe you."

Robert threw his hands in the air and his face reddened. "I'm not calling you a fool. I'm talking about Shirley. And this has nothing to do with my issues. It's about the truth."

He dropped to the chair opposite Elsie and sighed heavily. With his hands fanned on the table, his voice softened. "I don't mean to hurt you, Elsie. I'm not saying this to upset you. And I'm not after your money, money doesn't buy happiness and I have money of my own, in fact that's all I have. Besides money, I have nothing. I have no one. I belong nowhere. But I care about you, Elsie, I don't want to see you hurt."

Robert covered his face within the palms of his hands and began to cry.

"You have me, Robert, and I hear what you're saying about Shirley, but I have to think. I can't believe anyone would be so manipulative. She's been with me for years, helping me, cheering me up, taking me for meals."

She gently touched Robert on the arm.

He looked up. Had Elsie believed him?

CHAPTER FIFTY-FIVE

Huddled beneath the eaves of Elsie's house, Robert inhaled the sweetness of his menthol cigarette, stubbed out the butt and lit another. Leaning against the wall he tried to calm himself. Stressful situations always had him searching for his smokes. He'd been smoking since he was sixteen and nicotine was an addiction he was yet to beat.

Suffocating humidity trapped sweat. Robert worried about Elsie, he wanted to protect her, but protecting was impossible if she didn't believe. His frustration grew. Tugging at the knot in his tie, blustery winds delivered thick sheets of rain. Darkened skies lit up as lightning cut through. Thunder rocked. Peering into the deluge, he sucked in one last drag and tossed his butt to the ground.

Inside, Elsie had moved into the lounge room and was resting on her couch with Missy G. The woman appeared far more relaxed than when he had retreated outside. As he walked towards her, he found it difficult to breathe and wondered if he should continue with their discussions. With another pull the knot in his red tie released, and now hung loose around the back of his neck and over his chest. Robert removed the tie, unbuttoned the top of his shirt and pulled at the fabric in an attempt to cool off. Taking a deep breath, he wondered how he should handle the situation. Elsie was stubborn, he didn't want to end in an argument and if he pushed the issue further, he feared that's how things would go. Resting against the dining table he remained silent. As he scrunched the tie within his hands and toyed over what to say, Elsie's steel-blue eyes stared up at him – wide and unblinking as if she'd seen a ghost. His focus was on his tie. He didn't see her place her hand softly in front of her mouth. Nor did he hear her gasp as she clutched her chest.

"Lord have mercy on my soul," she whispered.

Robert jerked his head in her direction. "What?"

"May 7th 1971." Elsie hung her head and continued to slowly stroke the cat.

Robert stepped closer. "What did you say?"

Elsie began to shake. She stopped stroking the cat and Missy G jumped to the floor and dashed from the room. Fumbling in her pockets she removed a tissue. Her breathing became shallow. Trembling fingers plucked at the paper, and tattered pieces fell to her lap. She closed her eyes.

"It was a rainy day. There'd been violent thunderstorms all night. Road closures everywhere. We had to go the long way. I thought I'd…" Pausing for a moment she took a deep breath and began to sob.

Robert stepped closer again. "What are you talking about?" Moving to her side, he placed a reassuring hand on her arm, her skin soft and tissue like. Her weeping eased. Staring blankly towards him, she cleared her throat and shifted on the couch. "I should have died! That's the day they stole my heart."

Removing his hand from her arm, Robert kneeled next to the lounge. "Who stole your heart? Was that when you lost William?"

Elsie looked away and did not reply. A heavy silence hung over the room.

Robert remained on his knees, scrunching his tie. "Elsie, I want to know why? Why would you say that date? Why would you remember the weather?"

THE BELONGING

Elsie lifted her chin and stared, clutching at the diamond encrusted cross hanging from her chain. "Because that's the date that changed my life."

Her eyes sparkled with sadness and regret as she released her cross. Reefing her hand into her pocket, she grabbed another tissue and wiped her tear stained cheeks. Heavy lashes blinked. "William was the love I never married, that date was the day I left my love."

Rising to his feet Robert placed his hand on his hip. The woman made no sense. "Elsie you're talking in riddles. I want you to tell me why you said that date."

Elsie looked to the floor, her voice became frail, and her body began to tremble. Robert remained silent, allowing the woman time and space.

"I feel so ashamed. It wasn't what I wanted. My parents forced me. I had no other option. You have to believe…" she whispered through quivering lips. One by one her tears fell to her lap. Shame and guilt besieged. She cupped her face within her hands, preventing herself from looking at him.

She flicked her hands. Tatters of tissue fell to the floor. "You have to go." Her voice was just a whisper when she spoke, and she kept her eyes down. "I want to be alone."

"Elsie, just tell me. What happened to William? It's about William, isn't it? You know what happened."

She looked up and narrowed her eyes. "I don't. You have to believe me. I don't. Please, Robert, I want you to leave."

Slumping forward, she buried her face in her hands and shook her head. Robert stared as he listened to the woman's staggered breath. Elsie's body rocked and he feared she might have been having some sort of medical turn.

"I'm not leaving you. I can't leave you. Besides—"

"Besides what!" Elsie glared towards him with

reddened eyes and shoulders tensed. "We all lose things in life, that's what life is. From the moment we are born we are losing! Losing time, losing moments. We think we are winning, we believe we'll find happiness, but before we know it it's gone, it's all gone and we're alone."

Tugging at his shirt, Robert stepped back and shook his head. "You're speaking in riddles."

"4:12am." She said it faintly, though loud enough for him to hear.

Robert froze. His heart raced and hands trembled. His red silk tie fell to the floor. *Impossible.* Surely it was impossible, but how could it be? Heat rose from within. Adrenaline coursed through his veins as demons from his past screamed. Frantic thoughts. Powerful memories. A sea of serpents churned within the depths of disbelief. Robert felt like he was going to be sick. Was Elsie the truth of his existence, the reason for his ambiguous loss?

He stared at the fragile stranger before him, the one he'd pitied only moments ago. He did not see his face in hers. Stepping back, he created distance. Rubbing his eyes, his breath quickened. A million thoughts ripped through his mind. Clasping his hands behind his head he didn't know what to do, where to look or what to say. Elsie sank back into the couch. Turning around he stormed towards the front door but froze in the doorway. How could he leave? He'd spent years dreaming of the perfect reunion.

Was Elsie Graham his mother?

Collapsing against the wall, he was not game to look back. Nausea swirled deep within his gut as he listened to the woman's gentle sobs. Swallowing became difficult. Unwelcome sensations invaded his sweat-covered body. Hands cold and clammy clasped his forehead. Every breath strained.

This can't be happening! She can't be.

But there had to be some truth to her words. Why

would she state the time of his birth? How would she know? Was this the first time she'd realised?

Robert jerked his head in her direction. His breath quickened. Eyes glared. "How do you know?" He rushed towards her with hands squeezed into fists and slammed them into the arm of the couch next to where she sat.

Elsie flinched. Tears streamed from her rapidly-blinking eyes. "You were beautiful. I never gave up hope. They never let me hold you. They whisked you away. But I saw and I never forgot."

Robert froze, hesitating with his response. "You saw what?"

Time appeared to stand still. Her eyes darted beneath her furrowed brow as if she were searching for an invisible escape, but she began to cry again. Her shoulders jerked.

Robert shot her a withering look. "What did you see? I want you to tell me what you saw?"

Elsie wiped her hands down her face and pointed to her chest. Her fingers tapped gently on the upper left side. Robert stared into her sunken eyes then moved his gaze to her tapping. After what seemed an eternity she stopped, her hand found rest on her chest. She stared towards Robert and cleared her throat.

"The red birthmark on the top left side of his chest. Australia, I thought… it looked like a map of Australia." Elsie gave a half smile then lowered her head. "It's funny isn't it, the small things we remember."

Robert's mouth dropped open as he reefed at his shirt, a button popped and dropped to the floor. Everything appeared as in slow motion. The old lady never broke her gaze.

Why am I entertaining her madness?

Robert's heart pounded. The hairs on the back of his neck stood on end. Why would Elsie say such a thing if it weren't true? How would she know details of his life he'd never revealed? He'd never before removed his tie and unbuttoned his shirt while in her presence. He loved that tie. It was the last gift from Julie.

Collapsing to his knees he stared at the red birthmark on his chest. A chilling wave of goosebumps encased his shaking body. Choked up he tried to speak, but words failed.

Elsie stared down at him. "You were born in Sydney Hospital, room 6," she said. "It was a rainy day. There had been violent thunderstorms all throughout the night."

She paused. Robert remained silent. Tears seeped from her eyes. Tilting her head, she leaned a little closer. Her eyes stared into his, as if begging forgiveness and understanding. "They stole you. You must believe me. First, they banished William. They sent me away. And they stole you, my angel... my darling Robert." She cried with outstretched arms.

Her words had to be true. But if so... How could it be possible?

Silence hung in the room as the words set in. Robert remained kneeling, not knowing what to do, while battling to get his head around the situation.

The nightmares from his childhood rushed back; the sleepless nights, the wondering. Moving from one home to the next. And now the person who claimed to be responsible had a name. She was within reach. Should he be repulsed or should he embrace her?

There had been times when he'd been angry because he felt abandoned. But he'd always tried to rationalise his birth mother's actions. She could have been a victim of circumstances. And that was exactly what Elsie was saying, she had been young and was forced to make a heartbreaking decision to appease her family.

Robert turned to ask her another question then stopped. A large knot formed in his throat as he stared. How could he have not known? Knowing who she was changed everything. One thing he hadn't considered was that he would know his mother as a person before he met her as his mother. And as a person, Elsie was kind and caring. She inspired and encouraged. She'd openly shared her stories of regret and encouraged hope, but most of all she believed in him. Would she do the same as a mother?

After what seemed like an eternity Robert finally responded. "Mum?"

Elsie nodded.

Again, her words were whispered and she watched his face closely as she spoke. "It's a miracle. God has sent me my angel."

Robert bowed his head and looked to the floor. Unable to contain his emotions, he burst into tears. "I have to go."

"Go where?" Elsie reached for his hand, but Robert pulled away. No longer in reaching distance, he struggled to his feet and stared. Elsie looked afraid and defeated as she plunked at tiny pieces of tissue. Her eyes swollen and bloodshot, make-up smeared across her cheeks.

"I'm sorry, Elsie, I can't think straight. I need to go. I have to do something." He turned and walked towards the door.

"What are you going to do?" she cried.

"The only thing I can do." And without another word, nor a returning glance he stalked out of the room.

"Robert! Robert!"

The front door slammed.

CHAPTER FIFTY-SIX

Shaking, Shirley slammed the front door behind her and slumped to the floor, hands clasped over her mouth. A thud followed by silence. Panting breaths. Cold air snapped at her lungs. Momentarily dazed. His words began to seep into her consciousness. High-pitched ringing filled her ears. Reality struck. She hammered her fists onto the floor and kicked her feet. Loud repetitive thudding filled the hallway. Wailing echoed.

Jai dashed towards his mother. "What's wrong, Mummy?"

Shirley grunted and groaned as she pushed herself onto all fours. Releasing a loud moan, she dropped to her haunches. Jai edged backward looking down at his mother. Shirley jerked her head in his direction and took a deep breath.

"How can this be happening after everything I've done? After everything I planned?" She slapped her forehead and released a crazed chuckle. She gazed towards the seven-year-old. "Why didn't he just leave?"

"Who, Mummy?" Jai stood over his mother shaking. "Who?"

"Robert."

"Robert's gone?"

"No, that's the problem. He didn't go."

"Where, where didn't he go?"

"Queensland," she roared. "He was supposed to go to Queensland. A fresh start would do him good. I even said we were thinking of going too."

Jai shook his head and his tiny body trembled. "We're going to Queensland?"

"No, you stupid boy. We're going nowhere. Do you hear me? Nowhere! I just told him Queensland was a wonderful idea, warm weather, great job opportunities." She glared at her child. "Leave me alone, just leave me alone. I need to think."

Jai remained silent as he retreated, leaving his mother on the floor.

CHAPTER FIFTY-SEVEN

My dearest Julie,

It's only been one day since I last wrote, but I want to share some mind-blowing news. Something astounding has happened. Elsie Graham claims to be my mother. I think I went into shock when she told me. I wasn't sure if my heart was going to burst out of my chest, get lodged in my throat or just stop altogether. And now I think I've made a huge mistake. I walked out on her, I walked out like a coward. All my life I prayed I would find my birth mother. I needed to know who I was and where I came from, but more than that, I hoped it would fill the massive hole in my heart, I hoped it would provide me with a sense of belonging.

And I walked out.

So much for a picture-perfect meeting. There was no spark, no feeling as though I had been born again. Instead the eccentric recluse whom I'd grown fond of overwhelmed me. And her face quickly disappeared behind the face of an unrecognisable stranger, an intruder and a thief. I felt like she robbed me of my heart-warming occasion. The happy meeting that was supposed to be filled with hugs, long embraces and joyous tears. Everything I had ever imagined vanished. And now, my love, as I struggle to let it all sink in, I find myself worrying about her and hoping she is okay, but

THE BELONGING

I'm too afraid and embarrassed to pick up the phone.

Before I walked out, she said our meeting was a miracle. I don't know how many times I've pinched myself to make sure I wasn't dreaming. But I wasn't Julie, I wasn't dreaming and I know many people wouldn't believe such a thing could be possible, but it was and I guess miracles do happen after all. It just seems so surreal. All my life I felt like I never belonged, but I was wrong. I do belong. I've always belonged. In fact, I was missed. I was loved. I was in thoughts. I didn't realise it, but now I know. I have answers. I finally feel like I have something to live for. I have a foundation on which I can build an amazing life.

It's so weird how things happen. On my way home I stopped to buy groceries. Amazingly, it was the first time I noticed the supermarket sparkle. Hundreds of bright and colourful eggs adored the shelves – Easter is just around the corner. Maybe I thought, this is a symbol of my clearing darkness, a celebration of resurrection and rebirth and a time when people come together. While I continue to struggle with my beliefs, I can't ignore the extraordinary sequences of events and the timely revelations. Maybe this is in fact a time of rebirth and clearing. I feel my thought patterns changing.

Since you left, I've been plagued by the question as to how my life would end. I've stared out to the garden we once danced in. I've gazed towards the heavens where I'm told you are waiting and I've wept in all the places you no longer visit. Unbidden tears touched my eyes when I listened to your voice on the answering machine. Frustration and confusion, that is until today.

Today I listened to your words with an open heart, I heard your words with calm encouragement and peaceful confidence and I now know what I must do. I'm so sorry my sweetheart, for I cannot change what has happened, I wish I could, but I can't. I can no longer live in the past. Dwelling on what might have been is fruitless. I'm sorry I failed to protect you and our precious baby, but I realise now it wasn't my fault. It was an accident. We never know what, when or who will change our life until it happens. That is why we must love and appreciate those we have while we have them.

Please know I love you. I will always love you. I will always miss you. In my living, I will honour your memory. Each day, I will celebrate life. I will be unafraid of crying and sharing my emotions. Everyone's life has a purpose, even mine. I just had to be patient for it to appear, and now I know I can survive even when I don't think I can. Life can be sad, but with life there is hope. There is always hope.

Thank you for sharing in precious moments. Thank you for loving me. You were and always will be my angel. Without you I may never have met my mother. Who would have known all those months ago that your insistence for me to help a lady in need would result in something so mind-blowing? I feel so privileged to have had you in my life. You are truly an angel. Miracles do happen, if only we believe. Until we meet again...

Love always and forever,
Robert

CHAPTER FIFTY-EIGHT

Robert raised his eyes to the darkening skies and watched the swirling clouds. Lightning flashed on the horizon and darkness covered as far as the eye could see. He wondered if Julie was watching and thought about what she used to say. *"If you're going to do something, make it count, commit, or don't bother at all."* It was time to follow her advice.

Tossing his cigarette butt to the ground he stomped in out and walked inside. Picking up her letter, he kissed the paper. Folded and enveloped, he stacked it on top of the others he'd neatly placed in his desk drawer. There was still so much he needed to do.

Next on his list was a phone call, he dialled a number he had rung so many times before.

"Hello, this is Robert Jackson can I speak to Gloria... Hi Gloria, this is Robert Jackson... Yes, I'm well, thank you... I wanted to speak to you-.... Yes, yes I can hold."

Walking towards his open window with the phone pressed to his ear Robert listened to the soft music and peered outside. Shades of black and grey intensified. The time between thunder and lightning reduced and the earthy smell of rain filled the air. A gust of wind, his curtains flapped like an angry flag. Another gust, hot air rushed through his house and his front door slammed. Robert snatched the flailing fabric and reefed the window shut. The curtains dropped. Rumbling cannons exploded within the heavens as he stepped back into his lounge room.

Let it rain. Let it cool and cleanse the earth.

"Yes, yes I'm here… That's okay… No, no nothing's wrong… I'm just phoning to let you know I will no longer be able to accept the position in Brisbane… No, no just a change for personal reasons… Yes, I'll hold again."

Bloody Nora.

Robert dropped to his couch, then rose again and began pacing, clicking his fingers.

I don't have the time for this! I need a drink.

A large crash from outside, Robert jumped and rushed to the window to look out. Visibility was almost zero, but he could see a large limb from his eucalyptus tree had snapped and swayed precariously in the wind. The heavens opened, pelting rain pummelled. No one in his or her right mind would be out in this kind of weather. The limb would have to dangle. He gripped the phone, pulling it closer to his ear.

"Yes Gloria… No Gloria… Before you continue… Please Gloria… Uh-huh…Uh-huh… If you'd let me finish… Thank you… I quit… You heard me… No, I'm not talking about Queensland, I resign… Yes, altogether… Of course, I'll put it in writing… Today, effective immediately. Thank you, Gloria. Goodbye."

Slamming the phone on the receiver, Robert dropped to his couch and let out a huge breath. Closing his eyes, he bowed his head. A slow smile. A slight moan. Slumped forward he listened to cracking of thunder. One violent burst quickly followed another. His closed eyes unable to block out the incessant flashes of lightning that snaked across the sky and lit up his lounge room. It was done. He was now free to act, unburdened by the commitment to an employer and under no further obligation to see Elsie Graham.

But Elsie Graham was one person he couldn't stop

thinking about. Scurrying thoughts filled his mind, the way he'd walked out after hearing her claims, the struggles of not belonging, of wondering, of wanting to know the truth and meaning of his own existence. Elsie Graham held all the answers. But how could he face her? What must she be thinking? Was she elated by her realisation? Did she feel a connection?

For Robert the moment he'd spent years dreaming about had left him bewildered and crushed. What happened to the instant connection, the sudden recognition, the uncanny likeness and intense emotion that was supposed to secure a future bond?

Opening his eyes, he straightened and rubbed his whiskered face as he gazed around the room remembering Elsie's voice and how she had stumbled for words. If Elsie Graham was his mother, was William Honeysett his father? Robert leapt from the couch and dashed into his bedroom snatching up the shoebox he'd forgotten to give Elsie. Flinging the lid to the floor he plucked at the snapshots from William Honeysett's life. Throwing away images of places and random people, Robert continued with his frenzied shuffling. And then he stopped. His knees weakened, and he dropped to the floor.

Diastema! Oh my god! He has diastema.

Robert knew the medical term.

Propped against the wall he studied every section of the incredible photo, all the while running his tongue back and forth behind his teeth. Memories of the teasing he received as a child came flooding back. Most people couldn't stick their tongue between their two front teeth, but as a child he could.

Oh my God! William could too.

Robert's hands trembled as he stared in disbelief. Gapped and rotated inwards, William Honeysett's two front teeth were freakishly similar to those Robert had as a youngster. In his twenties, Robert had undergone a dramatic and life-changing transformation. Numerous orthodontist appointments, years of wearing braces and retainers had fixed his aesthetic shortcoming and erased any similarity. Had Robert discovered a genetic link? It was a likeness only those from his childhood would recognise. The finding was momentous. Scientists believed a specific gene was accountable for gapped teeth. Medical researchers noted this gene as dominant, and his orthodontist had claimed his condition was likely to have been inherited. William Honeysett had to be Robert's father. As for the dissimilarity between himself and Elsie, well that could be determined by the amalgamation of genes.

Hours passed, the storm had moved on and so many photos had glided through his fingers. Two piles sat on his bed, those of significance separated from those with little meaning. Strolling outside Robert looked skyward, admiring the sparkles of hope. After a quick smoke it was time to return inside. Tears flowed as he wrote one more letter. With a bottle of bourbon Robert walked into his bathroom, grabbed a jar of sleeping tablets and went to bed.

His decision had been made.

CHAPTER FIFTY-NINE

Hours after Robert's visit, Shirley was still sobbing. Sprawled on her bed surrounded by a sea of damp, discarded tissues. It looked as though she had been thrown into a washing machine, transferred to a clothes dryer and dumped on the floor. Her face reddened and blotchy, eyelids puffy and eyes bloodshot while her hair shot out in wild directions.

Sudden ringing cut through her reflective sorrow.

Digging around in her handbag, she snatched for her phone. Shaking fingers tapped the button.

"Hello," she said attempting to gain composure.

"Oh, hello dear… I'm sorry to phone so late. I just looked at my watch and noticed it was nearing ten o'clock. But you did tell me you were somewhat of a night owl so I thought it should be fine."

Shirley recognised the voice; she squeezed her eyes closed dreading what was to follow. The caller continued.

"Oh, sorry dear, it's Elsie."

Shirley rubbed her eyes and pinched the bridge of her nose. "Hello, Elsie, is everything okay? Do you need me?"

Elsie laughed. "Oh no, dear. Everything is fine, actually everything is beyond wonderful."

Shirley clenched her jaw and tightened her hand around her phone. She felt like jumping through the phone and throttling the old woman. "That's great, Elsie, so what do I owe the pleasure of this call?"

Elsie laughed again. "Oh, I thought you were never going to ask. I know you've been so concerned about my welfare. So many questions about family, you wanting to be assured I'm looked after. I don't know what I would have done without you."

"I'm concerned about you, Elsie, we've known each other for years. I consider you family," she exclaimed, her voice increasing in volume.

The line went silent. Shirley could hear faint breathing.

"Are you there, Elsie?"

"Yes, yes, I'm here, my dear. I wanted to tell you something, something of great importance. I was going to wait until tomorrow, but I need to tell you now." She paused panting into the phone. "Shirley, I want you to listen to everything I have to say."

"I will, Elsie, but you're scaring me. Is everything all right?"

Elsie made a muffled grunt as she cleared her throat. "Everything is fine, dear. I just want you to listen. You need to listen."

Shirley bit her lip. Elsie's tone was stiff and weary, but perky. It made her nervous. The old woman was obviously unaware of Robert's earlier visit.

"I will," she said, straightening herself on her bed. Maybe there was more to what Robert had said. Biting her nails, she waited for Elsie to speak.

"I want to thank you so much for everything you've done. I want you to know how much I appreciate you. You have been my number one carer." Elsie paused. Shirley could sense a but coming. Elsie continued. "I feel like I'm babbling. My emotions are so fluttery at the moment. I know you said you would come to the solicitor with me and I know I stated some intentions regarding my will, but things have changed." Elsie paused again.

THE BELONGING

Shirley heard her ragged breath, but remained silent.

Elsie continued. "I've discovered my son. I never told you I had a son. But by some miracle I've found him. It's Robert, Shirley. Robert is my son. I've found my long-lost son."

Shirley rolled her eyes and braced herself for what was to follow. "Oh wow, that's fantastic, Elsie," she squealed, through clenched teeth.

"It's… it's a miracle, a wonderful miracle that wouldn't have happened without you, Shirley. I want to thank you. You are truly my angel of mercy. Without you this wouldn't have been possible. You steered Robert towards me. It was you. I've found my son all because of you, and words cannot express how much I appreciate all you've done. I want to show you how much I appreciate you. I've been sitting for hours mulling over how I could ever repay you and then it came to me, something Robert said."

Elsie paused. Shirley racked her brain. What had Robert said that could have Elsie so excited?

"I want to give you a huge gift just as you have given me a huge gift. I want to open your life to endless possibilities and make your dreams come true." She paused. Shirley straightened on the bed, her heart pounding in her chest. Elsie continued. "Robert mentioned the transfers to Queensland and how you would like to move there and have a fresh start. He said your main hurdle was lack of finances. I've heard your struggles and witnessed your sadness. My dear, finances or lack thereof should never restrict one's dreams. You made my dream come true and therefore I want to make your dream of moving to Queensland come true too."

Shirley's eyebrows raised, her breaths quickened as her hand strangled her phone. She couldn't believe what she was hearing. Swallowing became difficult, her mouth void of moisture.

"Shirley, my dear, I am the answer to your prayers," she cried. "I want to be your angel of mercy and I won't take no for an answer." She paused again. Shirley could hear her faint breathing. Why was the woman taking so long?

"Now, Robert told me you have an office in Brisbane. He's so concerned about you, and we both want to see you happy. That's why I want to pay for your relocation costs."

"Oh, Elsie." Anger boiled from within as Shirley threw her weight back into her pillows and slammed her hand onto the bed beside her. Was that all she was worth? What were relocation costs but a drop in the ocean. Two days early she was going to inherit a fortune. She wanted to scream.

"That's not all, my dear."

"Oh?" Shirley's tense muscles relaxed, her boiling reduced to a simmer. Maybe there'd be a silver lining to the conversation.

"I know moving would mean finding a suitable property, having money for a bond. Well I am again the answer to your prayers, my dear. You see I have a rental property in Paddington, just north of Brisbane. You've told me how Jai loves football; well Paddington is a stone's throw from Suncorp Stadium. Jai will be able to attend sports matches. Moving up there will rid him of the bullying he has endured. It's perfect, so perfect and so close to your work, vibrant cafes, and trendy restaurants. It's everything you could want for in a new start. I'm going to contact my estate agent and tell him it's yours, you won't have to pay a bond. The place is furnished. I will have the papers drawn up when I go to my solicitors with Robert."

Shirley's face lit up as she fist punched the air.

A house. I'm getting a house. It's probably a mansion.

"Oh wow thank you, Elsie, thank you so much. A new life is something I've dreamt of for so long."

"I know, my dear. And I am going to ensure your rent is capped."

THE BELONGING

Shirley's face dropped. "What?"

"Rental costs, my dear. Rentals can be so expensive up there, so I am going to reduce my price. Your rental costs will match what you pay here. And on top of that, just to show you how much I really appreciate you, I want to give you a few thousand dollars so you can add some personal touches and treat Jai."

"Reduced rent, a few thousand dollars," Shirley whispered.

"I'm sorry, my dear, I can tell my generosity has been overwhelming. I'll let you go. Thank you, you really are my angel of mercy. Sleep. Good night."

The phone clicked.

"Nooooo!" Shirley threw her phone and collapsed to her bed burying her face within her pillows. High-pitched anger ripped through the house.

This can't be happening. How can this be happening?

Her body thrashed, legs kicked and fists punched. Bitterness stung, blood boiled and grievous wailing tore through the house. She jumped from her bed and paced the room, feet stomping, muscles tensed.

How can this be happening after everything I've done? Picking up after that whingeing woman! Being at her beck and call! Smiling and nodding when all I felt like doing was knocking her to the ground. For years, I sacrificed myself. For years... and for what? Nothing, that's what!

Half an hour later, her room had been destroyed and an exhausted Shirley lay still on her bed, throbbing hands clutching her aching chest.

What am I going to do?

CHAPTER SIXTY

Night quickly became day. Dashing footsteps. The toilet flushed. Jai was up and getting ready to go to school. Shirley had not budged. Torn pillows propped behind her back. Weary eyes stared beyond her inconsolable grief. Hopelessness swayed as her body rocked back and forth. Dreams vanished. It was gone. It was over. Her free ride had kicked her to the kerb. As in the past, Shirley would find herself standing on the side of the road watching those who had more, glide by. Struggle street; that's where she came from, and there is where she would stay.

Fresh tears seeped from her bloodshot eyes as she contemplated her next move. Despair weighed heavily upon her shoulders, her chest ached, her breath delivered in gasps. Bowing her head, her eyes settled for a moment on her mobile phone that lay beside her. The thought of picking it up and calling, but who? Elsie had been cheerful in sending her on her merry way. Robert, adamant when he had said she was not included within his plans. And as for her parents who she had kept secret, why would she crawl back to them? Only a fool would return.

Shirley jumped. The front door slammed closed. Had Jai left? She hadn't heard the door open. Soft footsteps drew nearer. Out of the corner of her eye she saw movement. Jai poked his head around the corner then disappeared. Silence. Shirley straightened her back, wiped her eyes and watched the open doorway.

After a while, small fingertips wrapped around the doorframe. Jai's face appeared from behind the wall. "Are you okay, Mummy?"

He stepped out into the centre of the opening. Shirley forced a smile and nodded. "Yes, Jai, Mummy's just upset. I've made a huge mistake." She patted the bed next to her. "Come and sit with Mummy, I need to talk to you."

Jai inched forward, paused, and looked around her room. She patted the bed again and signalled for him to come closer. The boy appeared uneasy, he walked to the bed with faltering steps and sat next to his mother.

"I think its time for a change. A new house, a new beginning with new friends," she said.

Jai's head tilted to the side, his fingers touched his lips. "A change. What do you mean?"

Shirley smiled then turned away, adjusted the pillows behind her wiping the clamminess from her hands. Why was her seven-year-old son not excited by the prospect of moving and new friends? Jai sat waiting for her answer. She turned towards him. Another brief smile.

"Well, you know Mummy and Robert have been talking about moving to Queensland. Well, I think we might move. What do you think?"

Jai leapt to his feet as if he were on a trampoline and squealed. "Wow! We're moving to Queensland with Robert."

Shirley grabbed the boys flapping hand and shook her head. Jai stopped his bouncing and dropped to his knees. His smile vanished within his mother's gaze.

"No, Jai. We are moving. Robert is staying here."

"Why? Is he mad at me, Mummy? Did he find out what happened?"

"No, Robert isn't mad at you, Jai. No one knows what happened. I told you it was our secret."

"But I thought you said we were going to be happy together."

"I did, but things have changed."

"Why?" Jai's eyes brimmed with tears, a slight gasp; he looked away.

"Sometimes things just change."

"Is it because of what I did? I'm sorry, Mummy. I'm sorry. I didn't mean to let the cat out." His voice was soft and strained.

Shirley tugged at Jai's hand. His body flopped forward and he spun around next to her. Wrapping her arm around his shoulder, she pressed her hand against his tiny arm and pulled him close.

Jai looked towards his mother. Fumbling for words she studied his face, his eyes appeared dull as if life and joy had vanished. His chin trembled, and Jai broke down. Shirley squeezed a little tighter. His body pressed against her as she embraced him. His sobs muffled by her chest.

"It's not your fault. Mummy shouldn't have taken Tinkerbell."

"But... but if I didn't let her out—"

"Shhh." Shirley stroked his back. She could feel the shudders of her son's sadness. She could hear the sting of his regret. She watched as he pushed away. His face crinkled by guilt and remorse.

"I'm sorry I make you cry, Mummy. I'm sorry I didn't listen."

"You don't make me cry."

"But Tinkerbell's dead because of me."

Shirley reached out, turning Jai's chin towards her. "No, Jai, Tinkerbell died because Mummy did the wrong thing. Mummy should have been honest, but instead I chose to lie."

"But you didn't do the wrong thing, Mummy. I opened the door."

"And Mummy was dishonest. Mummy lied and nothing good ever comes from lies, I want you to remember that. We should never lie."

"Why did you lie?" Jai said, wiping his tear-stained face with the back of his hand.

Shirley took a deep breath to steady her voice. "Tinkerbell was sick. Now I want you to listen to me and I want you to promise this stays our secret."

Jai nodded then stared at his mother, sucking in staggered breath.

"As I said, Tinkerbell was sick."

"Did she have a cold?"

"No, she had worse than a cold. She had lost a lot of weight and become listless."

"What's that?"

"She had no energy and a squirty bum. Then Mummy found blood in her poop."

Jai flopped to his back, nose wrinkled, hands covering his mouth. "Yuck."

"Yes, it wasn't nice and Elsie had also been sick so she hadn't noticed the change in Tinkerbell. Mummy didn't want Elsie to worry. I wanted both of them to get better. I thought if I could take Tinkerbell to the vet and get her well then everything would be fine."

Jai sat back up, his eyes tight and worried. "Did you take her to the vet?"

"Yes, and that's why she was here. The vet said she had something called 'Giardia'. Mummy had to give her medicine and keep her quarantined until the vet said she was well again. That's why I had her locked in the laundry. She needed to take the medicine and I had to give her a bath then go back to the vet for another check up. I had to clean down and disinfect her home so when she went back, she wouldn't get sick again."

"Yuck."

"My point is, Mummy should have told Elsie about Tinkerbell being sick. If I'd been honest none of this would have happened. If I had told the truth, Tinkerbell may still have been in our laundry. Because of my lies, Elsie worried. Because of my secrets, you opened the laundry door. You wouldn't have opened the door if I had explained everything, especially if you were worried you would catch something. So now do you understand why it's important to tell the truth and also listen to what you're told?"

"Yes, Mummy."

"I never want to hear you blame yourself again. The car hit Tinkerbell because mummy lied. Without my lies none of this would have happened. We need to put this behind us. Elsie has a new cat. We are moving to Queensland. There will be no more talk about Tinkerbell."

"Yes, Mummy."

"And when we get to Queensland maybe you could look at getting yourself a pet, how about a dog?"

"Really? I can get a puppy?" he said, his voice full of excitement.

Shirley smiled and nodded. She knew she had to keep her son on side and, more importantly, he had to keep his mouth shut about the cat.

"Only if you promise no more talk about Tinkerbell."

"I promise, Mummy, I promise."

"Then off you go and play in your room."

Shirley watched as Jai dashed from the room then rolled her eyes and shook her head.

Stupid child. No wonder he still believes the great Santa Claus lie.

She chuckled. Jumped from her bed and quietly closed her bedroom door. Sneaking over to her bedside cabinet she looked over her shoulder and listened. All was silent. She opened the bottom drawer.

"There you are." Her eyes wide and staring, her

smile exaggeratedly smug. She bit her lip then chuckled again. She snatched the tattered shoebox from the drawer. Unable to contain her joyous triumph, she popped the lid and squealed, jumping up and down. The sweet scent of polymer filled the air. Shirley ran her fingers along the tightly stacked notes.

Oh yes! There has to be over a hundred grand. I'm rich! I'm rich and the old bag can't prove a thing.

Spinning and twirling, she danced across the room and collapsed to her bed with the box close to her chest. Grabbing handfuls of fifty-dollar notes, she threw them in the air while laughing hysterically.

She probably won't even realise it's gone and if she does, so what? I'll be long gone. Might even find myself a nice sugar daddy.

"Woohoo!"

CHAPTER SIXTY-ONE

Robert sat within the comfort of his car. Clammy hands wrapped around his steering wheel, the armpits of his shirt drenched with sweat. At last he had arrived. His long, silent journey was over. Taking a deep breath, he tried to ease his racing heart. It was time. His mind said to move, but his body would not budge. Staring into the distance, he watched the trees sway in the breeze. The summer sun danced overhead, providing warmth. It was going to be another hot and humid day.

Infinite blue with dashes of pink and grey created an amazing canvas above the distant mountain range. This was it. Raking his fingers through his hair, he bit his lip. Sitting still would get him nowhere. A field of long wispy ryegrass danced between him and his final destination; a large man-made lake with an island. His decision had been made. Tears welled in his eyes, the ache of saudade overwhelmed as he thought of the last time he had walked through the fields. It had been a day of pure bliss. He'd been with Julie. They'd laughed and joked, enjoyed a picnic, walked barefoot on the sand, swum within the cool water and sunbaked in the warmth of the sun. Both had felt such a deep connection to the place. It was beautiful. They were in love and being there filled them with a sense of serenity.

Reminiscing would get him nowhere. He stretched and yawned as he grabbed the bag he'd placed on the passenger seat then hopped out of his car.

He stretched again, and took in a healthy sniff of the fresh country air. The mixture of damp earthiness with a slight hint eucalyptus imbued a sense of hope, a chance of new beginnings. Holding his breath for a moment, he was filled with an overwhelming feeling of peace. What he was doing was right. Removing his shoes and socks, he could feel the soft grass on the soles of his feet. Robert opened the rear door, threw his shoes and socks onto the floor, and whipped the blanket from the back seat. There it was, just as he had placed it. Picking it up, he tossed it over his shoulder.

No accidents.

Robert walked warily to the water's edge, his fingers wrapped firmly around the handle of his rifle, his eyes darting between sticks and grass. He'd never seen a snake, but the last time they were there they had been warned of their presence. It was better to be safe than sorry.

Finally, he made it to the clearing on the edge. Gently he placed what he had been carrying to the ground. He knelt down, reached over the edge, cupped his hands within the cool water and took a mouthful of freshness.

The place was amazing, entrancing water, so clear and blue. Not a soul to be seen, everything was so peaceful. Picking up a stone, he threw it to the centre. It splashed, ripples in widening circles appeared, and then they were gone. All was still. All was quiet. The smile on his face was tinged with sadness, if only that last day by the lake had lasted forever.

Robert removed the note from his pocket as he stepped off the embankment. Fine sand squished between his toes; cool water swelled at his feet as he stepped forward. He unfolded his note, inside was a treasured photo of Julie. Pressing his lips against the photo he gave his beloved a kiss and placed her safely in his pocket. His eyes glistened with tears. Doubt entered his mind. Was this the right thing to do? Was he ready?

Looking over his shoulder, he glanced at his rifle. Prior to leaving home he had been positive in his decision, apprehension had surfaced within his journey, confidence had faded, and now he was reluctant. Robert raked his fingers through his hair as he gazed at the magnificent view. Taking a deep breath, he reminded himself to remain focused, it was imperative he maintain control.

Robert turned his head as if peering towards an invisible person over his shoulder. His heart was in his throat; eyebrows raised then lowered, while he narrowed his eyes deep in thought. Taking a ragged breath, he turned and faced the lake. Absorbing the beauty of his surrounds, he nodded repeatedly acknowledging his decision to continue as planned. Clearing his throat, he held his note with both hands and began to read.

My dearest Julie,

I hope beyond hope in some strange and unknown way that you can hear my words and feel the love I have for you. There are so many things I never got the chance to say while we were together, and for that I am truly sorry. You were my gorgeous woman, my world, my forever girl; you were the one I was never meant to say goodbye to. So how do I say goodbye to the one person I thought would walk by my side for the rest of my life? I don't know if I will ever be ready to say goodbye. I don't want to. For in my heart I am sure we will meet again. We will recognise each other. We will feel that special spark reignite. I always said, 'I love you forever and a day plus more', and I meant every word. So, when we least expect it, it will happen. In another time, and another place. My sweet Julie, I look forward to that wonderful moment.

You may wonder why I believe this to be true? Well that's simple. The strength of my belief is supported by my fundamental understanding that love does not diminish or die just because someone has left. Love is endless. But for the moment my sweet, gorgeous woman, I want you to know what you meant to me in this lifetime. You were all the corny cliches and more. You were my light on a dark and stormy night. You were my rock. You were my everything. You supported my decisions, applauded my successes, and picked me up when I felt down.

When I lost you, I was heartbroken, suspended with pain, unsure how to escape or move forward. Our special moments were replaced by moments of emptiness and longing to be with you. I want you to know I am thankful we met. I am thankful for the moments we shared. I am thankful for the love you showed. You brightened every day. Your smile was contagious, your laughter infectious, your touch so warm, I embraced you with open arms, accepted and appreciated all of you. I am so grateful for the precious time we shared. Never in my life did I ever imagine I would experience so many wonderful moments. For all of those, I thank you too. I love you, Julie. I will always love you.

So, for now, my gorgeous sweetheart, I will say farewell, see you later, ta-ta, toodle-pip and until we meet again. Please know where there is forever love, there is never-ending love. Where there is never-ending love, there is life. And where there is life, the possibilities are endless.

I love you forever and a day plus more and I will miss you, until our souls reconnect...

Tears saturated Robert's face as he folded the note and returned it to his pocket. His body trembled as a tumultuous wave of conflicting feelings overwhelmed him, sadness for his loss clashed with love and appreciation. Julie had lived an amazing life. Robert felt privileged and honoured to have shared in her love, and hoped they would one day meet again.

He picked up the silver urn that contained Julie's

ashes, removed the lid then paused for a moment of quiet reflection.

All was silent.

All was still.

Turning the urn upside down, he released Julie's ashes to the place they had both found tranquil before turning and returning to his car. Sitting in his car, he wiped his eyes and smiled; it was a beautiful celebration. Julie would forever be in a place she loved.

As Robert drove home, he thought about his new life complete with amazing revelations, he was determined to make the most of every opportunity and was steadfast in his belief to live a life Julie would be proud of.

Knowing where we belong provides us with two things; one is roots, the other is wings. I am an eagle. I am strong with a powerful heart. I will fly, I will glide, and I will soar. And one day, my dearest Julie, I will open the café of our dreams. I will call it, 'Julie's café'. That is my promise to you.

Toodle-pip, my sweetheart, until we meet again.

THE BELONGING